CW01085072

ABOUT THE AUTHOR

Originally from Northern Ireland, Jacqueline Harrett has lived in Cardiff with her husband for over thirty years. Her two grown-up children also live in the capital city.

A multi-genre author, Jacqui has published non-fiction; *Exciting Writing,* (Sage), *Tell me Another…* (UKLA); children's stories; and short stories in anthologies. She has co-authored a novel with Janet Laugharne, *What Lies Between Them*, (Dixi, 2022) as well as flash fiction and blog at www.jlharland.co.uk.

The Whispering Trees is the second novel in her DI Mandy Wilde detective series.

Jacqui has already started work on *With Grave Consequences*, the third Mandy Wilde book.

Published in Great Britain in 2022
By Diamond Crime

ISBN 978-1-915649-18-8

Copyright © 2022 Jacqueline Harrett

The right of Jacqueline Harrett to be identified as the author of this work has been asserted in accordance with the Copyright, Designs and Patents Act 1998.

All rights reserved.

No part of this publication may be reproduced, stored in a retrieval system, or transmitted in any form or by any means without the prior permission in writing of the publisher, nor be circulated in any form of binding or cover other than that in which it is published.

All characters appearing in this work are fictitious. Any resemblance to real persons, living or dead, is purely coincidental.

Diamond Crime is an imprint of Diamond Books Ltd.

Thanks to…

Steve, Phil and Jeff whose patience, hard work and good humour is much appreciated. Also, to the Diamond Crime team of authors. Members of the Criminal Fairies: Linda, Gwyneth, Duncan and Jan for reading a very rough first draft and giving me constructive criticism.

Writers Enjoying Words for constant encouragement and interesting conversations.

The Welsh crime collective Crime Cymru who are an amazing group of friendly and supportive writers. I am delighted to be a member.

For all the lovely readers who left reviews for *The Nesting Place*; a special thank you. Reviews are like gold for writers, more important than readers realise. I hope you enjoy Mandy's latest adventure in *The Whispering Trees*.

Cover photo: Ebba Thoresson

Book cover design:
jacksonbone.co.uk

Also by Jacqueline Harrett:
The Nesting Place

And coming soon from With Grave Consequences
The third D.I. Mandy Wilde Novel
To be published by

DIAMOND
CRIME

For information about Diamond Crime authors
and their books, visit:
www.diamondbooks.co.uk

For Doug, Douglas and Felicity

The Whispering Trees

A D.I. Mandy Wilde Novel

JACQUELINE HARRETT

CHAPTER ONE

DI Mandy Wilde sighed. She picked through the files on her desk. Tedium. What she needed was a good homicide. Her eyelids felt heavy and her throat dry. The summer in Cardiff had been a series of burglaries, drugs, domestic violence, mixed with a bit of fraud. Plenty to do but all routine. Nothing interesting. September had dragged and now it was the first week in October and the year was turning around. As if he'd read her thoughts, Superintendent Withers appeared, glowering.

"Wilde, get moving. Body found in Nant Fawr. Male. SOCOs have beaten you to it."

"On my way, sir." With a nod to DS Josh Jones, she grabbed her coat.

"Nant Fawr. What do we know?" Josh threw a nicotine mint into his mouth as they piled into Mandy's Juke.

"Nothing much yet. Death in the woods though. Bodies beat burglaries any day." Mandy started the car.

"You been told you're weird?"

"All the time, especially by Withers."

Josh smiled. "If you will nick his friends..."

"How did I know the bloody guy was a golfing chum? Fair play, Withering sticks with the law regardless. Besides the idiot deserved what he got. The poor woman

9

was shit scared." She grinned at him as they sped past Roath Park Lake. "Which end of the Nant Fawr corridor?"

Josh checked the map on his phone. "I think if you park along Rhydypennau Road we can walk from there. Nice little coffee shop close by too. We can pick up lunch after."

Mandy glanced at him. "Do you ever think of anything other than food? Maybe a dead body will put you off. Depends how long it's been there."

"Not long, I wouldn't think. Popular area. Bet you a fiver it's a dog-walker found the body."

"Ha, no way. It's either a bloody dog-walker or a runner."

There was nowhere to park near the entrance to the woods. "Shit. How many vans do they need for one body? I'm going up on the pavement. Stick a sign in the window in case we get a ticket. Withers would love that." Mandy laughed. "It'll be muddy there. Glad I invested in a new pair of wellies." She reached round behind the driver's seat and pulled out pillar box red wellington boots.

"Paddington Bear." Josh snorted.

"Well, at least I won't have to get my nice suede shoes dirty, will I?"

Josh glanced down at his feet and groaned. "They'll be for the knacker's yard by the time we get finished here. Lisa will kill me. I only had them last week."

They pushed their way through a small crowd gathered on the pavement. At almost six feet, Mandy had the advantage of being able to see over the heads of most of the rubberneckers. A uniformed officer, arms crossed, stood blocking the way into the wooded area. Mandy waved her badge at him.

"Which way?"

"Straight ahead, Ma'am. Over the bridge. You'll soon see them."

The trees were showing the first hints of autumn. Crimson, ochre, cinnamon and paprika leaves peppered the branches and the ground underneath. The wind whispered through the branches, rustling as it picked up speed. A storm was coming. The crunching of acorns disturbed a squirrel which scrambled up a tree and peered down at them, wary and suspicious. As they moved away from the pathway the ground became spongey underfoot. The smell was damp, rotten, ominous. The sky darkened and the rain started, drops pattering at first and then more persistent, drumming into the stream which bubbled away in the background. Mandy pulled her hood up. Her hair was frizzy enough without getting it wet. Josh yanked at his collar and shivered as a sudden gust of wind whipped around his neck.

They approached the SOCOs behind the cordoned off area. "Who found him?"

An officer pointed to a group of three lads clustered together a little way from the scene. Another uniformed officer was standing with them.

Mandy looked at Josh. "I should have taken your bet. It looks as though we were both wrong. Sneaking out of school for a quick fag and they find a stiff. Serves them right."

The body could be seen, chest downwards, sprawled across the undergrowth. Dark hair and skin the colour of bleached wood. His face was turned to the side, eyes and mouth open. The left arm was pinned underneath the body while the other stretched out above the head. Rishi, the pathologist, was there.

"Nice start to a Wednesday, Rishi. Got to keep you busy."

Rishi nodded.

"What you think? First impressions." A hint of impatience.

He glanced over at her, taking in the bright red wellies, almost smiled, held the look just long enough. "Male. Twenties. No sign of attack. Let's turn him over." One of the SOCOs helped and Rishi continued with his examination. He gestured for Mandy and Josh to approach. Putting on protective foot covers they moved closer. Not close enough to contaminate the scene but where they were able to view the body more clearly.

"I won't know what killed him until I do the post-mortem. Nothing to suggest what happened. There's a bruise here on his forehead. It seems consistent with him hitting the ground. No marks on the back of the head, no stab wounds, defence wounds or anything else."

"ID? Do we know who he is?"

Rishi checked the pockets. "Well, you can rule out robbery." He handed over a roll of notes tied with an elastic band. "Looks like a lot there. Nothing else on the body."

"You're right. I reckon at least a grand, could be more. Pity it's evidence as it would give the missus a nice treat, eh?" She winked at him. "Or send the mother-in-law away for a week's holiday."

"Indeed. Somewhere far away with no telephone. I have constant earache from her."

"She doesn't appreciate your talents like we do, Rishi." Mandy glanced around the area. "Not much evidence of a scuffle either. A few footprints. I suppose those belong to the lads who found him. He's not far from the stream here. Josh, go and ask them to widen the search. See if anything was dropped. Mobile phone, wallet. Maybe he was chased, fell and hit his head. And tell those lads we'll want a word."

Mandy studied the body. The victim looked young, late twenties as Rishi said, and well-dressed in a rust-coloured woollen overcoat, smart trousers in dark grey and brown brogues. The soles were barely worn. New perhaps. How the hell had he ended up dead and, more to the point, who was he?

Josh returned. "They've cordoned off this part of the woods. We'll need a bigger team to comb the area."

"And we'll want a door to door on those houses," she pointed to a row of houses whose gardens overlooked the woods, "plus any close to the entrances. We'll get a photo of the victim. Send it over to the tech boys. They can tidy it up. Remove the bruise and stuff." She bit her lip. "Get a team out here. Find out if anyone recognises him, or if they've seen or heard anything suspicious. And a couple of uniforms out in the morning asking any regular users the same questions. And keep the bloody press away. We don't need them tramping over stuff and making wild assumptions."

"Good point."

"Right. Let's see what see no, hear no, and speak no have to say for themselves." She indicated the boys with a nod of her head.

CHAPTER TWO

The three lads were standing, out of sight from the crowd, whispering to each other as they watched proceedings. Mandy and Josh flashed their badges and introduced themselves.

"Okay, names first. Who phoned in?" Mandy looked from one face to the other.

"Me. I'm Luke. This is Asif and Daniel." Luke was fresh-faced with dirty blond hair flopped over one eye. He bit his lip while Asif shuffled and stared at the ground.

Daniel, dark curly hair and the beginning of a stubbly beard, met her eyes. "We've a maths test at ten. Can we go now?"

It was a challenge which Mandy ignored. Why was he in such a hurry? "I'm sure, under the circumstances, your teacher will understand." No way was she going to let some smart-arsed schoolboy tell her what to do.

Asif raised his head then. "You mean you're going to tell the school. And… and our parents?" His dark eyes were shadowed with concern.

"I'm afraid it's inevitable. You've found a dead body. What did you think would happen? There'll have to be an investigation. Now, who wants to tell me what you saw?"

Asif swallowed and looked as if he was going to be sick while Daniel rolled his eyes. Cocky little bastard could do with a slap. Just as well she wasn't a teacher.

"We came into the woods for a smoke before school and spotted him lying there." Luke's voice was shaky, although he seemed to be in control of himself.

"Did you touch him? Move the body?"

"No. We could see he wasn't moving. I rang 999 straight away."

Daniel snorted. "Problem is, Lukey boy here watches too much telly and thinks he knows it all 'cos his dad's a pig."

Mandy gritted her teeth. She was tempted to ask Daniel to empty his pockets, pretty sure she'd find something to wipe the contemptuous look off his face. Too much trouble. Instead, she turned her attention to Luke. "Well done. Most people would plough on in without realising they were contaminating a crime scene."

Luke coloured.

"Did you see anyone or anything suspicious or find something around the area? A mobile phone for example?"

All three boys shook their heads.

"We'll need to see you all again and take statements. I assume you all go to the same school. What form are you in?"

"We're all in lower sixth. Now can we go?"

Mandy took a deep breath. Daniel needled her and she wanted to rattle him, but she needed to rise above it. After all, they were still kids. They thought it their duty to take the piss.

"Give your names and addresses to one of the uniformed officers and we'll be in touch later. You may wish to have a parent, or responsible adult, present when we interview you to take formal statements."

As Luke nodded, Asif looked as if he was going to cry. Mandy guessed his parents would be furious with him at sneaking out of school with the others. Who was the leader of the little group? Daniel? He had the confidence and arrogance to drag others with him. Luke seemed a decent kid. She'd find out later where his dad worked. Which station. Background checks. Always good to know who you were dealing with.

When the boys had shuffled off, Josh asked, "Should we arrange for counselling or something for them? I mean, it's a shock. Perhaps they need support?"

"What? They couldn't wait to get out of here. Do you think the school will have somebody?" She frowned. "I hadn't even thought about it. Bloody hell. Not our job, babysitting kids."

By then the body was covered up and ready to be transported to the mortuary. The crowd was going to love it. A bit of gossip and intrigue. She hoped they could get it away before they had the reporters out or, God forbid, a TV crew.

"What time for the PM, Rishi?"

"Noon?"

Mandy nodded. The post-mortem would provide more clues. The first step was to identify the victim. She hoped someone would be able to throw some light on it. Strange not to have any identification.

* * *

Two new files on her desk. She rolled her eyes at DC Olivia Wyglendacz. "Not more bloody burglaries. I reckon we've got two gangs on this. Teenagers probably. What's the latest?"

"Two more break-ins around the Llandaff area. Owners out. Mainly tech stuff taken, it was. Computers, cameras. Easily transportable." Olivia blinked from behind her owl spectacles.

"And easily sold. Forensics been?"

"Yeah. No prints. Neighbours on one property heard something. But they didn't see nobody."

Mandy sighed. "There's got to be some link. Sift through and see if you can find anything. Do it by area. Sometimes it's in the little details. Time of day. They all use the same hairdresser or whatever. We'll get them in the end. These things piling up are pissing me off."

Olivia grinned at her. "Could be worse. We had one woman who reported a large sum of money stolen. Thousands it was. Then she rang back an hour later to apologise. She'd made a mistake, she said, and forgotten she'd put it in the safe."

Josh laughed. "Now I've heard it all. Demented or too much dosh. How do you forget where you've put your money?"

"Not everyone is scraping for every last penny like us lot." Mandy picked up the new files. Better get on with some work before the PM of the mystery man.

CHAPTER THREE

Mandy passed the Vick to Josh as they entered the mortuary at the University Hospital of Wales, or the Heath, as the locals called it. Nothing like a suspicious death to get the grey matter going. Maybe it wasn't suspicious. It was always better to wait for Rishi's opinion.

There was something heavy about the mortuary. Bleak, with the unmistakable stench of death and formaldehyde which clung to clothing long after they left the place. Josh rolled his shoulders and put a hand to cover his mouth. God, he wasn't going to gag, was he? It always felt slightly weird in there. Cooler than the rest of the hospital, artificial light, no windows, refrigerated drawers to hold the bodies. She wondered how many of those drawers were full. The sound of pipes and other clunking noises seemed to echo. The world of the dead.

The body was on its back, naked, exposed. He looked younger than she'd first thought. Vulnerable. The bruise on his forehead contrasted with the paleness of his limbs.

"What have you found, Rishi?"

"Nothing significant on the body – yet. He's clean. Nothing under the fingernails or toenails. If you sniff his hair, you can detect the faint aroma of shampoo. It looks as if he showered not long before his death." Rishi took a breath. "I think he's Eastern European. He has typical Slavic features, high cheekbones, a pointed chin and narrower eyes. Romania. Croatia. Albania. Somewhere around there, I think."

"And cause of death?"

Rishi shrugged. "I won't know for certain until I open him up. Do you want to stay?"

Panic crossed Josh's face. Mandy supressed a grin. She hesitated to see if he would bolt, before shrugging her shoulders.

"It's okay. We'll wait for your report. Anything we can use to identify him? What about the clothing? It all looked expensive to me."

Rishi went over to a bench where the clothes were laid out. "You're right, Inspector. Designer labels. A good quality coat at least. Some cat hairs present. Grey shorthair, probably. The rest from good old Marks and Spencer."

He paused. "This is something you will find interesting though." He picked up one of the brown brogues and waved it at Mandy. "What do you see different about this shoe?"

"Is this a trick question? Looks fairly new to me. Size nine or ten? Bit of mud on them." She shrugged her shoulders. "What?"

"The mud is consistent with where he was found." Rishi pointed to some specks of grey. "There are particles of road dust too. What else do you see?"

"Bloody hell, Rishi. I'm not an expert on shoes." She could see a faint twitch at the corner of Rishi's mouth. "You're bursting to tell me something."

"These are very expensive shoes."

"Right. We're assuming this guy was minted? Designer coat, smart shoes, a roll of notes in his pocket. Two grand. More than I thought…" Her voice trailed off as she frowned. What the hell was Rishi getting at?

"Not merely expensive shoes. Custom made." He indicated with his index finger. "Look at the label. There's a mark inside."

Mandy inspected the stamp inside the shoe. "Best. And a little crown. So what?"

Rishi pulled himself up to his full height and beamed at her, the opportunity to display his knowledge irresistible. "My dear Inspector Wilde, those are the most expensive shoes you are likely to have the pleasure of examining." He paused for effect. "Best is the name of the firm, a name synonymous with quality. Members of the Royal family go there to have their shoes custom made. Hence the crown."

He gestured with his free hand, almost as though he expected applause, as he glanced from Mandy to Josh and back again. "Each shoe is made to fit the customer. It takes months. They make a wooden last of the customer's foot and keep them in their workroom for future reference."

Mandy smiled. "What you're telling us is that if we can find whose shoe this is, we'll have the identity of our man. It's like a fingerprint for feet. Like Cinderella."

Rishi nodded. "Exactly."

"Rishi, I could hug you." Her arms spread wide.

Rishi stepped back, shaking his head. "Better not. My wife would not approve."

Mandy said, "Come on, DS Jones. We've got some shoe shopping to do. After we interview those lads. Get Olivia on to it first. She can ring the company. Send them a photograph of the shoes and see what they come up with."

* * *

Josh's stomach was rumbling as they headed from the hospital to the school. Mandy glanced at him.

"Have you got the cleaned-up photo yet?" Josh checked, showed her. Then, remembering, she said, "Sorry, I didn't give you the chance to pick up something at the coffee shop. Doesn't Lisa make you sandwiches or something to take in with you?"

"You've got to be joking. She says if I want sandwiches then I should go and get them myself."

"Does she take stuff with her to work?"

"Yeah. An apple and a banana. Permanent diet." His stomach grumbled again.

"Look, there's some cereal bars in the back. I get them for when Tabitha needs a quick bite. Not exactly healthy, but they fill a gap. We can't have you rumbling away like Vesuvius when we're trying to talk to these boys. Daniel especially. Cocky little bugger."

"Well, it's easy to see why you never had kids." Josh was quick to respond.

Yeah, never had kids. Too busy doing this bloody job to have time for a relationship. A fleeting thought about Lucas. Would it have worked out if they both hadn't been so focused on their careers? And the other complication.

"Sorry. I didn't mean, you know."

"Forget it." Mandy said, "I've got Tabitha to think of now, thanks to my elusive twin sister."

Josh was crunching at the second cereal bar, dropping crumbs over himself and the Juke. How did Lisa put up with him?

"No word from her? Joy, I mean. Your twin sister." Josh asked.

"Nah. She came back to Cardiff end of May, when I eventually found her. Less than two months back home, lover boy rings and off she goes again. Can't blame her, I suppose, except it's messed up Tabitha's head again. She doesn't say anything. I can see it in her eyes."

"She's lucky she's got you to look out for her."

They arrived at the school and pulled up in the carpark. Lunch was over although there were a few stragglers about. Mandy gave a grunt of disapproval. "Don't they do anything about keeping these bloody kids in school? There's no-one around to ask them what they think they're doing when they should be in class."

"Could be they've got free lessons."

"Huh. At least when we skipped lessons, we kept a low profile. Got out of the place pronto." She pulled back her shoulders. "Right. Let's see what these clowns have to say. You can take the lead. Down with the kids, like." Mandy did a mock slouching walk and gave Josh a thumbs up.

They waited for someone to open the door, showed their identification, explained the reason for the visit, and were asked to wait while the headteacher was informed.

"Do all schools smell the same? Cabbage, feet and pheromones. "I think I prefer the mortuary."

It seemed to take an age before the receptionist, or whoever she was, signalled for them to follow her along the corridor. She ushered them into an office lined with books and filing cabinets, not dissimilar to Withers' office at the station. A dark-haired woman with tortoiseshell spectacles sat behind a desk which seemed to dwarf her. She stood up when they came in. An air freshener dispensed a cloying waft of artificial scent. It was worse than the institutional smell in the corridors.

"Joanna Sharpe. Our head is in a governors' meeting. I'm his deputy and authorised to speak to you."

"Detective Inspector Wilde and Detective Sergeant Jones. You'll have been told the reason we're here?"

Joanna Sharpe pushed her specs further up her nose. "Yes. I knew nothing of this. I saw the police vans this morning, however, I'd no idea any of our pupils were involved."

"We need to speak to the boys again. To get some further information. Probably best in a familiar environment than the police station, don't you think?" Formal statements would have to be taken later anyway. "Would it be possible for a member of staff to be present?"

Flushing, the little woman came around the desk. "Of course. Who do you need to see?"

Josh consulted his notebook. "Luke Roberts, Asif Khan and Daniel Levin."

"I see. Daniel's father is one of our governors. He is probably in with the headmaster now." She took a deep breath.

Mandy kept her eyes fixed on the woman's face.

Ms Sharpe held herself upright, her mouth a thin line. "They are all in lower six so if they are not in lessons, they should be in the common room." She had a precise way of speaking, formal, no doubt honed by years of dealing with stroppy teenagers and their parents.

Mandy and Josh exchanged looks. More likely those three had sneaked off to the local pub.

"If you'd like to take a seat, I'll go and find out. You may use this office for the interviews, and I shall stay to hear what they have to say." Despite her stature this was a woman used to giving orders and demanding respect.

"We'd like to see them together, please." Mandy tried a friendly smile as the deputy head bustled out of the room.

"A bit up herself, isn't she? Daniel's father is a governor. Interesting. Might be why he's such a little prick. Privilege and entitlement going hand in hand."

"Could be. We'll see how he behaves with her watching. Maybe he'll be more docile."

Mandy snorted. "His type thinks the rest of us are here to serve. I bet the father is equally as obnoxious."

The clicking heels returned and Joanna Sharpe entered followed by the three lads. Time to talk.

CHAPTER FOUR

Ms Sharpe indicated to the boys where to place their chairs and Mandy and Josh adjusted theirs to face them. Joanna Sharpe retreated behind her desk again. Mandy studied the boys. Luke was sitting upright; Asif on the edge of his chair, hands clasped together between his knees and Daniel slouched with an air of boredom, real or contrived. It was hard to tell.

"So, you're all in lower sixth. I hope you made it in time for your maths test," said Mandy.

A murmur of assent.

"I take it you're all over seventeen." She glanced at the deputy head who nodded.

"It was Asif's birthday yesterday and he's the youngest," Ms Sharpe said, in a formal tone.

"Daniel." At the mention of his name, the lad looked at Mandy and gave an overdramatic yawn. "I believe your father is in a meeting somewhere in the building." Mandy continued, "Would you like to have him present while we talk to you?"

For a second Daniel's eyes widened and then, wary again, he shrugged. "Not bothered."

Despite the indifferent response, he looked at Ms Sharpe. Neither of them moved. Time to crack on.

"Right. We need to get the facts straight. What time did you go into the woods this morning?"

"About quarter past eight, I guess." Luke's gaze was steady, his eyes guileless. "We usually meet up outside school about the same time."

"And do you walk or get a lift?"

"I usually catch up with Asif on the way. Dan meets us outside. He comes from the other direction."

Asif nodded while Daniel seemed more interested in the books on the shelf by the door. A front or was he really so unconcerned? It was hard to tell. Bloody teenage boys. It didn't matter. They had their home addresses so could check the information.

"Do you normally go into the woods before school or was there a special purpose this morning?" It was easy to guess what they'd been up to, but she wanted to see the reactions.

"What's that got to do with anything? I thought you wanted to ask us about the body."

Daniel's voice was challenging, and Mandy could hear Ms Sharpe take a breath, almost a gasp.

"Well, it would be useful to know if it was routine or not. You may have seen this man before, if he was in the habit of walking in the woods. He may pass through there on his way to work. All sorts of reasons."

Asif, biting his lip, shifted in his seat and gave a sideways glance at Daniel.

"We went to have a quick fag before school. Alright? It's not something we do every day, but then we had this test. It was to relax us a bit." Daniel's eyes narrowed as he spat out his answer.

Satisfied now she had succeeded in needling him, Mandy carried on. "Am I right in thinking you went into Nant Fawr from the pathway leading from here," she waved towards the front of the school, "rather than any other entrance? There are several routes you could have taken."

They all nodded.

"Good. Did you see the man before you found him on the ground? Even from a distance?"

They all shook their heads.

"Did you see anyone?" She hoped for more information, not three stooges.

"Yes. There was a woman with a dog. A black Labrador," said Luke. "She passed us. She was on her way out as we were going in. I don't know her name, but I see her sometimes walking around the lake. The dog's called Joel. I've heard her calling him."

Mandy smiled at Luke. It was something. A regular walker in the woods. If they could locate her, she might be able to provide further details.

"Anything else? Any unusual noises, someone running off, anything at all. Even small details could be vital."

The boys said nothing, so Josh took out his phone. He scrolled to find the picture and passed it to Luke first.

"This is the man you found this morning. Have you seen him anywhere before?"

Luke frowned before passing it to Asif who swallowed and shook his head. Daniel took the phone.

"So, this is the bloke we found. Looks pretty ordinary." He passed the phone back to Josh.

"He didn't have any identification so the first thing we need to do is find out who he is. I'm surprised you didn't check for a pulse or something before you called the police."

"Asif was shitting himself." Daniel had a smirk on his face, despite the loud tutting from Ms Sharpe.

No doubt she'd reprimand him afterwards although Mandy suspected he didn't give a toss.

"We stood waiting to see if he moved. When we couldn't see any sign of breathing, I called for the police and an ambulance." Luke coloured. "I don't know if we should have done anything to help."

"Yeah, Mr CSI here," Daniel said, nodding towards Luke, "wouldn't let us go near in case we," he raised his hands and made quotation marks in the air, "'contaminated the scene.' As if we'd be so stupid to—"

"Quite right," Mandy interrupted. It didn't look as if they were going to gain anything further. "If you remember anything else, no matter how insignificant it seems, please let us know. You've been very helpful."

"Do you need to tell our parents?" Asif said, almost in a whisper. It was the second time he'd expressed the same concern. Said something about his upbringing.

Mandy turned to the deputy head. "I'll leave it with Ms Sharpe for now although I suggest you let your parents know about this morning. You'll need to make formal statements. And sometimes the shock of these things can affect you more than you expect and for longer. I'm glad the school are aware and I'm sure they'll support you if needed." She fixed them with a stare, took a card from her pocket and passed it to Luke. "This is my number. If you want to speak to me about anything, give me a buzz. If I'm not there, leave a message and I'll get back to you."

They stood, and with a word of thanks to Joanna Sharpe, left. A lead at least. The dog walker might have seen or heard something useful. They could hope.

CHAPTER FIVE

Back at Cardiff Central they caught up with the team and the latest news.

"Well, Olivia, what about those shoes? Did you ring the company? Ask if they'd be able to identify who they belonged to? It would be good to give Cinderella man a name."

"I rang them, and some bloke told me they couldn't give out personal information. Right up himself he was. He said someone would have to speak to his manager when he got back from lunch."

Mandy resisted the urge to thump the desk. "Bloody jobsworth. You did tell him they were found on a dead body, didn't you? I'm sure the bloke in the mortuary isn't going to complain." She sighed and rubbed her forehead. "Right. Give me the number. I'll give them both barrels."

She saw Josh exchange a glance with Olivia before he left the room. He knew her too well. It didn't take long before Mandy was speaking to the manager. She smiled at Olivia. She'd show her how to get results. The smile soon disappeared.

"I'm sure maintaining the privacy of your clients is a major concern, sir. However, we have a dead body, and he was wearing those shoes. Data protection does not cover the dead, so I'd be obliged if you'd forget the confidentiality bit and give us the name and address, now." She almost shouted the last word, fist clenched, and teeth gritted. "We need to inform his relatives of their loss before they hear it through the media."

A muffled sound from the other end of the line.

"Yes, sir. It's a dark brown brogue style. Size ten. Hardly worn so could have been purchased quite recently. I can send you through a photograph. Right. I see."

More mumbling.

"Yes, the person concerned died in Cardiff, although we think he may be Eastern European." Mandy rolled her eyes. God it was painful. Talk about pompous. He was a shoe seller not a member of the Royal family. The arse and crockery her Gran used to call the upper classes.

"What if we courier the shoe or send a member of the team to bring it to you? Could you identify the owner then and give us details? Right. Someone will come to see you, with the shoes, tomorrow. Thank you so much for your help." Olivia tried not to giggle.

Mandy slammed the phone down and a pen rolled off the desk. "Hell's bells. We have to take the bloody shoe to them so it can be identified by the last they made. Apparently, the style of shoe is the most popular and they have recently," she made quote marks in the air and mimicked the man's superior accent, "'diversified and are producing less expensive models.' Those shoes still probably cost more than my month's salary."

"Who'll take the shoe to London then?" Olivia flushed. "I don't like it there. I always get lost, I do." A little pause. "I'll go if you want me to."

"I'll ask Helen. She's got an aunt there so will be glad of an excuse. We need a name and address. She can charm Mr 'I'm so much better than you.'"

Josh came back, frustrated. "I've been to see if any reports had come in from the door-to-door. Not a dickybird. Nobody heard or saw anything unusual. Nobody remembered seeing a guy of his description. The uniforms on duty saw a couple of women with black dogs. None of them Labradors. Zilch."

Mandy sighed. "Rishi's report?"

"Here it is." Helen appeared, folder in hand. "He rang to say he had preliminary findings for you."

"And?"

Helen handed the folder to Mandy. "Natural causes. He had a weak heart. Rishi wants to do some more tests on blood and organ tissue to be certain. He says its likely SADS."

"What's SADS?" asked Josh.

"Sudden Adult Death Syndrome. It can be inherited so we need to find his family. They should be tested to see if they have the same condition." Helen's dark eyes held concern. She doubled up as family liaison officer for the team. Possibly having children had given her an edge on the empathy factor. Although if she had a child anything like Daniel Levin, she might not be so sympathetic towards others.

"What about the mark on his forehead. Where did he get it?" Olivia asked.

"Rishi reckons he hit it when he fell. There's no evidence of any sort of foul play," Helen replied.

"Finding his identity is priority then, if we aren't looking for a motive. Helen, how do you fancy a trip to London tomorrow? Visit your aunt, do a bit of shoe shopping?" Helen frowned as Mandy explained. "We need someone polite and persistent to go to Best, the firm who made Cinderella man's shoes, and get us a name and address. You can collect the shoes from Rishi. Tell him we'd like those other tests done as a priority, please."

"Don't know why she gets to go to London for the day. I'd have gone."

Oh God. What a pain in the arse Josh could be sometimes.

"I sent Helen because she knows her way around London and because I think with her winning way, she's likely to get further than any of us." She smiled at Josh. "You were great with those lads this morning. I itched to knock Daniel's head off. Little prick. We work well as a team because we're all different and we use those differences." She gave them a moment to consider it. "Okay, pep talk over. Now, all of you buck up your ideas and let's see if the Super will agree to a media splurge."

* * *

Superintendent Withers was reading a report when Mandy knocked the door. He glowered at her over the top of his gold-rimmed specs. Oh hell, he was still in a piss.

"Well?"

"The body in the woods, sir. I thought I'd give you an update."

He put the file down and steepled his hands in front of his 'I'm eating cat-shit' face.

"Anything interesting?"

"Rishi says he thinks it was natural causes. Sudden Adult Death Syndrome. He's going to do some further tests to make sure. There were no external signs of a struggle." No reaction. "The body was clean, well-nourished and the position he was found in, indicated he gripped his chest before collapse. His arm was under his body, across his chest, so we assume he felt pain before death."

"What else?"

"No ID on the body just a roll of banknotes. Two thousand, in fifties and twenties."

Withers sat up straight. Good, he was interested. For all he was a miserable bastard at times, he was still a detective at heart.

"Two K. Do you think he could be a fence for these robberies or linked to them?"

Oh, bloody hell. Same old tune.

"I don't think so, sir. We'll keep an open mind. We do have one lead and Helen is going to London to pursue it tomorrow." Don't ask. Present it as a fact.

"London. Why does she need to go there? It'll cost." The glower deepened. You could hold a pencil between those frown lines.

Bloody budget again.

"Shoe shopping, sir." She watched his face change as he struggled to understand. She had an urge to smile at confusing him. "Cinderella man, our unknown body, was wearing handmade shoes. Best, the company, make shoes for royalty and are very cagey about giving any information. To help, they need to see the shoes. They'll check against the lasts they have in stock and, we hope, give us a name."

Withers nodded. She could almost see him doing calculations in his head. At last, he grunted at her. "Was there something else?"

"Yes. We'd like to involve the press. Give them the photo and make an appeal for information. Somebody must know who he is."

A raised eyebrow, a hairy caterpillar crawling up his forehead. "Let's see what DC Probert finds tomorrow. We could have an identity by the morning and then we can release a statement. Once the press is asked to do anything they want something in exchange. Let's keep it quiet for now."

"Of course, sir. There'll be local speculation with the area cordoned off. Police presence indicates something has happened…" She tailed off at the look on Withers' face. Relationships with the press were not always pleasant although he was an expert at avoiding tricky questions.

"Let them speculate. We'll tell them what we want to tell them, and when it suits us, not them. Low profile. Right? Got it?"

"Sir."

Mandy exhaled as she closed the door behind her.

CHAPTER SIX

Mandy hung her coat on the pegs in the narrow hallway of her house in Brithdir Street. The radiator gave a welcoming warmth. Tabitha's shoes were stacked neatly to one side and Mandy kicked hers off as well. The tiled floor was cool underfoot then gave way to warmth as she entered the carpeted lounge.

The previous owner had knocked through, combining the rooms so it was more spacious. It was a welcoming room, painted a pale blue, restful and minimalist with a sofa and chair at the front and dining table towards the back. A footstool doubled as a coffee table and shelving in alcoves held a few books and a couple of tired looking plants. Tabitha was sitting at the dining table poring over her laptop.

"How's my favourite niece?"

With a smile, Tabitha looked up. "Your only niece. You're home early." She pointed to the screen. "What do you know about algebra? I'm stuck."

"Precious little. I scraped through my maths. I doubt if I'd be much help to you. Sorry." She peered at the screen over Tabitha's shoulder. "Nope. Not a clue. Why don't you leave it for a bit? Sometimes resting your brain helps." She patted her niece's shoulder. "I'll cook something. I popped into Lidl and got some chicken breasts and salad stuff. I thought I'd do my special chicken a la Mandy tonight."

Tabitha laughed and closed the computer, moving it to one side. "I'll lay the table."

"No rush. It'll be forty minutes or so. Relax. Have you been at your homework since you got in?"

"Yeah. All done except one last problem. You're right. I can't think straight now." She paused. "Mum rang earlier." Tabitha got up, rolled her shoulders, made for the sofa, slumped into a corner and pulled her feet up. She looked young and vulnerable curled up, scrolling on her pinging phone. Messages from friends, no doubt. One of them could solve the maths issue.

"So, why didn't she ring me? Or wait until she knew I'd most likely be home? What's the news? What does she want now?" Despite herself, Mandy couldn't stop the edge to her voice. Her niece shrugged and looked at the floor.

"She said she's had an e something. Peel or pith and knee. A word I wasn't sure about. I didn't know if it was some sort of beauty treatment or what."

"Epiphany?" Despite her annoyance, Mandy's mouth twitched at the idea of the beauty treatment. Much more Joy's sort of thing than any insight into her behaviour or its consequences.

"Yeah. That's it. She was sorry and all. Usual stuff. So, what's an epiphany?"

"A moment of coming to your senses. Well, if it's true, it's taken her nearly forty years. What else did she say?"

"Not much. She had an idea and would talk it through with you. She's going to come back soon. Zac or Zorro, or whatever the latest man is called, isn't who she thought he was." Her voice wobbled a little as she stared at the fireplace. Although Tabitha pretended it didn't matter, Mandy could see through the act to the vulnerable teenager below.

"Oh well. I'll have to wait to see what she has to say. It doesn't have to worry us, Tabs." She plonked herself down on the sofa beside Tabitha and patted her leg. "I'm here for you. No matter what. Always remember."

Mandy took a deep breath. She loved her twin sister although there was no denying Joy was a total liability. Walking out on her daughter was one thing. To keep bouncing back, and bringing trouble with her, was another. They thought, when she'd cleaned up her act and got a steady job as a care assistant, albeit with false references, that she'd changed. Wrong. When the lover phoned and begged her to go back to Greece, she'd dropped everything. Bloody Joy brought nothing but shit with her. What flaming scheme did she have in mind now?

Cooking was a relaxation Mandy didn't always have time for. She hummed to herself as she stood in the kitchen. Like the rest of the house, it was neat and tidy. Tabitha had poured herself some fruit juice when she'd got in and the glass was in the sink. Mandy bent to put it into the dishwasher, almost dropping it when next door's cat leapt on to the windowsill and meowed.

"Satan. Cut it out. No treats today after scaring me."

The cat gazed at her, pacing up and down and pawing at the window. In the end, Mandy gave in, and threw a few treats out of the back door. The black cat leapt down and hoovered them up. He licked his lips and leapt back over the wall again.

Before long the aroma of fresh herbs and cooked chicken filled the room. Over the weekend she'd make a vegetable lasagne for the freezer and a big pot of curry. Home-made ready meals for when the job demanded long hours. As she cooked, Mandy pondered on Cinderella man. Some things didn't fit. How could a young man from Eastern Europe afford handmade shoes? Why was he not carrying any identity? Where had the money come from? It wasn't counterfeit, although so much money raised her suspicions. Was he involved in something dirty? Drugs? Let's hope Helen's mission proved a success.

The cat was back. A light rain had started, and he was scratching at the back door.

"Oh no, Satan. You can't come in. I know it's wet out there. Tough luck."

"Who are you talking to?" Tabitha had appeared with her phone in her hand. What was it about teenagers and their phones? Needed to be surgically removed they were so attached. Josh was the same though, and he was a lot older, at least in some ways.

"It's that bloody cat. I gave him treats and now he wants to take up residence. He'll be sitting with us at the table next."

Tabitha padded up to the door. "Poor puss. Go home. You can't come in. Aunty Mandy might cook you."

Mandy was laughing as the black tail disappeared over the wall again.

"Have you seen this?" Tabitha held her phone where Mandy could view the screen. "It's a short video... it looks sort of real."

They could hear singing, "If you go down to the woods today, you're in for a big surprise," then a blurred video of a man lying face down. "Guess what we found in the woods today? Beware. There could be a killer about." A ghoulish face appeared, and the video stopped. It had been posted by someone calling themselves Dan the man.

Mandy thumped the work surface. "The little sh... now the media will have a field day and Withers will have me on the chopping block. Is it possible to take it down?"

"I think whoever put it there can do it. What's it all about? Is it real? Is there a killer in the woods?" Tabitha had paled as she tucked her hair behind her ear.

Should have checked their phones. Damn. Mandy put her arm around her niece and gave her a hug. "No Tabs, there's no killer in the woods. We found a body. It was a young man with a weak heart who had died of natural causes. If the video goes viral, we'll have an awful problem with the media."

"It's had thousands of views and comments."

Mandy closed her eyes. "Too late then. The wrath of Withers tomorrow. He won't remember he was the one who didn't want press involvement. No prizes for guessing who will get the blame? I'll get Josh to deal with Daniel. I might be tempted to violence if I go near him."

CHAPTER SEVEN

THURSDAY

Superintendent Withers was waiting when Mandy arrived at the station the next morning. Red-faced, tight-lipped and curt.

"Wilde. Office. Now."

Josh had followed Mandy into the building and hurried to a desk before he was caught in the Super's wrath.

"Close the door."

Bad news. It meant a major bollocking. She could guess why, even though it wasn't her fault. She steeled herself for the onslaught.

"Certain members of the press have been on to me this morning. About a killer in the woods. Why haven't they been given a statement about the body?"

"You suggested we kept a low profile, sir. I did ask for the photo to be–"

"You know what the press are like. They were bound to find out. You should have thought about it." He was almost hissing the words.

Bloody marvellous. She was going to get the blame for all of it. Gritting her teeth and holding her head high, Mandy said nothing. Let him rant until he'd worn himself out and then she could get on with her job.

"The reporter who's always hanging about, whatshisname, says there's a video. Something about a clock ticking."

Todd Blakeney, the sneaky bugger. Reporter who was always after a story. A bubble of laughter rose inside her despite the seriousness of the situation. A clock ticking. Well, the Super wasn't down with the kids then. Should she explain or let him carry on?

"What's it about? What video?" His voice was getting louder by the second. "Who the hell has made a video and what can we do about it?"

"It's a social media site called TikTok, sir. Younger people use it. I've seen the video. I know who posted it. I'll make sure we see the individual concerned and have it removed." And roast his balls on a platter.

"What does it show?"

Should she let him see the video? Would it make things worse? Difficult to judge when the Super was in one of his moods. Of course, he'd be getting flak from higher up as well. No doubt the chief would be on his back.

"It's a little blurry. A shot of the body and someone singing the teddy bear's picnic." And a warning about a killer. Plus, it had gone viral. Best not let him see it.

"Get it sorted. I'll draft a statement for the press. Any update on the identity?"

Christ, she'd only come through the door. Did he think she was bloody psychic or something?

"Not yet, sir. DC Probert has an appointment at nine with the shoe company. We're also looking through missing persons' files. He's a bit of a mystery."

"Keep at it. I don't like mysteries."

"Sir."

As Mandy left the office, she rolled her eyes at Josh and Olivia.

"Withering is in a right piss. You've seen the video?"

They both nodded.

"Well, he's going spare over it. All my fault for not briefing the press, despite him telling me to keep things quiet. Frigging stupid. You know who did it, don't you?"

"Dan the man," said Josh. "Kid's got problems."

"Problems? He's got more problems now. Interfering with a police inquiry for a start. Come on then, Josh. Let's see what our little friend has to say for himself. Is he at school this morning or off trying to find another body? Olivia, keep checking those missing persons, will you, please? It's a long shot but you never know."

Mandy powered out, followed by a tired-looking Josh. Either he'd had another row with Lisa and slept on the sofa or the reconciliation was going better than expected. Whatever. None of her business as long as it didn't interfere with his work. He needed to take the lead with Daniel.

* * *

If Ms Sharpe was surprised to see them, she didn't show it. She probably knew about the video. No doubt it had caused a stir. School had started so, apart from a few dawdlers in the corridors, it was relatively peaceful. A quiet hum in the background and the sound of laughter now and again. Mandy shuddered. Give me a dead body any day. All those teenagers. No way. Dealing with one was hard enough. And peer pressure. God, the memories.

Daniel came into the room and sat down where Ms Sharpe indicated. He didn't look so tough this morning without his buddies to back him up.

Josh nodded to him. "I guess you know why we're here, Daniel." Straight to the point.

Daniel said nothing, looked at his feet. Then, with a sigh, he met Josh's eyes. "It's the vid, isn't it?"

"Bit of a prank, was it?"

Daniel swallowed and nodded with a sideways glance at Ms Sharpe who sat upright behind her desk, disapproval written in her stance. It was possible she'd already spoken to him about it.

"You realise your little prank has not helped our inquiries, don't you?" said Josh. "In fact, scaring people into believing there's a killer on the loose is irresponsible. You could be in serious trouble."

"I don't suppose your father knows," said Mandy.

Daniel sneered. "As if he'd care. He doesn't notice anything I do. All I get is nagging about passing exams, getting a good job. If he knew about it, I'd get a bollocking and then he'd ignore me again."

Josh and Mandy exchanged a glance. Mandy heard Ms Sharpe sigh. Josh could be right. This kid, despite his privileged background, was troubled.

Josh leaned closer to Daniel. "You know my old man was the same. Constant nagging to do better until I switched off. Didn't listen. Never felt I was good enough. Then, when he died four years ago, I found things that showed he'd been secretly proud of me. He just couldn't show it."

He paused and leaned back. "I'm sure your Dad only wants what's best for your future."

"Whatever." Despite the nonchalance, Daniel seemed to be listening. "Funny way of showing it."

"That's parents for you. A nuisance at times. Just don't assume, like I did, that he doesn't care. It's a mistake I'll always regret."

Daniel looked away. They waited until he broke the silence. "I'm sorry. I was a dick. Sorry, miss." A quick look towards Ms Sharpe who inclined her head a little. "Thing is. I think I recognise the dead bloke."

Something new. Mandy held her breath.

Josh bent further forward and almost whispered, "We still don't know who he is."

"I'm pretty sure it was him. Couple of weeks ago. I was on my bike. Paper round." He looked towards the ceiling and then back at Josh. "He was with another bloke. Same age. Looked similar. Bit foreign, like. I nearly bumped into them, and they said something in," he shrugged, "some sort of language I didn't understand. It didn't sound too friendly, so I didn't hang about."

"Can you tell us where this was? Better still, show us the exact spot on a map."

When Daniel responded with a smile, Mandy could see the boy behind the façade of indifference. Well done, Josh.

Google Maps identified the place where Daniel claimed to have seen Cinderella man. It was a sort of alley between houses in the north of the city. Not far, as the crow flies, from where they had discovered the body.

"Dan, you're a star."

For a second, Mandy thought Josh was going to do a high five and cringed at the thought.

"Do you think you could talk to someone to put together an e-fit picture of this other man?"

"Sure."

The stroppy teenager had gone.

When they got back into the car Mandy turned to Josh. "I didn't know about your old man."

"Doesn't matter. Before I joined the team. Why would you know?"

"You were bloody brilliant. I'd never have got through to him. We've got another lead. I'm proud of you, DS Jones."

Josh scrambled in his pocket for a nicotine mint.

"I hope Lisa appreciates you. You'll make a wonderful dad."

"God. What's the matter with you? Going soft or something?"

They were still laughing when they exited the school gates.

CHAPTER EIGHT

As they were approaching the station, Helen rang.

"Good news and bad news. Which do you want first?" Helen's voice sounded disembodied, as if she were talking from a tunnel or something.

"Give me the good. A possible identification and a name would be great."

"Well, I've got a name and address in Cardiff." Mandy gave a thumbs up to Josh.

"Yes. Excellent, Helen. I knew you'd wheedle it out of those stuffed shirts one way or another. What's the bad?"

She could hear Helen draw breath and then, "It's not our man."

"What do you mean? How do you know?"

"The guy I spoke to remembered the client in question, as it was his first pair of handmade shoes. Apparently, this client said he'd always wanted handmade shoes. He was having problems with his joints so decided to treat himself for his birthday."

"And?"

"His seventieth birthday."

"Shit."

"Sorry. I showed the picture of the deceased to him. He was adamant. He didn't recognise our bloke and the

49

shoes were definitely made for a man in his late sixties. Medium build, grey hair, thinning on top, about five foot ten. Nothing like Cinderella man."

"Shit. Shit. Shit." Mandy slapped the steering wheel. "So, our bloke was wearing someone else's shoes?"

"Seems the case. Do you want the address anyway?"

"Yeah. We'll check it out." Josh made a note of the address. "I don't recall anyone reporting stolen shoes in these burglaries. Never mind, we'll pop up there now. Thanks, Helen. Enjoy the rest of your day."

Mandy turned to Josh. "Why would someone spend so much money on a pair of shoes and then get rid of them? It's not making sense. The address is off Cyncoed Road, isn't it?"

* * *

Set back from the road, the detached house they pulled up in front of was in a quiet area. They rang the doorbell and heard the chimes before a tall, steel-haired woman appeared. Mandy and Josh produced their warrant cards and introduced themselves.

"Mrs Price-Williams?" asked Mandy, "We're here to see your husband, please. Is he at home?"

"No."

The curt response fitted with the hostile look in the woman's grey eyes. She had the appearance of someone who knew how to look after herself. Hair and nails immaculate, dressed in casual, well-structured, clothing and wearing gold earrings and matching necklace as well as a wedding ring and large diamond solitaire. Her imperious look didn't worry Mandy. The questions had to be answered.

"When is he likely to be back? We'd like to ask him a few questions. He's not in trouble of any sort. It's part of an ongoing inquiry and we think he may be able to help us."

Mrs Price-Williams sighed, and her shoulders sagged. She no longer sounded aggressive or suspicious when she replied, "My husband is beyond questions. You'll find him in Thornhill cemetery."

Josh stepped in. "Our sincere apologies, Mrs Price-Williams. We were unaware of the facts. We're sorry for your loss. Do you think we could come in, please? We can explain this intrusion on your privacy and bereavement."

Mrs Price-Williams opened the door and indicated for them to enter, before leading them, with a slight limp, to a spacious and bright lounge at the back of the house. A hint of expensive perfume wafted behind her. Something like Chanel or Givenchy, no doubt. No chance Mandy would have a clue. Perfume was for nights out – a rare enough event. Bifold doors looked out over an immaculate garden and a large summerhouse at the bottom, the size of a double garage or bigger. The room was furnished in an understated classy style, brown leather sofas and rosewood side tables. Above the mantlepiece, where a mock log fire danced in the grate, hung a huge silver-framed mirror. It reflected the vibrant colours of the paintings on the walls, watercolours and oils, which looked like originals. No Ikea for Isobel Price-Williams.

"May we?" Mandy indicated the matching sofas.

Isobel Price-Williams nodded. "Perhaps you can explain why you wanted to speak to my husband. I can't imagine him being in any trouble."

"Of course." Mandy cleared her throat. "I don't know whether you heard about the young man's body found in Nant Fawr?"

"Yes, yes, I heard something." She frowned, "I don't see how it is connected to my late husband."

Taking a deep breath, Mandy said, "The dead man was wearing handmade shoes. We've been to see the makers in London, and they're certain those shoes belonged to your husband."

Mrs Price-Williams slumped back in her seat and placed a hand on her chest. She exhaled with an audible sound somewhere between a sigh and a groan. With a shake of her head, she stared at them both, incredulous.

"Have you any idea how it could have happened, Mrs Price Williams?" Josh asked.

"My daughter sorted out all my husband's clothes and shoes. I couldn't face it. Much too painful. George died very suddenly. It's been quite a shock," she shuddered, "Clare, my daughter, took some things back to Coventry with her, I believe. Some shirts and pyjamas, new, unworn, for her husband. Everything else she bagged and passed to one of my neighbours, well she used to be a neighbour. Ruth downsized and moved."

Mandy nodded as Mrs Price-Williams stared into space with a glazed expression. "I think she was going to take things to the charity shop. I really don't know where the shoes went. He paid a lot of money for those.

George always wanted handmade shoes as his feet bothered him especially as he grew older." Her eyes filled with tears. "Then he didn't get a chance to wear them."

"I'm so sorry if we've added to your distress. I'm sure we don't need to bother you further. If I could have the name and contact number for your friend?" Mandy asked. "She may be able to tell us which charity she donated the bags to. It would be very helpful."

"Of course. I'm sure Ruth won't mind." Isobel picked up her iPhone from the side table, scrolled through, and gave them the full name and address.

Josh made notes while Mandy gazed out over the garden. A man emerged from the summerhouse and made his way up the pathway to the house.

"There's someone in your garden."

"Oh, it's Simon, my son. He took over the business when George died. He was already involved although George kept a tight rein. The office is down there. I didn't want messy paperwork hanging around the house."

"What business, madam?" asked Mandy.

"Wine import. Williams' Wonderful Wines. You've probably seen the lorries. We bring in wines, mainly from France. I do think the French know about wine, don't you?" Isobel paused then carried on. "He sells to restaurants, small outlets around the country and so on. I don't know a lot about it. Best to leave these things to them. Simon goes to France a couple of times a year. He drives the lorry himself. It allows the men to see he's not afraid of hard work and helps him to make valuable contacts in the trade. It's good to keep it in the family."

A definite glow of pride accompanied her words. Isobel Price-Williams was still a force to be dealt with. Her husband's sudden death had shaken although not floored her.

Simon, who must have spotted the strangers in the room, appeared seconds later. He didn't have his mother's patrician looks, his features ruddier and his frame more thickset although with his height, he carried it well.

Isobel introduced them and said, "Your father's shoes were on the body of the man found in Nant Fawr. These detectives are trying to find out who he is, poor soul." Her face was impassive. Simon exchanged a look with her before responding.

"You gave everything away, didn't you? I thought Clare sorted it." He seemed perplexed by the situation, a little crease forming between thick eyebrows. Dark brown like his curly hair.

"Yes. She took some stuff and asked Ruth to deal with the rest. I don't know where it went."

* * *

Back in the car Josh popped a nicotine mint into his mouth. "A dead end."

"Not necessarily. We go and see this Ruth…?"

"Crozier. You want to go now? The address she gave us is only about a mile or so away. In Rhiwbina."

"Yeah. Let's do it. What did you make of it all? Price-Williams?"

"Business must be doing well. That home office is as big as our house."

"Yeah. And what about wine, Josh? What's your opinion? Do you think French wines are superior?" Mandy mimicked the woman's accent.

"Dunno. We have whatever's on offer in Lidl at the weekend. Don't care where it's from as long as it doesn't make me puke up. Lisa loves the fizzy stuff – Prosecco. I told her it's only white wine with liver salts. She insists she likes it. All it does is give me wind. Rather have a good pint of Rev James any day."

"Well, I bet Williams Wonderful Wines doesn't sell anything cheap and cheerful. Not if their house is anything to go by."

CHAPTER NINE

Rhiwbina village was busy as they drove through. A mixture of shops, charities sitting side by side with boutique art, craft styled premises and the usual mini-market, coffee shops and restaurants. Ruth Crozier lived in a nondescript bungalow at the head of a cul-de-sac with a garage to one side and a stretch of lawn bordered by flowerbeds with plants in varying stages of decay. She was getting into her car when Mandy and Josh arrived.

Mandy had expected someone about the same age as Isobel Price-Williams so was surprised to see a woman in her forties, dressed in typical office clothing of a navy trouser suit, white blouse and smart court shoes with a low heel. Her blonde hair was shoulder length and shaped around her face. Like the other woman her nails were painted a pearly pink, not a chip in sight, or a showy ring, just a plain gold band.

Thank God her job didn't demand such a degree of personal grooming. Mandy patted her frizzy hair and straightened her jacket.

"Ruth Crozier?"

Mrs Crozier seemed startled at first when she saw their warrant cards. Then she relaxed a little. "Is this about the attempted break-in?"

"Break-in?" Josh exchanged a glance with Mandy.

"In the shop."

"Shop?"

Ruth scowled at them. "Yes. My estate agency. Movers and Shakers. I think someone tried to get in on Sunday night. I reported it. A young constable came and took some notes. I was hoping you had news."

"I'm afraid not, Mrs Crozier. We've come about a different matter." Mandy watched Ruth's face as she continued, "Your friend, Mrs Price-Williams, gave us your contact details."

"Isobel? Why? Has something happened to her? To Simon?" She put a hand to her throat. "Why are you here?" Rapid fire questions as she glanced from one to other.

"Nothing serious. Purely an enquiry. Better have a quiet word inside," said Mandy, nodding towards the net curtains of the neighbouring house where she had spotted movement.

"I haven't got long." She glanced at her watch. "I popped home to check something and there's only a temp in the shop."

"Two minutes."

With an overdramatic sigh, Ruth Crozier opened the front door and they stepped into the hall, Mandy catching the floral tones of the woman's perfume. Mrs Crozier made no attempt to take them any further into her home. The hallway was narrow and afforded a glimpse of the kitchen at the back and doors to other rooms.

"It's about the bags of clothing Mrs Price-Williams gave you after her husband died." A little pause to let the information sink in. "She said you were going to take them to the charity shop.'

"Clare, her daughter, asked me to do it. She said her mother was too distressed to deal with the stuff. If I'd known how much of it there was, I'd have made some excuse. Clare forgets I have a business to run." Her lips pursed before she continued, "Although, of course, I was glad to help Isobel."

Interesting. No love lost between Ruth and Clare though some sympathy towards the mother. And she'd asked about Simon.

"Did you look at the contents of the bags?"

"And when do you imagine I would have time to look through what amounted to a jumble sale?"

"Do you remember which shops you took the bags to?"

"Albany Road. Some of it is still in the garage. I passed on some of the bags to a couple of friends of mine. There was a ton of it. At least two carloads. What is this about? I can't believe the police are searching for charity stuff. Surely the pay's not so bad?"

It was almost a sneer and Mandy straightened, making the six-inch height difference between the women seem more. "We're investigating a death, Mrs Crozier. A young man was found dead in Nant Fawr woods yesterday. I'm sure you've heard something about it. We're trying to discover his identity. He was wearing shoes belonging to the late Mr Price-Williams. We're endeavouring to find out how he got them." Mandy smiled, a polite smile which didn't reach her eyes. "Now, the names and addresses of your friends, please. And a list of which shops you donated items to."

Josh made notes as Mandy scrutinised the woman. Close up she could see the wrinkles on her hands. Nearer fifty than forty, well preserved. Another widow. Wonder what her husband died from. A tongue lashing perhaps. She could imagine Ruth Crozier making everyone jump to attention. Had she always run the estate agency? Idle thoughts. What was more important was tracing those shoes.

As they emerged from the house again there was the invasive sound of a pneumatic drill, then hammering and builders shouting.

"Looks as though someone's busy," Mandy said.

"There's always building work going on here. I thought it would be quiet. Since I moved in it seems all my neighbours have decided on home improvements. And those builders," she shook her head, "start at first light even on a Sunday. Is there some law to stop them doing it?"

"It's a code more than a law." Josh replied. "Speak to your neighbours first and the council."

They made a hasty retreat, as did Ruth Crozier, zipping out of the cul-de-sac in her blue mini. Mandy's phone rang when they got back into the car. Withers. She rolled her eyes at Josh as she answered and put it on speakerphone.

"Wilde. I'm being pestered by the press over this body in the woods. Do you have anything?"

No. Except what is probably another dead end. "We've spoken to the widow of the chap who owned the shoes, sir."

"Widow. He's dead then?"

God he ought to go on Mastermind with those skills. "He died a few months ago, sir. His daughter bagged his clothes and shoes and gave them to an ex-neighbour. We've just left her home. Ruth Crozier, the ex-neighbour, distributed some of the bags to friends and took others to charity shops. We have the names and addresses of the other ladies, and we'll talk to them as well."

Withers groaned. He asked, "So, nothing much then?"

"Some leads. Unfortunately, no indication of the identity of Cinderella man. Sir."

"Okay. I'll issue a statement saying we are pursuing several lines of inquiry. Meanwhile there's been another burglary. At least try to get some results. Our stats are down this month. I'm getting hassle about it and all I can do is fill in the forms and pray you lot catch the weasels."

Mandy raised an eyebrow at Josh and finished the call. "Bloody burglars and bloody stats. Let's find a sandwich somewhere before we track down the names on Ruth's list."

They'd got their takeaway orders when Mandy's phone rang again.

"Got it. We're on our way." Mandy turned to Josh. "Your food will have to wait. They've had a call about something suspicious up in Pantmawr. It could be our little gang of thieves. Let's head up there now and see if we can nab them."

Five minutes later they were at the address they'd been given to find an empty house and no sign of a break-in. The neighbour was digging a flowerbed, replacing the summer bedding with winter pansies and heather.

Josh approached him. "Excuse me, sir. Did you report a break-in?" He waved his warrant card and nodded towards the adjoining house.

"No." The man stood up and leaned on his spade. "Why would anyone break in there? Been empty for ages. Nothing in there to pinch."

Had they got the right address? Mandy rang the station to check and then frowned. "We're at the right place. We'd better have a look around the back and check things out."

The search was fruitless. Everything was secured and the back windows had been covered with metal sheeting to provide an extra layer of security. Who had rung in with the information?

"We'd better pop back to the station and see what's going on. The call can be traced, or the postcode is different or something. Let's see."

"Can I have my sandwich now?"

"Eat your bloody sandwich. I don't need you passing out from starvation."

Back to Central where Olivia had bad news for them. "Seems the thieves have been at it again. A house over in Radyr about the time we had the anonymous tip about Pantmawr."

"Little buggers. It was a decoy and we fell for it. Let's sit and work out the pattern again. See if we can anticipate where they'll strike next. Plus, we need to organise a trawl of the charity shops on Albany Road and see if any of them recognise Cinderella man."

"What about those names Ruth Crozier gave us?" asked Josh.

Mandy pointed to the clock. "I doubt if we'll get overtime. If it's death by natural causes the Super will be watching the budget. Let's write up what we've got from Ruth Crozier and start again in the morning. Did she say anything much about the friends? I was studying her. What age would you say?"

"Sixty?"

"What?" Mandy laughed. "You haven't a bloody clue, have you? I reckon mid to late forties. She looks after herself. It's the hands. They are the giveaway. Hands age faster."

"She said something about widows. I think her friends are all widows too."

"Well, I reckon she has a look that could kill at fifty paces. Okay, the merry widows tomorrow and see what they've done with the stuff from Price-Wiliams." Turning towards Olivia, Mandy asked, "Any sign of a mobile yet? Did they widen the search?"

"Yeah, they did. Nothing. The stream level was high so they're going to look under the bridge tomorrow. Maybe they'll find something."

"I hope so, otherwise it will be visits to every sodding charity shop in Cardiff or hope someone sees his picture and calls in. Surely to God, somebody will give us a clue to the poor bugger's name." She sighed. Maybe he was a refugee. They should ask the immigration people or the Jobcentre. Then again, with two grand in his pocket. What was it all about?

CHAPTER TEN

Tabitha had left a note on the dining table saying she'd gone round to Kelly's for a while. The friendship had continued despite the debacle in the spring when they'd been in danger. Kelly was the sort to attract trouble.

Tempting though it was to loll in front of the television as darkness descended, Mandy decided to give the bathroom a thorough cleaning. Rishi should have the tests back after the weekend. From the evidence, it all pointed to a heart attack. Dreadful in such a young man. She thought again about the information Daniel had given them. Who was the other guy with Cinderella man and why, when the press was full of the news, hadn't he come forward? It was very odd. Unless...

Bathroom cleaning abandoned and grabbing a pencil, she scribbled on the back of an old envelope. Thoughts and actions. Door to door in streets close to where Daniel had spotted Cinderella man with someone else – also eastern European; speak to Ruth Crozier's friends and follow any leads; chase up and check reports from the area where the body was found. She stopped. There was something else. Yes. A dog walker. A woman and a black dog called Joel. Had they found her yet?

Grasping at straws. It's the way it was sometimes. She really needed to learn how to switch off from the job.

A creak of hinges followed by a clunk as the front door shut again, indicated Tabitha was home. A distraction from work worries.

"Hi Tabs, how's things?"

Tabitha sighed, kicked off her shoes and dropped her bag at the side of the sofa. "Okay, except we've got course work to be finished over half-term. So much for having a break."

"You'll fly through it. No problem, honey. Have you eaten?"

"Yeah. Kelly's mam did a pasta thing with chicken. I wouldn't mind a cuppa and biscuit though. Fancy a green tea? I'll put the kettle on."

Without waiting for an answer, she disappeared into the kitchen and Mandy could hear her rummaging in the cupboards and the grumbling of the kettle. Tabitha looked pale and stressed. School or something else? They both settled on the sofa.

"Has your mam rung again? I thought she was going to talk to me."

"No. Nothing more. She said the weekend. Do you really think she'll come home for Christmas? I mean…"

They both remembered the previous year and broken promises. No point in telling lies.

"I don't know, Tabs. Really, I don't." It was best to be straight. "My sis is as unpredictable as a dog's hind leg. If she doesn't ring me over the weekend, I'll call her. You're okay, aren't you? You'd tell your favourite auntie if anything was bothering you, wouldn't you?"

Mandy nudged Tabitha and grinned at her. Damn Joy. Didn't she have any idea what all this uncertainty was doing to her child? Perhaps she should apply to adopt Tabitha. After all, she was the one who'd been doing the parenting. Even when her sister was around, she behaved like a teenager. Almost forty and behaving like a fourteen-year-old. She felt Tabitha sit up straighter and fidget a little.

"Would you mind if I joined a drama group? My English teacher is starting a group for fifteen to eighteen-year-olds in the north Cardiff area." Eyes wide while biting her lip, Tabitha continued. "She wants to put on a play to make links with other secondary schools. She suggested I go along and see. Kelly too."

It was a bit of a surprise. No doubt Kelly would be hoping to join as the route to stardom. From what Mandy had seen she was a wannabe. But Tabs? It would do her good. Take her out of herself. Give her some confidence and self-esteem.

"Sounds a great idea. When does it start?"

"Saturday morning. We're going to meet at a church hall in Roath." She seemed to perk up as she spoke.

"Brilliant." Mandy paused. "On one condition."

Tabitha nodded, unsure what was coming next.

"When you become famous, I want to be your escort on the red carpet. I'll buy the biggest ballgown I can find in silver lamé and wear six-inch heels so I can see over everybody."

They both collapsed in giggles before settling down to watch a crime drama on Netflix. Mandy was amused at how the detective in the series always got his man, no matter what difficulties and red herrings he passed on the way. If only it was so easy.

* * *

"We have to go to the police, Igor. Tell them about my brother."

"Are you mad? What do you think will happen then? You think they say, 'Oh thanks to you so much, sir. Have a nice day.' You know we can't do it, and you know why." It was harsh, uncompromising.

Paskal paced up and down the room. It was minimalist, not in a fashionable sense, furnished with an old worn sofa, two equally battered armchairs and an empty wooden wine crate where a small television perched, linked to a DVD player. The three other men in the room stared at the screen trying to ignore the growing argument. The volume was so low they had to lean forward to hear it above the raised voices. Although Paskal was younger and taller, there was no doubt who was in charge. Igor stood, legs apart, and glowered at him. His fists were clenched, ready for a fight. His thin lips curled in a sneer, revealing stained teeth, the front one chipped.

"You've had it too soft. Look at you." Igor gestured with a dismissive wave. "Hands like a girl. All soft skin and clean clothes. You need to keep a low profile. Like boss says. Come with us tomorrow. See what it's like to work for a living. Get your hands dirty instead of using your dick."

A muffled laugh from the sofa made Paskal spin around. He knew there was no chance of defeating Igor.

"You ask me to deny my brother. They'll put him in some unmarked grave or worse. Burn him and Mama will never know where her son lies. How can I do as you ask?"

Igor moved closer, hissed. "Because if you don't do as I tell you I swear you'll be sharing a coffin with your brother. Now, get some rest. The van comes at five. Wear warm clothes, not those fancy things they gave you. You'll have to use your strength in other ways until things calm down. Understand?"

After a moment, Paskal looked away, nodded. There was no choice. To admit he knew the dead man whose picture was all over the media would be to sign his own death warrant. It didn't make things right. Elio was lying alone in a cold mortuary with no-one holding vigil over his body. All he could do was pray for the soul of his older brother and for his own life. When they'd left home, he never imagined what way their lives would turn out. He looked in distaste at his companions and his surroundings. The house itself was secure. They had limited heating and hot water, but it was no better than the refugee camp they'd lived in before coming to this country, foul air and stagnation. The promise of a better life was a lie. Paskal groaned as he thought again about his brother and his hopes for their future.

"Don't worry. I have a plan." Elio had become more animated. "One of the clients has a soft spot for me. Look at the things she's given me. Clothes, extra food and money. There are several expensive things sitting, waiting to be taken."

"Stealing?"

"What do you think they are doing to us?" Elio's face had hardened, distorted with anger, the excitement gone in a flash. "You think I haven't stolen before. How do you think I've kept your belly full and away from danger?" He stabbed Paskal on the shoulder with his fingers. "How many times do you think I've had to do things to keep us safe? Things you don't have to do."

"What I do..."

"There are harder ways to earn money, little brother. It's distasteful, demeaning. It could be worse. Some of our companions who are not so pretty eh," he'd patted Paskal's cheek with affection, "do not have such work. They break their backs all day working until their skin breaks with blisters. Is that what you want?"

"No. They all lied. This is not how they told us it would be."

"Everybody lies. Don't worry. I have a plan. I'll get us the money to get out of here. A bus to London and then we melt into the crowds. We'll escape this... this situation and life will be ours to decide. Trust me."

Money. A different life. It had all seemed so possible when Elio had talked, now... what hope was left? Grief for his dead brother mixed with despair.

"I'm going for a smoke," he told Igor as he opened the back door and stepped out into the overgrown garden.

It was quiet out there, hidden from prying eyes by overgrown hedges full of brambles. Two glowing dots alerted him to the animal prowling in the undergrowth. It emerged, a shadow, from under the hedge and approached, meowing.

"No food today, *mace.'*

With a disgruntled hiss the cat disappeared around the side of the house. Paskal finished his cigarette and stubbed it out on the ground, the taste lingering in his mouth. It looked as though his schedule of work was changing so he needed to rest. Sleep would not come easy, and he would pray for the soul of his brother. Had someone killed Elio? The man on the television didn't say. If he had been caught stealing perhaps it's what happened. He didn't trust Igor. Best keep his head down and do as Igor said. One day there would be a chance. One day.

CHAPTER ELEVEN

FRIDAY

The team meeting on Friday morning was a recap; Josh tapping away on his computer, checking for anything new. They had contact with the woman with the black dog.

"Uniform spoke to her this morning. She'd been away on business on Thursday so someone else had taken the dog out. She was back on her usual early morning walk today." Helen read from her screen. "She doesn't recall seeing anyone fitting the description of Cinderella man. There was another dog walker she sometimes sees with a grey lurcher. He wasn't about on Wednesday."

"Nothing from the door to door either. Few houses with no reply, now. Couple empty, they said. So, a bit more trotting about." Olivia pushed a purple strand of hair behind her ear as she blinked over her glasses.

"Have they looked in detail at houses close to the alleyway Daniel showed us on the map?"

"Yeah. It's where they've got to go back. Checking on the ones with no answers, like."

"Right. So, nothing much then." A sigh. "What about the search of the area where the body was found? Bring up anything?"

The phone rang and Olivia picked it up while Helen shook her head. Olivia waved at them and then put the phone down.

"They've found a mobile near the bridge. It's been sent to forensics. They can't guarantee they'll get anything from it. Been in the water, so..." Olivia shrugged, and Mandy groaned.

"Bloody hell. Days drying out. We can't rely on it for info. It might not even be his. Okay. Carry on with the charity shops. We'll need to extend our search across the city if any of them send stuff to other branches."

"Sometimes they put clothes and shoes on eBay as well," said Helen. "Expensive stuff. He could have bought them from there."

"Thanks, Helen. God, perish the thought. It's our best lead so far. Josh, let's go and see if we can talk to Ruth Crozier's friends. Maybe they can help. Then again maybe I'm hoping for the moon and the stars. Let's get out of here before Withers corners us over the burglaries again. Whose first on the list? Nearest?"

Josh took out his notebook. "They both live in Llanishen. Not far from Nant Fawr woods. Then it does stretch a bit. Down almost as far as the lake and up to the reservoir the other way."

* * *

Their first stop was a white-faced house in a quiet side road. The front garden, despite the rain and wind of the previous week, looked immaculate. Not even a leaf from the fading maple tree littered the ground. A wooden wind chime made a pleasant sound as the breeze danced around it.

"Looks as though it's been clipped with manicure scissors," said Josh, surveying the lush green of the lawn.

"Mine's lucky if it gets a strimming twice a year. Artificial?"

A blackbird landed on the lawn and, after a bit of tugging, flew off with a worm in his orange beak.

"Don't think so."

There was no doorbell. Instead, the front door had a brass knocker in the shape of a dragonfly. Mandy rattled it and was rewarded by a cough and the sound of muffled footsteps approaching. The woman who opened the door was about fifty, ash blonde hair and dressed in skinny black jeans and a loose jumper in shades of pink. Mandy had seen a similar one in John Lewis with a gasp-worthy price label.

"Beverley Bowen? DI Wilde and DS Jones. Do you mind if we come in?"

Unlike Ruth Crozier, she gave them a welcoming smile. "Ruth rang to say you might be calling. Do come in and take off your shoes, please."

Josh caught Mandy's eye. He coloured as he struggled to undo his laces. They should have brought plastic shoe covers. Less undignified. Was it designed to make them feel uncomfortable? Mandy smiled when Josh removed his left shoe, exposing a hole in the toe of his sock. No wonder he looked ill at ease. Beverley raised one eyebrow and said nothing, leading them into a room overlooking the front garden with a bay window draped with silk curtains in eau-de-nil. The carpet was a light honey. She was wearing what looked like soft leather ballet pumps. Slippers? Shoes? Whatever. Shoeless cops were still able to ask questions.

With a wave of her arm, she indicated for them to sit down. She plumped the cushions on the chair opposite before easing herself into it. Crossing her ankles she sat upright, waiting. The fragrance of lavender filled the room. Furniture polish probably. Dare a speck of dust land in this house. Everything seemed to be in shades of cream and honey except for the white walls which were covered with bright and bold paintings. Originals, not prints, Mandy noted. Catching her appraisal of the art, Mrs Bowen smiled.

"You are admiring the collection, DI Wilde. My late husband's passion. He died of MS about three years ago. He was a talented artist himself before the illness robbed him of the ability. His father, Alexander, was quite famous."

She stood again and pointed to a small oil of a woman. "This is Alexander's portrait of Fonteyn. The ballerina," she added, meeting Mandy's blank look. "It's worth a small fortune. I won't sell it though. I've been selling off some of the others to raise cash for the charity I'm involved with. Helping the homeless. I'm so lucky and it's good to be able to help others."

She plumped the cushion again and flicked something invisible from her jeans before looking up at them again. "However, you haven't come here to talk about my life. You want to know where I took the bags Ruth gave me. Do you know, I've been trying to remember? I can't even recollect how many there were.

I know I took one bag, or maybe more, to Caerphilly."
She looked towards the ceiling as she ruminated. "You
can park there near one of the shops and drop off. I may
have given some to the homeless charity too. Goodness,
one doesn't always recall every little detail, does one?"

She looked from one to the other, blinking with a
fixed smile. She held both hands clasped on her knee,
diamond rings glinting when caught in the light.

"Did you notice a pair of shoes in any of the bags?"

"Shoes? I suppose there could have been shoes. I was
given black bags and asked to pass them on to charity. I
think Ruth was surprised at the number of bags Clare had
given to her to distribute. It's why she asked Rebecca
and I to help."

"And how do you know Mrs Crozier?"

Beverley Bowen shifted a little in her seat. A hint of
pink touched her neck, almost matching one of the
shades in her jumper.

"We met at a bereavement gathering. Rebecca, Ruth
and I. The three of us seemed to get on well together and
we started meeting for drinks and dinner once every few
weeks. We all miss our husbands," she sighed. "Ruth has
been such a rock. She understands the frustrations of
being a widow. The sort of expectations, almost stigma,
attached. People don't always understand."

Not a clue here. No husband to worry about and, for
all Mandy knew, in certain society it could be met with
disdain. Losing a husband in your fifties seemed almost
careless. And what do you do with the rest of your life?
Beverley Bowen seemed to have found a cause. Ruth
Crozier had her job and Isobel Price-Williams had a

family to support her. Now they knew Rebecca Hubert was also a widow it would be interesting to find out what got her out of bed in the morning. Did you lose your purpose in life if your life-long partner died? It was something Mandy didn't have to worry about.

CHAPTER TWELVE

Rebecca Hubert's house was also detached, and the front garden had been covered with a brick driveway. A red BMW with a new number plate sat in the middle. A planter by the front door held one of those tiny cypress trees which gave a faint aroma of lemon.

Mrs Hubert showed no surprise when they introduced themselves. Ruth Crozier had forewarned her friends. She was dressed in old jeans and top with an oversized man's shirt over it. Although she looked respectable enough, Mandy noticed her nails were bitten, and she was barefoot.

"Come in. We'll go down to the kitchen. I was about to have a ciggie. The patio doors are open so it's a bit chilly, I'm afraid."

Another large house which seemed to be in good condition. How the other half live. Mandy wondered if this is the sort of house Lisa, Josh's wife, aspired to own. She seemed intent on pushing her husband up the ladder. The kitchen was a mess, much to their surprise. Glasses and empty bottles littered the draining board and the round table by the open patio door was covered with old newspaper and beads, string, glue and other odds and ends. Rebecca made no apology for the mess.

"Cuppa? Tea? Coffee? I'll put the kettle on. Bit early for the vino. Even I have standards." She gestured towards the half-empty wine rack in the corner.

Josh opened his mouth to say something. Mandy pre-empted his response. "No thanks. We've a lot to get on with. We're trying to find out the identity of the man found in Nant Fawr woods."

"Yes, I heard." She moved away from them and filled the kettle. The pipes made a gurgling sound. Mrs Hubert rolled her eyes. "The central heating playing up. Another thing needs fixing."

The dripping bath tap and overgrown garden in Brithir Street entered Mandy's mind. Jobs to be done over the weekend. Rebecca interrupted Mandy's thoughts.

"Ruth said you were trying to trace the clothes from Isobel. I can't help much. She gave me two big black bags to get rid of. Said she had tons of the stuff. I put it out in the first charity collection I could. We get dozens of the damned collection bag things here. They think because you live in a big house you throw things out all the time." She picked a packet of cigarettes from the table and waved them. "Do you mind?"

She lit up, moving to stand by the open doors. As the smoke rose in a spiral from her cigarette, Mandy could hear Josh inhale deeply. So much for the nicotine mints. Mandy looked more closely at the table contents.

"You make jewellery?"

"Yes. I've got to do something and I've no skills to speak of. It was a hobby when my husband was alive. Now it's a bit more. My darling husband, childhood sweetheart, didn't want me to have a career."

There was an edge to her voice, and it wasn't clear why she was telling them about her husband. "He

78

earned a packet, his own IT consultancy. John liked life in the fast lane. Fast cars, fast bikes and, as it turns out, fast women. When he had the accident, he had another woman riding pillion – and him no doubt. Lucky for me he had good life insurance. At least he did something right. Now… well, now I take my pleasures where I can."

She pulled on the cigarette as if her life depended on it and glanced out over the garden with its overgrown bushes and untidy borders. They still hadn't established where the bags had gone.

"Can you remember which charity was collecting when you put the bags out?" Mandy asked.

Rebecca Hubert shrugged. "Nope. As I said there's always someone wanting something. Sometimes two or three times a week. So, sorry DI Wilde. I have no bloody idea where the stuff went."

"What about the date? Would you remember which day or week?"

Rebecca threw the butt of her cigarette to the ground outside. A slight frown appeared between her eyes as she thought about it. "Sometime around August or September. A few weeks ago. It was dry when I put it out at night and still dry in the morning. I remember because I thought if it rained, they probably wouldn't collect and then I'd be left with it. The bag had gone before the rain started. Actually, it was the day storm something or other descended on us. I can't remember the name. Bloody stupid giving names to storms, don't you think?"

Another roadblock to progress. They'd have to find out the date of the storm, who had charity collections in the area on the date, and then ring to find out what they did with their collections. Another tangle. They thanked Mrs Hubert and left.

As they got into the Juke, Mandy asked, "What did you think of our merry widow then, Josh?"

"Bitter, isn't she, and hitting the bottle, as well as the fags, judging from the debris in the kitchen."

"I got the feeling the husband was controlling. Could be it's her way of dealing with it and the thought she wasted years on an adulterer. What struck me was how different she was from the others. She didn't care the house and garden looked neglected. Her personal appearance wasn't immaculate like the other two, or Isobel Price-Williams. A bit odd in some ways. What do they have in common?"

"They're all about the same age, well not Mrs Price-Williams, and they're all widows."

"You're right. They've been precious little help to us. We still don't know who our mystery man is, or where he came from. Bloody useless. Did anything at all come from the door-to-door yet?"

Josh checked his messages. Helen had said she'd update them on progress. "Nothing significant. Some empty houses, others with 'For Sale' notices and nobody recognised our man."

Mandy thumped the steering wheel and crunched the car into gear. "We should go back to the station. First, I want to go to where they found the body. See if we can identify where he could've been coming from. Not all the paths are on the map, are they?"

"No. Some criss-cross and others are overgrown."

"He had traces of mud and gravel residue on the shoes so we can assume he didn't tramp through those really muddy parts. He wasn't too far from the bridge either. Do we know exactly where the phone was found?"

"Tangled in some weeds in the stream close to the bridge."

"Let's go and have another look."

They parked on Rhydypennau Road and headed to the spot where the body had been found. The remains of the police tape flapped in the wind. They could smell more rain in the air. No time to waste. It was late afternoon, and the dog-walkers were out again. They passed a couple of runners panting to reach home before dusk settled in. Lights were on in some of the houses, and they could see interiors and people busy getting on with their lives.

Mandy stood for a minute, imagining herself in Cinderella man's shoes. He'd come into the woods, early morning, felt unwell, nauseous even, and stumbled off the path where he'd collapsed. What had happened to the phone? Had he dropped it? Thrown it away? And the money? Where had he got the money? At first, they'd thought he was rich. Now they knew they were wrong. Dressed in a dead man's shoes and possibly his clothes as well. Something didn't add up.

"Why was he here, Josh? Where was he coming from or going to? Why no ID? There are too many gaps."

"I know what you mean. He came into the woods from either north," pointing, "or south. It's early, so maybe he crossed the bridge if he saw someone coming. He wanted to avoid being seen."

"Do you think he'd stolen the money? It would be a good reason to avoid people. Or was he being followed?"

Josh considered the question. "Could be. Either way, he had a hand to his chest because he felt a pain and staggered off the path, collapsed and died." He surveyed the area. "Do you think he was disorientated or something? I don't think he was being followed. There's no evidence and the only reason would be if someone knew about the money."

"And they'd have taken it, not left it in his pocket. Poor bugger. Still doesn't explain why the phone was in the stream… how far away?"

"Couple of hundred yards."

"It doesn't make sense." Mandy shook her head. "If he dropped the phone then it would've been on the path or beside him. Unless he wanted rid of it."

"Somebody tracking him, you mean?"

"Oh shit. I don't know. Too many ifs and buts for my liking. It might not even belong to him. Let's get back to the station. It's Friday afternoon and we've hit a wall. By Monday we should know more if the tech guys can get anything from the phone. Plus, Rishi can confirm cause of death with more certainty."

"What if someone gave him something, a drug say, to cause the heart attack? Would the tests be able to identify those things?"

"I'm pretty sure Rishi has thought of it." Mandy changed the subject as they walked back to the car. "Plans for the weekend?"

"We're going to Ikea tomorrow. It seems we need a new wardrobe."

"Well, you guys really know how to live dangerously." A snort of laughter. "Ikea on a Saturday. I think I'd rather chew my feet."

"Yeah. I know what you mean. Roll on Sunday and a day of rest. Well, I hope."

The traffic was rumbling out of the city centre, so they were back at the station after five. Mandy exchanged a few words with Helen and Olivia, wrote up her report and headed home. No overtime had some compensations.

CHAPTER THIRTEEN

SATURDAY

Tabitha was up early on Saturday morning and Mandy woke to the smell of toast and the sound of her niece singing in the kitchen. Quick shower, something to eat and then, after dropping Tabs to drama group there'd be more than two hours to make a start on clearing some of the dead plants in the garden. The dripping tap needed a professional. Some friend of the desk sergeant's, a qualified plumber, was going to call late afternoon to take a look. Seeing Rebecca Hubert and the state of her house had spurred Mandy into action.

Once she found her rhythm in the garden, she enjoyed the work. It was physical and relaxing; pitting herself against the stubborn weeds and overgrown hedgerow was therapeutic. It was also back-breaking. A bonfire was burning somewhere close by, and the pungent smell of smoke wafted towards her.

After an hour and a half Mandy stopped, stretched and made a cup of green tea. As she sipped, she started thinking about the case. The poor bloke in a drawer in the mortuary. You'd have thought someone, somewhere would come forward.

A quick wash and change from her gardening gear, and Mandy was ready to collect Tabitha. She'd be able to teach her niece to drive in a couple of years. If Joy didn't try playing happy families again. Much as Mandy loved her twin, she sometimes hated her in equal measure for the way she treated Tabitha.

Several cars were parked outside the hall when she got there. Mandy managed to find a space between a Volvo and an Audi. The sound of laughter greeted her as she wandered into the foyer. It had the strange smell of dust and neglect although the floors seemed clean and there was an overtone of toilet freshener.

Other parents waited, some chatting to each other. Mandy didn't recognise anyone. She read the notices on a board by the door. Jigsaw afternoon. Yoga for the over fifties. Mindfulness. She could do with some of that. Creative writing. Film club. Book club. Bereavement group. Could it be the place where the merry widows met? Somehow, she couldn't see those three here in this understated venue. More likely some fancy hotel or church. She should have asked.

The doors to the hall opened, with a smiling Ms Thomas inviting them to enter.

"We've had a lovely morning. Thank you so much. These sort of cross school interactions are so important. Please, do come in and collect your offspring."

The parents shuffled into the hall which, considering the shabbiness of the foyer, was bright and welcoming with a raised stage to one end and a polished floor. Chairs were stacked to the side and what looked like a cage with mats and various other pieces of equipment. The young people were in groups talking – excited chatter. Mandy spotted Tabitha who was in an animated conversation with a boy. So, now she knew the attraction. It was bound to happen sooner or later.

The young man turned, and their eyes met. Daniel Levin. An unexpected meeting. She thought Daniel would scarper when he saw her approach. Although his smile faded, he stayed by Tabitha's side.

"Hi Daniel. I didn't expect to see you here. Isn't it the sabbath?"

She predicted a smart Alec response, surprised when he maintained eye contact.

"My grandfather was Jewish, hence the name. Dad married out. Saturdays are no big deal." He looked from Mandy to Tabitha.

"I didn't know your mum was a detective."

"I'm Tabitha's aunt, not her mam. She lives with me. How've you been, Daniel?"

He shrugged. "Okay, suppose. You find out who the bloke is yet?"

"No. We followed up on your lead. Thanks for the info. Nothing yet."

He nodded and looked at the floor, shuffling his feet. "Did you not find his phone then? You were looking for it, weren't you?"

Something about his body language, the awkwardness and the lack of eye contact made Mandy suspicious. Daniel Levin knew something. How to get it out of him? Could she persuade him to open up? She wished Josh was with her. He'd know what to say.

"We found the phone. It's drying out. We don't know if it'll be any use. It was in the stream." Should she have even shared the information? "All confidential, of course. You won't blab anything, will you?"

Daniel bit his lip and looked at his feet. Guilt. Mandy was sure of it. From the video thing or something else? She needed to find out. Tabitha was standing right by them, wide-eyed and listening, so she couldn't push it.

"You've got my card with my number so if you remember anything…" Mandy stopped, giving him the opportunity to speak.

He nodded and glanced at Tabitha. So, he didn't want to say anything with Tabs listening. Okay.

"Tabitha, do you think you could see if there are any leaflets about mindfulness. They've a poster in the foyer and there should be more information somewhere. Could you ask someone?"

"You? Mindfulness? You've got to be kidding me." Tabitha's eyes, dancing with laughter, met Mandy's and then darted to Daniel. The smile faded. Clever kid. She nodded her agreement and with a quick, "See you next week, Dan," left them to talk.

"Did you want to tell me something, Daniel?"

He shifted from foot to foot and looked around to make sure no-one was within hearing distance. "Yeah…well…am I going to get into trouble?" His eyes met hers and she saw anxiety in the look.

"Why would you think you'd be in trouble?"

"The day… in the woods. I found a phone."

She knew it. The little sod. "And?"

"It could have been that bloke's. It was near the bridge. I put it in my pocket and then not long after we spotted him – the body."

If it was Cinderella man's phone, then they could charge him with obstructing the course of justice at least.

However, finding out what Daniel had to say at this point was more important. She had to keep the desire to slap him under check.

"Do you think it was his phone? What did you do with it?"

Daniel looked at the floor again. "Thing is, I had weed in my pocket when Luke rang for the cops. I was afraid they'd search us or something. I told the others I was going to get rid of the weed and I threw the phone in the stream. I hid the weed in the hollow of a tree. Did they find it?"

Daniel's face was flushed now. All the defiance gone – was it just a defence mechanism? Bugger. Now she had an extra problem. If vital clues to Cinderella man's identity were on the phone and had been lost…

"Go on. Tell me. I'm in the shit," Daniel said. "My old man won't be able to ignore this. He'll ground me for months. No more drama group. No more football. No more anything I enjoy."

What to do? Procedure told Mandy she should take him in and get a statement and give him a warning at least. Then he'd never trust her again and he had given them something. The door-to-door could still yield valuable information. To hell with it. Worth the risk.

"Anything else you forgot to tell me?"

"No." A long sigh. "What happens now?"

Mandy let the question hang while she considered what to say to him.

"Right now, I'm going to take my niece home and do some thinking. I may need to speak to you again. For now, we'll keep this between us."

Daniel's face brightened. She needed to make sure he knew the possible consequences.

"But, and it's a big but, it could go further. I'd leave the weed where it is. You shouldn't be messing with that stuff."

Daniel grunted his thanks and headed for the door. As she followed him, she could see Tabitha in the foyer. They exchanged a few words. Tabitha's gestures, the twirling of her hair and her sparkling eyes gave the game away. Tabitha fancied Daniel Levin. Could she have chosen anybody more unsuitable? Teenagers. Give her criminals any day. She knew how to deal with them.

Daniel was riding off on his bicycle as they emerged from the hall into the car park. No parent to collect him. Tabitha's eyes followed him until he turned the corner, out of sight, before she turned to Mandy.

"Is Dan in trouble or something?"

"No. He remembered something about the day he found the body in the woods. Did you know he was one of the boys? Did he say anything?"

Tabitha shuddered. "Yeah. Sounded gruesome. We had to do an exercise, in pairs, where we showed a reaction to something horrific, and he told me about it."

No doubt to impress. Well, it had worked. As Tabitha chattered on about her morning with the drama group it became even more obvious; she had a crush on Daniel.

CHAPTER FOURTEEN

SUNDAY

Joy rang at midday. Tabitha had gone around to Kelly's. No doubt to drool over photos of Daniel on Instagram or TikTok. Mandy was preparing a vegetable casserole and the aroma of fresh herbs permeated the kitchen. She'd been feeling nauseous for days and thought it was her diet. Police work often involved rushed meals or no meals at all. In the garden the birds were pecking at the breadcrumbs she'd left out. She hoped next door's cat was inside. Murder was one thing, just not in her back garden.

When she saw Joy's name appear on screen she sighed. Her sister lived her life as if she was in some sort of television drama. Always a crisis. It was wearing. And it was about time she grew up. Joined the real world where people dealt with problems instead of running away from them.

Mandy took a few deeps breaths before answering. "Well, you're up early. What time is it in Greece or wherever you are now?"

"Ha ha. Very funny – not. I told Tabs I'd ring. Didn't she give you the message?"

"Yes. She did. Since when have you ever been reliable?" Mandy tried not to reveal her irritation. Something of her annoyance must have filtered through.

"There's no need to get shitty with me. I'm being responsible. I've left Georgio. Did she tell you?"

"Until the next time he beckons with his little finger – or his dick."

"Look Mand, I don't need all this crap. I'm trying to sort my life out." A sort of whining quality accompanied the comment.

"I thought you were sorted in the summer when you were here. You had a job. Tabitha was glad to have you around. I thought we were good and then off you go again. Boomeranging back to your toy boy. When are you going to grow up?"

Mandy could feel the tension in her neck, and she tried rolling her shoulders to relax. This wasn't achieving anything. If Joy cut the call short, it could be months before she rang again. It wasn't fair on Tabitha. She'd have to apologise. "Look, I'm sorry, sis. I worry about Tabitha. She needs her Mum. I'm not really the maternal sort and I'm up to my eyes in a new case. I bloody love her to bits and want what's best for her. She was so excited you know. When you said you'd be home for Christmas she was over the moon."

Mandy could hear Joy breathing, taking her time to respond. God, sometimes her sister was a royal pain in the arse. She counted to ten before asking, "You *are* coming back for Christmas, aren't you?"

"I'm not sure you want me there." She sounded forlorn, wistful.

A wave of guilt came over Mandy. She'd let her anger take control. Start again. Try to make amends. "We do want you here. Tabs has made plans about what she's going to cook for you. All your favourites." No response. "And she's been buying little presents to do a Christmas stocking for you. You can't let her down. Not again."

At last, Joy spoke. Flat. Toneless. "I've booked a flight. Tenth of December. There's stuff we need to talk about."

"Stuff? What?" Shit. She wasn't into drugs again, was she?

"Yeah. Nothing over the phone..."

Her voice faded and Mandy thought she heard her sister sniffing. Before she could say anything else, Joy ended the call with, "Gotta go."

Something weird was going on. The number of times she'd had to pull Joy out of tight spots. And the number of times she'd had to shield Tabitha from the truth. It didn't bear thinking about. Another wave of nausea made her stomach lurch.

Tabitha came back soon afterwards. Mandy was pretending to read a magazine while her mind see-sawed between the case and her sister's problem, whatever it was.

"Something smells nice." Tabitha threw herself down on to the sofa beside Mandy.

"Veggie casserole and apple crumble for pud."

"Yummy. Did Mum ring?" Her eager face gazed at her aunt. Mandy forced a smile.

"Yes. She's booked her flight. She'll be home on the tenth December."

Tabitha's face lit up, she stood and twirled around the lounge.

"Yippee. She'll be in time to see our play. Miss is going to tell us next week what her plans are. She said we'd be putting something on in the middle of December."

"Nativity play."

A giggle from Tabitha. "No way. She says she's got a few ideas and we'll have to audition for the parts."

Mandy's heart filled with love for her niece with her twinkling eyes and flushed face. Don't spoil it this time please, Joy.

CHAPTER FIFTEEN

MONDAY

Monday was a relief. Back in control. Back to normal without catching Tabitha's face as she talked to Kelly on Facetime about the drama group and Daniel. It would all end in tears. Mandy was sure of it. All she could do was watch from the side and be there to mop up.

She entered the station, greeting the desk officer on her way. Nobody waiting in the foyer for a change. She was smiling as she headed up the stairs. At the top the Super was waiting with a face spelling trouble. All Mandy's good humour disappeared as fast as hot dogs at a barbeque.

"Wilde. In here. Now."

Mandy raised an eyebrow at Josh, who had settled down behind his computer screen. He shrugged. Oh well. Better find out what she'd done now. Grumpy old bugger.

Withers was standing behind his desk, a bookcase of files and framed certificates of his numerous awards behind him. He was an outstanding detective. Mandy often wondered if he missed being at the sharp end. Sitting behind a desk all day and directing operations instead of being at the thick of it must be hard. God, she'd be bored shitless. No wonder the poor bugger was miserable. His heavy aftershave didn't disguise the smell of smoke. A pile of papers littered the desk. He didn't sit and didn't indicate Mandy should either. It was going to be a short bollocking then.

"I take it you still don't know who our mystery man is?"

"No, sir."

"So, the trip to London was a waste of time?"

"It was a valuable lead. We know Cinderella man was wearing shoes which he either bought in a charity shop or–"

"Have you got any idea how much this little investigation has cost already? A team on door-to-door. Another lot searching charity shops. And where have we got? Precisely nowhere."

He was going red in the face, his jaw twitching, as he glared at her. Did he have any idea how frustrating it was to be restricted by budgets?

"We could do a television appeal." A pause. "Sir." Oops. Nearly forgot to be respectful. The Super was one of a kind. Everyone else used first names but he liked to keep that distance. It was weird. Maybe linked to his stint in the army before joining the force.

"We don't have much choice. I'll deal with it. Give me all the details and I'll ask the press office to organise something for this afternoon. I'll prepare a statement. An appeal for anyone with knowledge of the man's identity to come forward."

"Do you need me to be there, sir?"

"I think I can probably manage to speak a few words to the press myself, Wilde. You don't need to hold my hand. Find out whose body we have in the mortuary. It can't be beyond you."

Mandy clenched her jaw. Patronising shit. Sometimes she felt like telling him exactly what she was thinking. It wouldn't end well. She should try the mindfulness course. Or anger management... again.

"Well, what are you waiting for? Find out the identity of this Cinderella man."

He sat down heavily, and Mandy got out before he found something else to complain about. What would he say if he knew about Daniel and the missing mobile? She'd get the blame for poor interrogation techniques no doubt. It might be an idea to check out Daniel's story. If he was telling the truth, then they should find a bag of weed. He'd given her a good idea of the exact spot where he had hidden it, so she'd take Josh and have a look.

"Olivia, chase up Rishi, please? The lab results should be back today."

"Will do. What about the phone? Want me to have a word with the tech guys?" Her eyes were twinkling.

"Is your little friend in the lab still hankering after you?" asked Mandy.

"Yeah. Don't want to disillusion him, now. Keep him dangling." She grinned, her whole face lighting up with mischief.

"One day he'll find out he's been wasting his time." Mandy laughed. "How's the new girlfriend working out?"

Olivia jutted her bottom lip out and bobbed her head from side to side in a non-committal fashion. Policing wasn't the best job for forging relationships, was it? Never mind. Think of the satisfaction when they solved this case. Cinderella man's body reconciled with his family. If he had one.

"Right, Josh. Come on. We're going to do a bit of snooping. I've something I want to check."

The day was overcast, and a stiff breeze created flurries of leaves in the road and pavements. Cathays Park, opposite the police station, was a blaze of autumn colours. In the summer it would be full of people trying to find space to sit. Now it was almost deserted.

"I saw Daniel Levin on Saturday."

"Yeah, where?" A hint of surprise.

"I collected Tabs from this new drama group she's joined, and he was there too."

"Bit of a coincidence." He seemed unperturbed.

"He gave me some extra information which I've kept quiet. I don't want to put it into a report."

Josh turned to look at her. Mandy stared straight ahead. She could feel the tension. By telling Josh, she was compromising him too.

"He found the phone and threw it into the water."

Josh whistled.

"He found it close to the bridge, picked it up and then panicked–"

"Stupid little–"

"Because he had a bag of weed in his pocket. When Luke rang 999, he told the others he was going to hide the stuff. He threw the phone in the stream and hid the weed in the hollow of a tree."

Josh, shook his head, sighed, turned away and stared out of the window, watching the houses flash past as they made their way out to the suburbs. Mandy wondered what he was thinking.

"He told me where the tree is located so we'll go and check it out."

Still silence.

"Look, Josh. I know I should report it. Then the little bugger could be charged with something. He'd have a caution on his record and it's not going to help anyone. I'd like to wring his neck, but I think he's genuinely remorseful." She paused. Still no reaction. "And Tabitha has a crush on him, so I hope I'm right. I thought we'd have a look in the woods, retrieve the weed and then see if we can walk from there to where Daniel showed us the alleyway. Little trot around. There were a few houses with no response on the door-to-door so we could have another look at the ones close to the alley. What do you think?"

"I think you're pushing it. You need to tell Withers. Now. Today. He'll give you an earful, but he'll stand behind you. The one thing he does is support his teams. Daniel needs to give another statement and be given a warning. I thought we'd got through to him after the video incident."

"I thought reporting him might have a detrimental effect. If the others–"

"If that phone holds vital information, you could be facing disciplinary charges if the Super finds out."

"Unless they find vital information, time sensitive, on the mobile I think it's okay."

"Your call. I don't agree but you're the boss." He looked out of the windscreen.

"Look. If anything happens and it comes out, you know nothing. I did it all off my own bat. I'll take any consequences. Got it?"

"As I said. Your call."

Mandy parked, they both got out and walked in silence to the bridge. A few people were out. Couples, a runner, a woman with a pushchair and the usual dog walkers. No-one paid much attention to them. The odd nod as they passed. Mandy thought they must have looked a strange couple. Josh shorter and stockier and Mandy with her untameable hair.

The path was littered with acorns, crunching under their feet, and the damp smell stronger after the rain earlier. The tree Mandy was looking for wasn't far from the path; the hollow small enough for a squirrel to hide his nuts. Putting on a glove she delved into it hoping it didn't hold a nest of ants or spiders. Too late in the year for wasps, she hoped. Her gloved fingers searched, touching what felt like twigs and moss before she found something more man-made. With a satisfied grunt she pulled the plastic bag from its hiding place.

"Well, part of the story was true."

She showed it to Josh before putting it into an evidence bag. He raised an eyebrow.

"Evidence bag? What you going to do with it?"

"Good question. I don't want to give it back to him. If we find the identity of our man, I might be able to bury this somewhere in the reports and shove it in with something else." That didn't help.

"Why not tell Withers?"

"Are you bloody joking? That's the last thing I'm going to do. Not now, anyway."

"Sometimes…" Josh shook his head in disbelief and gave an exasperated sigh.

Their raised voices had attracted the attention of an elderly couple who approached the bridge.

Mandy smiled at them and said to Josh in a quieter voice, "We can talk about this later. Let's see if we can find the way to the alley. Is it feasible our man was coming from there or going to the area?"

"I'll ask Helen to send through the list of house numbers with no response. Might as well ask some questions while we're at it," said Josh, as he took out his mobile.

She pulled her collar up around her neck. The breeze had an edge to it, and those grey clouds scudding across the sky meant more wet weather. Their path led out of the woods into housing. They trudged along until they found the alleyway Daniel had identified. At the other end of the alley was a row of houses stretching several yards to right and left.

"Okay," said Mandy, "have you got the list?"

"Yes."

"Let's take a little walk," said Mandy. "See if we find anything out of the ordinary. This is the sort of place where people might notice what's going on."

"Or prefer to ignore it."

Mandy thought of the smell of weed which sometimes made its way through the party walls into her house. She could have played the heavy with those students… but, what the hell. It didn't happen often and not worth getting into an argument about.

"I'll take the right and you do the left. Meet back here."

Josh nodded and set off. Moody bugger.

CHAPTER SIXTEEN

The road they were in formed a sort of crescent with the occasional cul-de-sac. The report had identified nine houses in total where there had been no response. Mandy surveyed the properties as she passed them. Some large, detached houses and then a couple of semis seemed to be the general pattern, all of different styles despite being built in the same era. 1950s, she reckoned. Solid and dependable. A few showed evidence of ongoing building work and many of them had been extended or garages had been converted into living space. It was quiet – too quiet. No-one moving about and several empty drives, people were out at work.

It was easy to see why there had been no reply at number twenty-six. A skip sat in the drive and scaffolding cradled the house. Plastic tarpaulin covered the roof, flapping like some large, blue predatory bird. The builders were nowhere to be seen. Perhaps the owners had run out of money, or the team was working somewhere else. Her feet crunched on the drive as she went to take a closer look. The rooms were empty, except for a few pots of paint and a stepladder. It should have been recorded. No way Cinderella man lived there. Unless he'd been visiting someone in the area?

The next house she called at was shrouded in net curtains. No reply. Then a neighbour came out and was about to get into her car. Mandy seized the opportunity.

"Excuse me. Police." She waved her badge. "I'm looking for your neighbour."

"Best look in the Heath then. Eric had a heart attack three weeks ago. He'd gone a bit...you know... confused. I think the family are looking to put him in a home. Doubt if he'll be back."

Another one off the list. No doubt Josh was finding the same. Building works and old people. Three to go. It took another fifteen minutes before Mandy admitted to herself there was nothing sinister about any of the houses reported as no response. So bloody depressing. She made her way back to the alley and waited for Josh. What the hell was keeping him? He had only four houses to check out. Should she should go and look for him?

She saw him trotting towards her and could tell from his wide grin he'd got something. He waved and indicated for Mandy to join him.

"What've you found?" Mandy asked.

"There's one house up here which looks as though it's empty. The neighbour across the road was putting out his bin and says he's seen men leaving in a van in the early hours. Could be squatters."

"Did you have a look around?"

"Not yet."

"Let's hit it then."

Somewhere a dog barked, distant enough not to disturb the peace of the neighbourhood. The house was almost hidden from the road by a high laurel hedge, curtains closed. Impossible to see anything. It was neglected, the windows dirty, paint flaking on the front door. Although the driveway was overgrown, a smear of oil and crushed weeds showed evidence of a vehicle. Someone had been there recently. A grey cat was sleeping in the front flowerbed. It slunk away when it spotted them.

Round the back of the house, the place looked even more dilapidated. Once it might have been a beautiful garden. Now, the brambles had taken over. The curtains were closed here too. No peeping allowed. The back door was frosted glass, so they were able to see shapes and colours and they had the impression there were items inside. By the back door a pile of cigarette butts had been discarded.

"Some of those look recent. Got an evidence bag, Josh? Let's send a couple to forensics. See if they can find any DNA link to our body. I've a feeling we could be on to something here."

"Should we get a search warrant?'

"Nah. Not enough to do it yet. Of course," she paused, "if the DNA is a match..."

"Then we get in there."

"No shit, Sherlock."

"Meanwhile, we have a little snoop in case there's anything else here." She pointed to a piece of wood, shaped like a pole sticking out from the brambles. "What you reckon it is? Looks like a For Sale sign to me. Can you get it?"

"It's in a bramble patch."

"And?"

Josh tramped through the garden until he reached the board. It was entangled in brambles, some sort of vine and tall nettles. As Mandy watched she could see him tugging at it, then, with a grunt, he wrenched it far enough out to be able to read what it said. She'd been right. For Sale. Not one of the local firms. An online firm she'd never heard of. She took a photograph and nodded.

"Better shove it back in."

"What the...?"

"We don't know what's going on here. Best leave things as we found them. We get the evidence and then a search warrant. Meanwhile, we find out who owns the property."

The fag ends could have been left by a builder or decorator working inside the property. Still, it was worth checking. Josh was quiet as they walked back. They passed a garden with fruit trees including a large apple tree. The apples lying under the tree were rotting and releasing a cider-like odour. A few insects swarmed around the remains. Mandy wondered if they got drunk from the pungent fruit. Their last supper. It reminded her about Rishi's report. She hadn't checked to see what he'd said about stomach contents. Cinderella man's last supper. She hoped it had been a good one.

CHAPTER SEVENTEEN

"There's been confirmation of cause of death," said Helen as soon as they entered the office. "Seems Rishi was right. The extra tests confirm it was Sudden Arrhythmia Death Syndrome."

"Is it genetic?" Mandy asked.

"It can be, according to the report."

"Do you have the report there, Helen? What did the stomach contents show?"

"Stomach contents indicated a meal of fish and salad and wine, consumed less than twelve hours before death."

"Sounds like a posh restaurant meal to me," said Mandy. "Seems nobody has responded to the photo. We can't start asking every eating place in the city. Let's hope the public appeal tonight will bring up something. Apart from the usual bloody nutters."

"Could be he's not been living in Cardiff. Down from London or something." Josh rocked back and forward on his office chair.

"Unlikely. His shoes and possibly some of his clothes are from a local charity shop, as far as we know. Plus, Daniel spotted him in the Llanishen area with another man a week or so before his death."

"If you can believe anything he tells you."

"What I don't get is why nobody's looking for him," said Olivia. "I mean he's not been living under a hedge or anything, has he? You'd think somebody would've said something. Reported him missing. Odd, isn't it?"

"Unless he was involved in something dodgy. Josh, check with the drug squad, will you? See if they've got anything. And don't forget those fag ends for DNA. Check against Cinderella man's profile. Tell them we need it, pronto." Mandy turned to Olivia. "You're right, Olivia. Somebody out there knows more than they're letting on. We've a possible lead. Josh and I had a little walk in the woods and traced our way up to where Daniel Levin says he saw Cinderella man with someone else. There were several houses in the area with no response from the door to door. We found a dodgy one. Looks occupied, and the neighbour says he's seen a van leaving, early mornings."

"Do we set up surveillance?" Helen asked.

"We haven't got the budget for it, and the Super won't allow us to get a search warrant without a rock-solid reason. Josh here," Mandy waved towards him, "scrambled through the brambles and found a discarded For Sale sign."

"Hooray," said Olivia with a smirk at Josh.

"It's for one of these online estate agents so I suggest we follow it up and see what it produces. There's a number and presumably a website. Josh will put the details on the board before heading off with the fag ends." Mandy nodded towards a whiteboard in the corner. "Meanwhile, I'm going to have a butcher's at the burglary info again. If we don't catch the little buggers soon, Withers will be breathing fire."

As if on cue, the Super came into the room.

"You're looking very smart, sir."

Mandy couldn't resist the dig. He'd brushed his uniform and the jacket was buttoned up, stretched across his expanding middle. The smell from his aftershave was almost overpowering. Helen, who was closest to him wrinkled up her nose and took out a tissue, pretending to stop a sneeze. It was as well the whiff of eau de whatever wouldn't be conveyed on the screen although the journalists would get the full benefit in the airless room set up for the press.

"Did you put the file on my desk, Wilde?"

"Yes, sir. We may have a new lead."

"I don't want excuses. I want results and preferably before the press conference at four-thirty. Do you hear me?"

The whole station could probably hear. Josh concentrated on his screen. Olivia and Helen nodded. Bugger him. They were doing their best and if he couldn't see it, then too bloody bad. He stomped off to his office and they exchanged glances.

"Okay. Plan of action. Olivia, check over the estate agency and see what comes up. Josh, when you get back from the lab, write up our latest findings for the Super and you can have the pleasure of putting it on his desk. Helen, see if there are any more houses with no response and get uniform to have another look. I want to know if they're empty. Check the addresses against the electoral roll and land registry. Find out who's the registered owner. It'll be a process of elimination."

A while later, Olivia finished clicking on her computer and sighed. "I don't get it. There's a website with links to properties, no addresses or areas identified. When you press on the links you can't get any further. They've an online booking system. It's not working. All the requests for viewings are ignored."

"What about the telephone number?"

"I tried it, now. It's not connecting."

Mandy felt a thrill. "See if you can find out if it's genuine. Was it ever connected? Perhaps the firm went bust."

Olivia nodded. "What about the website? I've tried finding the IP address, it's not possible. Well, I can't seem to trace back far enough."

"A little trip to see your friend in the tech department again then, Olivia. Give him a big nudge about the phone as well. We need something."

"What about the press conference?" Helen asked, pushing a strand of hair behind her ear. "Shouldn't you be going?"

"No. It appears the Super wants the limelight for himself. Or he's scared of me putting my foot in it. Wouldn't be the first time, would it? Let's switch on the telly and see what Withers says. He's got all the info, so it'll be interesting how he takes a spin on it," said Mandy.

Helen found the remote and switched on as the news conference was about to begin. Withers looked larger than life, his blotched complexion and bulbous nose more pronounced than ever as his face filled the screen. The conference was held in a room on the ground floor and the Super sat, in full uniform, behind a table, flanked by the press officer. The symbol of the South Wales Police Force decorated the wall behind. As Senior

Investigating Officer Mandy should have had a place at the table. What the hell. Let him take the flak.

"You'd think they'd put a bit of make-up on, wouldn't you? Make him look a bit better." said Olivia.

A hush fell over the room as the Super began to speak. He coughed and paused to ensure all the members of the press were listening. Mandy gritted her teeth. Up his own arse, as usual. Whatever, they had to hope it brought results. Appealing to the public might work.

"As many of you are aware, a body was found in Nant Fawr woods early on Wednesday morning. There are no suspicious circumstances. The young man died from Sudden Arrhythmia Death Syndrome. This can have a genetic component therefore it is essential we find any relatives so they may be tested. Despite enquiries in the area, we have been unable to identify the man concerned. We are making an appeal to you all. If anyone watching knows anything about the identity of this person, or, has information they think could help, please do not hesitate to call Cardiff Central Police Station." He paused and looked straight at the camera as if he could see them all there watching him. "Our team will follow up any leads. Thank you."

"Why haven't they been able to find out who he is? It's been days." A reporter shouted above the others.

Withers glared at the reporter. "The young man had no form of identification on him. We are following several leads. A mobile phone has been recovered from the Nant stream. We are hopeful the information from the device will be useful."

A clamour of questions followed. Demands and shouts for answers. Withers stood to indicate he was finished and left the room. At the last point from the Super, Josh turned to Mandy and muttered under his breath, "Let's hope the mobile does give us something."

CHAPTER EIGHTEEN

"Somebody's been snooping." Igor's voice was gruff, deep and tinged with what could have been anger or anxiety. They were outside the back door of the house, having a smoke.

"How do you know?" asked Paskal. "It all looks the same to me."

Igor spat on the ground, "It's why I'm in charge here. Your brains are in your dick, not your head. Look at the weeds. Someone's been trampling over there. And the sign... see. It's been pulled out and shoved back in. I don't like it."

Paskal scowled. He said nothing, suspecting it was some kids. Plus, he'd seen the evidence of Igor's foul temper and didn't want to have it inflicted on him. He'd be no good with a broken jaw or a black eye. He was paid for his looks and... he grinned as he thought about the other reasons he was working. At times he thought it wasn't such a bad life. Couple of years he'd have paid off his debts, secured a more stable future and be able to return home a relatively rich man. Or stay here a while and reap the rewards. It all depended on how things panned out. He had his life ahead of him. No need to fret about it. Trouble was, he wasn't free. The root of the problem.

From the news it seemed the police were still trying to find Elio's identity. Paskal prayed for the soul of his brother and the forgiveness of his family. If they knew he had deserted Elio, refused to acknowledge his kinship... He crossed himself. Forgive me for I have sinned. If he did tell the police, he knew what would happen. There was no glory in it. Igor had told him what happened to men like him and he shuddered to think about it. He dragged on his cigarette, threw it to the ground and stamped on it. He was exhausted from the unexpected hard labour the day had brought and the next day loomed with more of the same. Best get some sleep while it was possible.

Asleep as soon as he laid his head down and awake it seemed minutes after, Paskal rubbed his bleary eyes. Igor was swearing and he heard another voice, more high-pitched, in English, protesting. Then everything went quiet except for the mumblings of Igor and the others. Dare he look? He rose from the mattress and crept downstairs to where he could see a light on in the kitchen. Igor was standing over a boy, strapped to a kitchen chair, and the others were grouped around him.

"What the hell?"

The boy's eyes turned towards Paskal and something like a flicker of recognition flashed across them. Then the boy flinched as Igor, towering over him, swearing, in broken English and Albanian, smashed his fist into the boy's face. A stream of blood spurted from his nose, dripping on to the floor.

"Stop! What are you doing? Where did he come from? Why's he here?"

"The little shit was creeping around outside. I told you someone had been here. I heard a noise, and this little snake was outside. Trying to peep in." Igor slapped the boy across the face again and the boy cringed with pain. He didn't make a sound.

"Christ, Igor. You can't go beating up kids. Someone will be looking for him. What are you going to do? This is big trouble."

"Not if they don't find him."

Paskal understood the implications. If Igor injured the boy – or worse. He knew he had to put a stop to it now.

"I'm not going to be a party to any of this. You're fucking mad. You know?" Paskal turned to the other men. "And what do you think will happen if he kills the boy then. Eh? You think they won't find us? You think the police will believe we weren't involved? No bloody chance. We'll all end up in prison, rotting. You want to go to prison? Well?"

The others looked at him and mumbled together. All the time the boy's eyes were fixed on Paskal. Even if he didn't understand the words spoken, the boy could feel the electricity in the air. He'd have to be stupid not to know his life was in the balance.

With a grunt Igor turned away, opened the fridge and took out a bottle of beer. "So, what do you suggest, pretty boy with his brains in his trousers?"

Paskal felt the tension leave him and his shoulders relaxed. He didn't have a plan. All he could think was the lad would be able to recognise all of them if they let him go.

"His phone. Switch it off in case they track him." Turning to the boy he asked, in English now, "Who knows you're here? Did you tell anyone?"

The boy swallowed and shook his head. He was biting his lip and winced as he moved in the chair.

Bloody hell. Igor had already given him a beating. As he looked more closely, Paskal could see a bruise beginning to appear on the boy's forehead as well as the bloody nose. Igor was right. They couldn't let him go. Not yet at least.

"You'll have to ring the boss. Say what's happened. Find out what we should do."

Igor sneered, one side of his mouth curling upwards in an ugly grimace. "I say we slit his throat and push him in the river." He leaned close to the boy and drew a finger across his throat. The boy flinched, still said nothing. With a grunt, Igor stood and took out a phone.

"The boss will not be happy. Bad news for all of us."

It didn't take a genius to work it out.

* * *

When Mandy spotted the message from Daniel on Monday night she didn't really register much except exasperation.

Think I no were dude hangs out. Go2C.

Trying to impress her because he had the hots for Tabitha. Really. Idiot. She ignored it.

CHAPTER NINETEEN

TUESDAY

Mandy changed her mind when Daniel Levin's father rang on Tuesday morning to say his son was missing and why the hell had he been involved in any of this mystery body stuff? The news Daniel was AWOL really got things humming. What had happened to him? Where was the little bugger? She'd skin him alive when she found him.

Withers was hopping about as if his shoes were on fire. "How is this Levin boy connected to this case? What's going on here you haven't told me about?"

It was a bad dream. Mandy closed her eyes. She'd wake up to find next door's cat sitting on her bed. No, Withers was still there going purple in the face and spit gathering around his mouth. Better confess. Best if he knows it all at this point.

"I had a text from Daniel last night, sir. It was late and I didn't think it was important."

The spit was flying now. "Not important. Not important! A boy is missing, and you think it's not important? What *is* important, DI Wilde, in your little world?"

Mandy swallowed. She really was in deep shit this time and no doubt about it. If anything had happened to Daniel... Oh God. It didn't bear thinking about.

"He said he was going to check something, sir. How was I to guess he'd be in danger? When was Daniel reported missing?"

"This morning. He didn't turn up for his paper round so they rang his home. His bed hadn't been slept in."

Great parenting. You'd think they'd have checked last night. Still, it wasn't going to absolve her from the wrath of Withers. "So, they have no idea when he went missing?" She could feel her stomach churning. With a missing person those first few hours were vital.

"The father's downstairs. Go and speak to him. Grovel if you need to. Mr Levin is a very important man."

Mandy didn't care about status. She was more concerned about the lad and what could have happened to him. She went downstairs to find Jacob Levin pacing up and down in the entrance. The desk sergeant, the portly Vincent, known as Gogo to his mates, indicated with a flick of the eyes he was glad to see her. At first glance, Mandy could see where Daniel got his looks from. His father was stockier and with an air of superiority stemming, she suspected, from a privileged background and possible public schooling. However, she needed to keep her prejudices to herself and make sure things remained calm and professional.

"Mr Levin. I'm sorry to keep you waiting. Will you follow me please?"

"At last. My son is missing. You should be out there looking for him. This is wasting time." She could see him assessing her and not being impressed by what he saw. Although she was almost eye to eye with him, he managed a look indicating he found her wanting in many respects, being a woman one of her many faults.

"On the contrary, sir. All the information we can glean from you and other sources will help us to establish a more focussed search area. Now, if you will." She turned on her heel and marched up the stairs, not waiting to see if he followed. There was a grunt and then his steady footsteps on the vinyl staircase as they made their way to an interview room.

Seeing the suppressed anger and frustration in the set of Levin's jaw she decided to get down to business. Josh arrived, ready to make notes.

"Right, sir. I believe you were first made aware of Daniel's disappearance this morning when, Mr Jenkins, the shop owner, rang to ask why Daniel hadn't turned up for his paper round. Is that correct?" Mandy met his eyes.

"Yes. Daniel knows he won't get his allowance if he doesn't earn a bit for himself. The discipline is important." Mr Levin had both hands on the table and his fists were clenched although he sounded calm.

"When did you or your wife last see Daniel?"

Mr Levin pushed a hand through his hair. "I saw him yesterday morning. He'd come in from his paper round and I was on my way out with my wife. She had to get the early train to London. She's still there at a conference. I haven't told her yet."

"Let's hope you don't have to. Let's hope Daniel turns up." Despite his spiky attitude Mandy felt sorry for Jacob Levin. His brashness probably hid the fear he must be experiencing.

"What time did you get home from work last night, sir?" Josh asked, pen poised over his notebook.

"I'm not sure. Late. I had paperwork to finish. About eight o'clock." He shook his head as if it would help him to remember.

"And was Daniel at home then?" Josh leaned across the table a little towards Levin.

"I'm not sure. His bedroom is in the attic. We had it converted so he had his own space. I don't usually go up there. I think I shouted to let him know I was home, then sat down with a glass of wine."

"Was there evidence he'd been home? Empty mugs, plates, shoes or bags hanging around. Anything?" They needed to establish a timeline.

"There wouldn't be. We've trained Daniel to be tidy. Everything has a place."

Mandy had to look down at the table to avoid showing how she was feeling. She sensed Josh stiffening in his seat. Poor Daniel. She thought about his attitude towards them. Arrogance covering a feeling of neglect. Poor little rich boy.

"Are you sure Daniel isn't with his friends?" Josh asked.

Jacob Levin glowered at him. "I rang the other boys I know he hangs out with straightaway. Sometimes he stays over at Luke's. He usually lets us know. The boys hadn't seen him since after school yesterday."

"Do you have any idea what he was wearing?"

Jacob Levin brushed a hand over his eyes as he tried to recall. "Jeans, dark blue hoodie, Nike trainers, probably. The school don't like them wearing jeans, even sixth formers so he could have been wearing anything."

Time to come clean about the text. "I had a text from Daniel last night after nine." She passed her mobile phone across the table. "I didn't see it until before eleven. I figured he'd be home by then."

"I knew it." Levin was simmering with rage, his face flushed and breathing fast. "He's been obsessed with this body they found. Fancies himself as a sleuth. This is your fault." He stabbed a finger at Mandy. "What has he got mixed up in?"

Or who? It was a valid question. She cleared her throat. "If Daniel thought he saw something it's likely to have been in the area where he does his paper round. Do you know where he delivers?"

"Llanishen. I don't know what streets. You'd have to ask Dewi Jenkins about it. Paper shop in the village. His bike was at home. I checked."

Mandy nodded at Josh who got up and left.

"Could you provide us with a recent photograph? We can distribute that and hope someone has spotted him."

Taking his phone out, Jacob scrolled through. "Will this do? It was taken on holiday in August."

Daniel stared back at her from the screen.

"Perfect. If you can ping that across, I'll make sure it goes out. Now, I suggest you go home and rest, sir. We'll keep you informed every step of the way. I'm sure Daniel will be alright. He's a bright and resourceful lad." She was tempted to cross her fingers although her smile and show of confidence seemed to work.

Jacob Levin sighed and stood up. "Find him. Find him before his mother comes home." He seemed weary as he left, shoulders slumped, ten years older than when he'd mounted the stairs.

"Right. Let's get on it," said Mandy as soon as she joined the others. "Josh." He was on the phone, waiting. "Get a list of the streets and if he has any idea of order of delivery. Olivia, get uniform to get out there as soon as we know. Helen, give Mr Levin a ring in an hour or so to check if Daniel's turned up. Doubt if he'd tell us immediately." She bit her lip. Jacob Levin was a potentially difficult customer. Need to keep him sweet. "And be ready to support the family if his wife comes home early. Silly bugger doesn't want to tell her. As soon as we have the delivery area, Josh and I are out there too."

Josh pinned a list and a map, crinkled and worn, on the noticeboard.

"Thought you only used tech. Google maps and stuff."

"Easier to see the big picture and we can colour the route he might take. Could help." He grunted and, using a coloured marker, started highlighting the roads where Daniel delivered the papers and magazines.

"I didn't think anyone read papers anymore." Olivia's eyes peered from behind her specs. "Get all the news you want on the internet."

"Well, it seems a few folks, mainly the wrinklies, still like the old tech, like paper. Can't be bloody bothered myself. Have you passed this on to uniform?"

"Yes. They're sending out a couple of patrol cars," said Josh.

"We need door to door again. With the recent photograph." The nausea was back. It wasn't good. He could have disappeared any time after school yesterday. Where had he been when he sent the text?

"Daniel's father sent a digital photo we can use."

"Good. Olivia, check social media and Daniel's phone provider. They should be able to use GPS to do some tracing. Keep us informed. Josh and I are going to have a snoop around."

* * *

A blustery wind was stirring the leaves and grey clouds sat on treetops, threatening more foul weather. A seagull had crapped on the bonnet of Mandy's car, a white splash across the paintwork.

"Bugger. It looks like an elephant shat on it. No time to deal with it now."

"It's corrosive you know. You can get special wipes to remove it gently. I read about it somewhere," said Josh, swinging up into the front seat beside Mandy.

"Josh, you are a constant surprise. Now, can you guess where we're going?"

"The house we saw. The empty one we thought wasn't empty. With the For Sale sign dumped in the garden."

"That's the one. It's on Daniel's route. Let's go and see if anyone's at home."

CHAPTER TWENTY

They passed a patrol car and a couple of uniforms heading the other way to the house. If Daniel wasn't with his mates, then he could be in trouble. God knows what he'd stumbled into as he was snooping around. It was a hunch, but a suspicious house and a missing boy, who was familiar with the area, spelt danger.

Making no attempt to be discreet, Mandy parked her car on the drive and knocked on the front door. She didn't expect a response.

"Go and ask next door and across the road if they've seen anything unusual in the last twenty-four hours."

Josh hurried off. She tried to peer through the windows at the front. The heavy drapes were closed, making it impossible even to get a glimpse of the interior. She sloped around to the back and was just able to see into the kitchen. It looked different from when they had been before. It still looked as if someone had been there; more fag ends in evidence than last time. Through the frosted glass of the back door the coloured shapes she'd noticed last time had gone. It was obvious no-one was moving about.

Josh appeared, excitement fizzing around him.

"The chap across the road said there was a flurry of activity late last night. He was going to bed when he heard car doors slamming. He looked out and saw activity at the house."

"And?"

"Lots of lights on and shouting in some foreign language. Five men or six men he thinks. Bags with them too. Looks like they've done a moonlight flit."

"They weren't too worried about being inconspicuous then. Did he get the make, model or number plate of the vehicle?"

"Nah. Too dark. Could have been black or navy or even a dark grey. Might have been a people-carrier or a van. He couldn't say. Didn't have his specs on and the streetlamp is out. Asked if I could contact the council to get it fixed."

Mandy gritted her teeth and pulled out her phone. "Olivia. Get a search warrant." She rattled off the address. "Any trace on Daniel's phone yet? No signal. Shit. Get records for yesterday. Who he rang, messaged and where he was at the time. Okay? And keep tracing the agency. There must be something, somewhere. A link. A connection. Pass me to Helen, please." She had another thought. Not a pleasant one.

"You alright?" asked Josh.

"We're working on the assumption Daniel's disappearance has something to do with Cinderella man. What if we're wrong?" The question dangled in the air. "Helen. Go and see Mr Levin, please. Ask him if he's got any enemies. Anyone who might want to get at him through his son. Any ransom demands. I should have thought about it earlier. We've been focussing on the idea Daniel got caught hanging around somewhere he shouldn't. Maybe we've got the wrong idea."

If only she'd taken more notice last night. Helen's calm approach should work with Jacob Levin. Another woman, one who at least looked more of a professional more smartly dressed than Mandy's casual style.

"There." Mandy stood, head to one side, pointing upwards towards the roof.

"What now?"

"Did you hear something?"

Josh listened; face crinkled with concentration. "Only the magpie and his mate making a racket."

"Are you sure? I thought I heard a noise from inside. I'm sure you must have heard it too." She watched a slow grin spread over his face and then disappear as quickly.

"Breaking and entering?"

"Technically. Well, it could take hours for a warrant and if there's someone trapped in there, in trouble – Daniel Levin, for example – they could need our help."

"How? It looks double glazed."

"Bloody hell. Thought you were a detective? Notice the little bathroom window at the side? Single glazed. Wouldn't take too much to get it open."

"And then what?" asked Josh. 'It's quite small. I don't think either of us could squeeze through that."

Mandy took her phone out again. "Olivia. Can you get up here, pronto? I think we might need to accelerate things. I'm sure there's someone inside. Yeah. We heard something. We may need someone more petite to climb through a window."

"What if there's nothing there? Still, I suppose we need to do something, in case... bit risky though."

"Life's full of risks." Mandy shrugged. "My gut tells me this house is connected to something. I'm not sure quite what yet. We'll see. Now, pass me the rock behind you. Let's get cracking," she laughed, "literally. Look away if it bothers you."

The crash of broken glass wasn't as bad as they expected. At least none of the neighbours appeared. They used the rock to break off any shards they could see still clinging to the window frame so Olivia wouldn't get cut or stuck. Mandy got an old rug from the car to lay across the sill.

"Let's hope they've put the seat down." As Mandy uttered the words, Olivia arrived. She looked like a child beside the other detectives with her purple-dipped hair covered in a beanie hat and sturdy gloves covering her hands. "God, Olivia, you'd make a great cat burglar."

"Miaow." She scrutinised the window. "Bit high for me to get at. Gimme a lift up then."

"Be careful. Any sign of danger you get out. Okay? I don't think there's anyone in there, but shit happens."

"Thought you said you heard someone, like?" The look she gave Mandy was conspiratorial.

"Nothing since we broke the window." Mandy kept her face straight.

Comprehension dawned. "Best get in quick then."

They helped her reach the ledge and watched as she slid through. There was the crunch of broken glass and a sort of grunt.

"You okay, Liv?" Josh whispered through the frame.

"Yeah. All in one piece, although I'm glad someone put the loo seat down."

Mandy gave Josh the thumbs up sign. "Open the door and let us in. Go cautiously, won't you?"

"Hey, I've got a black belt in judo, don't forget. See you in a minute."

They hastened to the back door and could see Olivia's shape as she fumbled with the key. As soon as she opened up, they entered and did a swift scan of the room. Someone had been living here until very recently. A half-eaten sandwich lay on a chipped plate and beside it a cup of something resembling oil, most likely coffee. A chair lay toppled over. No sound.

"Flannan Isle," Mandy said, the hairs on the back of her neck alerting her to something.

"What?" said Josh.

"It's a poem about a lighthouse where three men disappear, leaving a meal and a chair overturned." As she reached the kitchen table and could see more, Mandy stopped. Her stomach flipped. No. Was it?

"Do you see what I see?" She pointed to something on the floor. Olivia put a hand over her mouth.

"Call forensics," said Mandy. "Get a team out here now."

CHAPTER TWENTY-ONE

"Blood." Josh said.

"I'm going to look upstairs. I don't think there's anyone here now, although you never know. You two check the other rooms. Don't move anything."

Mandy crept along the hallway, glancing into two other rooms with minimal furnishing. Odd scraps of clothing, a pair of trainers, empty food containers and an empty bottle of spirits. The place had been occupied. The air stale and musty.

Testing each step before putting her weight down, she slunk up the stairs. Three bedrooms and a bathroom. She could see the toilet seat up and a grey towel crumpled on the floor. In the first bedroom she spotted mattresses and a sleeping bag. Same in the second. Dingy, dark places with heavy curtains blocking out the light and preventing anyone from seeing inside.

Only one door was closed. Locked. From the outside. The key turned with a faint click. At first it was difficult to see anything. As in the other rooms, the window was draped in blackout curtains. The room faced north so even the chinks of light around the edges gave little illumination. Silence so dense it was menacing. An animal smell alerted her to something in the corner. All she could see at first was another mattress heaped with a dirty duvet. It looked like a pile of rags and bedding. As she stood there, transfixed, Mandy spotted the top of a head. A body. She recognised the hair.

"Daniel." The word caught in her throat. No. No. No. Not Daniel. Please. Her breath shuddered before her training took over.

Dropping to her knees at the side of the bundle of bedding she pulled the top layer away and could see the blood dried on his face, rusty, flaky. Was he alive? She pressed her fingers to his neck and felt the pulse. Weak. Slow. Thank you, God.

"Josh. Olivia. Somebody ring for an ambulance. I've found Daniel. He seems to be in a bad way. We need help. Now!"

As she knelt by Daniel's side, Mandy stroked his face. "Come on, Daniel. Hang in there. You'll be alright." She didn't know if he could hear her or not. She knew people who were unconscious could hear, so she carried on muttering to him in little more than a whisper. "I don't know what they did to you. I promise when we catch the buggers, they'll suffer."

A meow from the doorway alerted her to the presence of a cat. A grey shorthair. How had it got in? Mandy's concentration was focussed on Daniel. The cat turned and padded out again, slipping past Olivia as she entered the room.

"We've called for an ambulance. Josh is waiting downstairs for them, and he's called in forensics too." She touched Mandy's shoulder. "They're on the way. Won't be long." Daniel's hands were tied, Mandy tried to loosen them, but the knot was too tight.

After what seemed to be hours, probably only minutes, they heard the ambulance siren blaring.

Olivia opened the curtains, the light revealing Daniel's unconscious body more clearly. He didn't stir, even when the paramedics cut the ties, lifted him onto a stretcher and carried him downstairs, Josh waiting by the open front door.

Mandy's throat was dry. "Has someone told his father?" God help them. No doubt Jacob Levin would be fuming.

"I rang Helen while we were waiting for the ambulance," Josh replied. "She was about to leave the Levin house. She's taken Mr Levin to the Heath to wait for the ambulance."

"I hope he's rung his wife. We'll have to talk to Daniel as soon as he comes round." Mandy ran a hand through her hair, making the frizz worse. "We need to find out what the hell's been going on here."

"Forensic team arrived." Another police van was at the scene. All the lights and noise had alerted the neighbours, some of whom were standing on the street, gawping.

"Good. Let's bugger off and leave them to it. Olivia, see if you can hurry things along a bit. Anything they find to give us a clue. Who was here and why? And get rid of the rubberneckers. Find a uniform to do it. There's nothing more for them to see."

Olivia nodded and scurried off. Mandy sighed. The adrenaline rush had gone.

"Amazing you heard anything at all, boss," said Josh. "Considering the state he's in."

"Okay smart arse. Very funny. I could do with a green tea before we do anything else. You're the café connoisseur. Where's the best place near here?"

"Follow me. Your shout, I think."

More bloody complications. Was Cinderella man part of the community of vagrants or whoever had been living here? His clothes and the shoes were tidy. And he was clean, still smelling of shampoo when the boys found him. This didn't look like the sort of place where Cinderella man would live. And the occupants had disappeared. Something dodgy was afoot. It didn't take a detective to work it out. Drugs? Money laundering? Maybe the forensics team would find something. Meanwhile, they had burglaries to solve and an estate agent to find.

CHAPTER TWENTY-TWO

Even Withers came out of his den to congratulate the team. "Excellent teamwork. Good result. Proud of you." He left them open-mouthed. Seems he was mellowing.

Olivia and Helen were checking CCTV after reports of another attempted burglary in Llandaff. This time they had reported sightings of a suspicious car, a dark coloured Corsa, and a partial number plate. Mandy's biggest concern was they had no links to Cinderella man yet.

"Anything from immigration?"

"No. They've run the photo through their database. No recognition. Want me to check with the counter terrorism mob?" said Josh.

"Might be good to flag it up with them but don't want them muddying it all so leave it for a bit. My gut tells me it's simpler than that. But what's he doing here? And why no ID and a shedload of dosh?" Mandy chewed the end of her pen.

"Must be an illegal immigrant."

"Well, it would fit the lack of identification... the money though, where the hell did it come from? It's a lot of dosh to have stuffed in your pocket. You've spoken to the drug squad?"

"Nothing there either. They've got their eyes on a gang. All home-grown and using county lines and young kids to get the stuff around by the sounds of it."

"So, we're in bloody limbo again. Waiting for Daniel to recover. Waiting for forensics. Waiting for the phone to dry out. Waiting for a trace on the dodgy estate agency. Waiting for land registry. What now?" With a sudden movement Mandy leapt to her feet. "Olivia, you said the website for the online agency had photographs of other houses."

"Yeah, not many though. About six there were. Maybe it's why we can't find them. Gone bust."

"Can't you stick photographs into a search engine, and see if it'll give you an address?"

"Yeah. Suppose so."

"Right. Let's do it. See what it comes up with."

"I don't get it," said Josh. "We still won't know who owns the houses. The tech boys are still trawling through it, aren't they?"

"Yes, but think about it. If the men who assaulted Daniel had to get out quick, they'd have to move to some other empty place, wouldn't they? It's a long shot, but my feeling is these bogus buildings for sale are a cover-up for something else. They might have been moved from one place to another nearby."

The building was suddenly filled with an ear-piercing screech. The fire alarm.

"What the...? Who thinks it's a good idea to have a fire drill in the middle of the afternoon without warning?" Mandy snatched up the phone.

Withers appeared from his office. "Everybody out. It's not a drill. I repeat. Not a drill." All the lights went out, the computers shut down and left everyone trying to peer through the gloom.

One of the uniformed officers appeared with a yellow tabard, nearly the same colour as her hair. She seemed to be relishing her task. "Assembly points please, everyone. I'm going to check the toilets. This is not a drill."

"Where's the fire?" Mandy grabbed her coat on her way out.

"Some electrical fault in the basement, Ma'am. It's smoking so we've closed down the main generator. They'll check it out and then probably switch to the emergency system. We'll have to see. Now, if you don't mind..." She held her arm wide indicating the stairs. Hell's bells. That's all they needed. A bloody fire.

Outside everyone stood in their designated groups while the fire marshals took a register.

"Anyone left inside?" Withers was in his element, taking command as the most senior officer in the building.

"No, sir. All present and correct," yellow hair replied, with a smug expression.

Mandy figured it was the most excitement she'd had all week. Probably all summer. They stood in groups, chatting, while the fire brigade investigated the building. As dusk settled it became colder and people started moaning. Mandy stamped her feet, glad she'd grabbed her coat. How much longer before they could get back in and on with their work? After what seemed forever, the firemen came out again and had a word with Withers. They engaged in a heated and animated conversation. At last, the fire crew left while everyone gathered around the Super.

"We can go back into the building and resume work. However, it seems the internet is still out of order and likely to be so for some hours. If you are able to continue your work at home, then you are at liberty to do so." He looked at his watch as the clock struck five.

Mandy turned to her team. "Looks as if it's quits for today. We'll make an early start in the morning. Plough on. Night all." She turned away again and headed towards her car. She could do the searching at home. There was no way to take any action until the morning. Unless…

* * *

The thought of going solo was dismissed as soon as she got back. Tabitha was in the hall to meet her as soon as the key turned in the lock.

"Is it true?" Her eyes were wide, and she looked pale, anxious.

"Is what true?" Mandy heaved off her coat, hung it on a peg and kicked off her shoes.

"Dan's friend, Luke, says Dan's in intensive care. It's all over social media. They think he might die." The words were spluttered, and then the tears started.

Shit. They should have thought about it. These kids did everything on their phones. News would spread like a rash and worse, the rumours would be twisting any sense of reality into nightmares.

"Yes. Daniel's in hospital." Mandy replied. "He's not in intensive care. He's in no danger. Honestly." She put her hands on either side of Tabitha's face so she could look her niece in the eyes. "He's a bit bruised and battered. We expect him to be well enough to talk to us in the morning. We don't know yet what happened or why."

Tabitha was crying, big heaving sobs which shook her whole body. She lurched, shaking into Mandy's arms. "I've been so worried. I didn't know what to think. And you didn't tell me."

"Hey. Hang on a minute. I only knew he was missing this morning. I'm the one who found him, and you can trust me, can't you?" Mandy stroked the top of Tabitha's head. "He'll survive. Maybe not as pretty as he was for a while but still in one piece. Okay?"

Tabitha tried to control her sobbing. "I thought…"

"Yes. Well people are very keen to speculate. He'll probably get out of hospital tomorrow, or the next day and you can see him yourself. Now, let's go into the lounge. My feet are freezing on these tiles."

Tabitha unwound herself from Mandy. "Do you think he'll be at drama club on Saturday?" She sounded hopeful.

"Oh, I expect so. I can see him enjoying the glory. Telling his gruesome tale." God knows what truth Daniel had to tell. He'd probably need counselling. At least it had focussed his father on what mattered. Jacob Levin wouldn't be too worried about bags and shoes hanging about the hallway or dirty plates on the worktop, for a while at least. Mandy's stomach rumbled and she felt a pang of hunger gnawing at her.

"Right then, Tabs. What's for dinner?"

"I… I didn't think…"

"… I'd be able to eat after finding your boyfriend? Rescuing people is hard work. I need food." She growled and tickled Tabitha under the ribs like she used to do when her niece was a baby. "What's in the fridge?"

"Leftover chilli and some veg. I was going to go and pick something up… I was too upset."

"Perfect. Baked potato with chilli filling coming up soon. You'd better text Luke and tell him to stop spreading rumours." Mandy indicated Tabitha's phone. "We don't want a big press story over this. It would alert whoever did it. They'd know we're looking for them. Got it?"

"Sure. I'll tell him. Did Dan not have his phone to call someone?"

"We don't know what forensics found and you know I'm not supposed to talk about things. As soon as we've spoken to Daniel, I'll text you to let you know how he is."

"Thanks Auntie Mandy. And Dan isn't my boyfriend. He's a friend."

"Oh yes," Mandy raised one eyebrow. Not a boyfriend – it didn't mean she didn't want him to be a boyfriend. Teenagers. It made her feel very old.

CHAPTER TWENTY-THREE

WEDNESDAY

A whole week since they had found the body and they were no closer to finding out who he was. A series of dead ends so far, unless this assault of Daniel was in some way connected. Then, a call from the hospital.

"Daniel Levin wants to see you," Helen had taken the call and, despite her calm exterior, looked relieved.

"Right, up to the Heath then. Josh, are you coming with me?"

Mandy whistled as she powered down the stairs. If Daniel could give them a clue, they'd have something to go on. What if his capture had nothing to do with Cinderella man?

They pulled into the multistorey car park at the hospital. The buildings sprawled over several acres and seemed to expand on a regular basis. A teaching hospital, it was always heaving with medical students as well as patients and visitors. Cars, buses, bikes and ambulance vehicles made it as busy as any part of the city It took a few minutes to get to the concourse. Mandy asked at reception and was directed upstairs to the ward.

"How does anyone find their way around this place?" Josh was puffing as they climbed the stairs. "Where is he anyway?"

"General medicine. Christ, you're panting like a horse in labour. You need to join a gym or something. God help us if you have to run after anybody."

"It's giving up the fags. I've put on weight."

"Well, if you don't stop wheezing like an asthmatic goat, they'll have you in a bed beside Daniel."

They asked at the desk on the ward and were directed to the left where Daniel was propped up in a bed by the window. Both his parents were there, though it wasn't visiting time. Jacob Levin throwing his weight around.

"We're waiting for Daniel's meds to arrive. They've said he can go home." Eva Levin was soft spoken but firm, with authority. Tall, blonde and immaculately dressed she was the perfect foil for Jacob. A dynamic pair who were the essence of success. Mandy introduced herself and Josh to Mrs Levin before turning to Daniel.

"You're looking better than yesterday. You're awake at least. And you've got a real shiner. The boys at school will love it."

Daniel started to smile and then winced as he moved to sit more upright.

"He's got a cracked rib," Jacob explained. "I hope you get whoever did this to him." His face was grim, his body rigid.

"Indeed, sir. We hope so too."

"Have you any ideas?" Eva asked, tilting her head a little.

"We have a number of lines of enquiry, Mrs Levin, and I'm hoping Daniel will be able to help us further." Turning towards Daniel she said, "I was told you wanted to speak to me?"

"I saw him there. The other bloke. The one I'd seen before with the dead dude."

Yes. At last. Something to go on. "Are you sure?"

'Yes. He was called Paskal. The fat guy who beat me up was called Igor. They were talking in some sort of language I didn't understand." He swallowed. "The fat one wanted to kill me. I got the message through his gestures."

"How many men were there?"

"Three others as well as Paskal and Igor. They looked a bit rough although only Igor hit me. I don't think they knew what to do."

"Can you tell us, right from the start, what happened and anything you remember?"

Daniel glanced from one parent to the other before he started to tell them what had happened to him. "I knew the house was supposed to be empty, then I saw a van driving away from there in the morning, as I was finishing my paper round. I had a look. There was nobody about, so I figured if I went back…"

"You'd find out if there was something dodgy going on." Mandy wanted to shake him. How could he have been so bloody stupid?

"Yeah. I waited until after eight and went to have a look around. It was all dark in the house, then next door's dog started barking. It happened so fast. I was grabbed from behind. I didn't hear him. He punched me and dragged me inside…" Daniel stopped and swallowed. His mother took a sharp intake of breath. It seemed the parents hadn't heard the whole story either.

"It's fine if you want to take a break. We can have a full statement later. Although the more we know at this stage the better."

Daniel moved and flinched. It was going to take a while before he recovered from the physical injuries.

"Enough for today." Jacob Levin stepped forward to intervene.

"No Dad. It's important I tell them. The Igor bloke hit me again about the head and strapped me to a chair. He shouted in my ear. The others were muttering among themselves." He paused. "Then Paskal came down the stairs and there was some sort of argument. Igor went off to phone someone. When he came back, they forced me to drink something. I don't remember anything else."

Mandy exchanged looks with Josh. Beaten up and drugged. Whatever the men had been doing in the house it wasn't legal.

A nurse came bustling into the room with a bag. She tutted at them. "Give Daniel some space, please." She put the bag down on the side cabinet. 'Meds. You can go home now, lovely, when you're ready."

"We'll give you some peace, Daniel. It would help if you could give us descriptions, though. Could you help put together an e-fit?"

"Not until he's had some rest. Now, if you've had enough?" Jacob's tone was firm.

Mandy came out of the hospital at speed, Josh trying to keep up. When they got to the car, she thumped the door. "We're going to get the bastards who did this to Daniel."

"It's given his parents a shock."

"Good. Maybe they'll realise their son is more important than an immaculate house. Bet you a tenner, bloody Jacob Levin will be on our tails too. Demanding justice. If I had hold of Igor now…"

"A charge of police assault wouldn't help Daniel."

"You're right. Let's get back and see what forensics have for us. If these men are linked to Cinderella man, we need to find them."

CHAPTER TWENTY-FOUR

"Good news." Helen held up a piece of paper when they arrived back at the station. "We think we've got a link in the burglary cases."

"Great. Keep the Super off our backs for a bit. Suspects?"

"A couple of possibilities. I could be wrong. We know whoever is responsible had targets in mind. It was systematic, not random. They were all over the city and the perps were cunning enough to divert the patrol cars to opposite ends."

"And?"

"I checked where the owners of the properties went when they left the house empty. It seems many of them are creatures of habit. Quite a few retired. It took a bit of time. I think I've narrowed it down."

Mandy could see she was trying to hide her excitement. Helen was a good detective. Quiet confidence, determination, and stamina. She'd go over evidence a hundred times if she thought she'd find the answer.

"There's a connection?" Josh asked.

"I think so. These people," she pointed to the page with highlighted names, "were all at a new driving range at the time the burglaries took place."

"And your theory is?"

"Someone at the range is tipping off the gang, lets them know when the people particularly retired couples, appear. They'll have their details on record. Easy enough to check if there's likely to be anyone else at the house. It'll all be online."

"Can we get a staff list without raising suspicions? If you're right, Helen, we need to be careful we don't chase them off."

"Sure thing."

Olivia came in with a couple of evidence bags. She put one bag down on a table. "Daniel's phone. It had been switched off and was under the bedding where we found him."

"Odd. You'd think they'd have destroyed it or something, to stop it being traced." Josh paused.

"I wonder if Daniel knew it was there. We'll have to ask him. I suppose if they drugged him and then buggered off, they could assume he'd come around again at some point. Maybe leaving it so he could get help. God knows how with his hands tied." A shrug. "He's bloody lucky. They could have taken him and dumped him somewhere else. He said the older one, Igor, threatened him. He thought he was going to be killed," said Mandy. "He must have been shitting himself. Not so cocky then. Check through and see if there's anything on his data, location, messages or calls. Could be significant. Did he have a hunch or follow someone?"

"He told us he'd spotted a van in the morning and went back later," said Josh.

"Playing Bloody Sherlock Holmes. I feel responsible. If I'd taken a bit more notice of my texts, we might have found him earlier."

Withers appeared. For once he wasn't scowling at them, a more benevolent expression on his face. Everyone turned towards him, not sure what was coming. In some ways Withers in a good mood was more unsettling.

"I believe the Levin boy is being discharged today."

"Yes, sir. We've spoken to him this morning and he's able to provide a good description of the men involved in his capture and assault. He'll help with an e-fit later."

"Good. Quick action there, Wilde, although I believe the entry to the house was unorthodox and without backup. Another of your hunches?"

Josh examined his shoes, saying nothing.

"I thought I heard someone shouting for help, sir. I decided speed was of the essence."

"So, you called Wyglendacz here before asking for backup. Was it wise, if you thought someone needed urgent assistance?"

Oh hell. What had started well was rapidly descending into a potential bollocking. "I didn't want to call a team out, sir, until I was sure it was needed, in case I had been mistaken about the sounds I heard. And being mindful of budgets, of course."

Withers' eyes narrowed. He seemed unsure how to respond and just grunted. "How Daniel Levin managed to shout when he was unconscious is something we won't go into. Suffice to say it was good work finding him. MISPERS are one of the worst things to deal with.

No closure for the family. My first case was a toddler, three-year old girl, who disappeared during a summer fair. Makes your stomach turn when you think of the possibilities. The mother was hysterical."

"Did you find her?"

"Yes, thank God. She'd crawled under the table in one of the tents. The sniffer dog found her, fast asleep. Best thing ever when it's a happy ending."

He looked almost happy at the memory, a trace of a smile on his lips. They remembered how long he'd been in the force. He'd have seen it all. A wealth of experience sitting in an office.

Then, it was back to business. "Any leads on the mystery man?"

"We hope so, sir. We think the men who assaulted Daniel are linked in some way. We don't know how or where they've gone."

"Well, don't let me hold you up." He turned on his heels to leave. "And don't forget those burglaries. We need to keep an eye on the statistics."

When he left, Mandy perched on the end of a desk and glanced around her team. Bodies relaxed again as soon as the Super had gone, and Josh exhaled. "Thought we were in for it then."

"And me. The results are what count. He can't complain. So, what's in the other evidence bag, Olivia?"

"They found a couple of receipts. Local supermarkets. And a few scraps of
paper with scribbling. Odd words, some foreign, nothing useful." Olivia showed them the items.

"Check the CCTV in the shops on those dates and see if we can get some images. Daniel's e-fit, coupled with video, will give us a good idea of who we're looking for."

Olivia made notes of the dates and times and headed out to check up on the surveillance in the stores.

Mandy was going through the other scraps of paper. "We probably need to get a translator to see if any of this is significant. Looks as if they'd started writing out a web address here and look," she pointed to a scribble in one corner of a ripped off sheet of paper, 'this is a name, Elio something. Is it a D or O or what?"

"Dunno. Not very clear."

"It could be Cinderella man's name. Maybe we need a graphologist to decipher."

"Expert help costs. Don't think Withers would be too keen," said Josh.

"Always sodding money. How we do a proper job without funding for expert help is beyond me."

"My Tom might be able to help." Helen looked up from her computer. "He did a course a few years back on deciphering handwriting and what you learn from it. Sort of interest of his. I can ask if you like." Tom was Helen's husband, a lecturer in social sciences at the university.

"Bloody brilliant. Take a photocopy and see what he comes up with. Every little helps and it's not as if a scribble is a state secret, is it?" She spotted Josh's disapproval.

"I doubt if Helen's old man has any criminal connections, Josh. Relax. It's the means to an end."

"As long as it's not the end of my career," Josh said, as he went out of the room.

"He's not a happy bunny," said Helen.

"Doing without the fags hasn't helped his mood or his waistline. Although he's right. Don't ask Tom. We'll get tech to look."

Wherever Josh had gone, he came back twenty minutes later and sat at his desk. Crisis averted, for now.

The tech team rang to say the phone found in the stream had dried out. There was only one number in the memory, and it was disconnected, untraceable. Another dead end. Mandy was relieved in some ways. If the phone had contained vital information, then Daniel's little chat with her may have needed to be disclosed. On the other hand, Cinderella man was still dead and finding the phone earlier wouldn't have made a difference to the outcome. Best keep it all hush hush and hope.

CHAPTER TWENTY-FIVE

Mandy brooded, fighting the nausea again. What the hell was wrong with her? Nerves? Anxiety? No. She was in control. She checked everything again. Those men knew the identity of the body in the mortuary. She was certain there was a connection. Pity they'd disappeared. For now. They circulated the e-fit pictures with a watered-down version of Daniel's imprisonment to the press and waited to see if any more information appeared. Somewhere in the pile of interviews and information there was a link, a clue staring her in the face, and she wasn't getting it.

"Olivia, check on your friend in the IT department, will you? It can't be that hard to trace back a number. You know, the one on the For Sale board."

"Yeah, you'd think it was easy, wouldn't you now? I got stuck. I'll give the lab a ring. Or I'll pop down there. See what's occurring."

This was the worst time in an investigation when everything seemed to be in limbo, waiting for the next piece of the jigsaw. Where did the gang go to every morning and why were they hiding out in what was supposed to be an empty house? They had to be illegal immigrants. It would explain why they hadn't come forward.

"Josh, do we have any stats on illegal immigrants? How many are caught and what have they been doing? How long they've been here? Are they automatically deported? Percentage involved in things like drug dealing."

"I don't think our guys were involved in any drug dealings otherwise they'd have had something more lethal for Daniel. There was no evidence of anything." Mandy's look was enough. "Alright, I'll have a dig. Got a mate who works in immigration. I'll give him a buzz. See what he has to say."

"Good plan."

Filtering through all the information took time and Mandy became lost in the process, the tapping of keyboards, muted conversations and an occasional cough passing over her. From what Daniel had said, the one man, Paskal, was different from the others. Not as rough looking and with quite fluent English, if heavily accented.

"I think I've got it. The link to the burglaries." A shout from Helen. "They've given me the list of staff for the golf range. There's a Lee Highman working there. He had a caution a couple of years ago. Some aggro over a girl. It was thought at the time he was mixed up with a gang."

"Good work, Helen. Ask uniform to keep a little eye on him. Known associates. I wonder if we've got enough to check out his phone records? Do you want to ask the Super? Give him one of your special smiles. I'm never flavour of the month and besides this is your breakthrough, not mine."

It was difficult not to laugh at Helen's response. The excitement faded to resignation. She stood, smoothed her skirt down, pulled her shoulders back and marched to the Super's office.

Wouldn't it be wonderful if they could catch the little buggers? Withers would be jumping for joy over the statistics, and they'd have more time for investigation of the mystery man. In theory. Withering wasn't playing. Helen returned in record time. They had suspicions but no evidence to look at someone's phone records and no manpower to conduct surveillance on someone who could be innocent. They'd have to concentrate on the car. There were several Corsas with the same partial number plate, including Josh's wreck. Three had been stolen in the twenty-four hours before the last robbery and would, no doubt, be dumped somewhere on wasteland or burnt out in the next couple of days.

Something had been niggling away in the back of Mandy's mind. She dismissed it and started with all the information about Cinderella man they had gleaned so far. Precious little.

Olivia returned. "Well, Stevie boy down in IT had some good news. They managed to link the number to a building based in London. Six businesses at the same address. It's hellish busy down there so I said I check it myself." She plonked herself down at the computer clicking away as she hummed a tune.

"Is it an office block?" asked Josh.

"Dunno." Olivia clicked on the address and got a visual of the building. "Nah. Looks like a semi-detached house. There's a sign above the door. I can't read it. Bit dodgy, do you think?"

"God knows. Check out the names of businesses registered there with Companies House. See if anything comes up."

It didn't take long. "Here we are. Rollins Inc. Nature of business listed as property development, now. All the rest are investment or shipping companies." Olivia leaned forward peering at the screen and mumbling. 'Filing history up to date. People... oh my God. Look." Eyes flashing in excitement, Olivia pointed to the screen. "The director of the company is Philip John Crozier."

"Is he? Bloody great. We've got a connection. At last. I wonder why Mrs Crozier didn't tell us about her little side-line?"

"Maybe she didn't know?" said Josh. "The estate agent business is different, isn't it? I mean it's a different name and all..."

"And I'm a fluffy bunny dressed in pink. Come off it, Josh. Do you honestly believe she knew nothing about her husband's development properties? It would all have come out after he died. She knew. I'd stake my new wellies on it."

"Funny it's a different name though, innit?" Olivia said. "And not much in the bank by the looks of it."

"What are we going to do? Interview her again? See what she comes up with?"

Mandy was scribbling something down on a notepad. At last, aware he had said something she looked up. "What?"

"Are we going to bring Ruth Crozier in for questioning?"

"Not yet. If we do, it'll raise her suspicions and we're unlikely to find anything out. Do we have a list of supposedly empty properties in the city?"

"Well, we've got the ones within a couple of miles of where the body was found. What are you hatching now?"

"We're going to play a little game. Olivia, do you have something super smart to wear – young executive style? And do you think your girlfriend would be up for a spot of sleuthing?"

"You bet? What's the plan?"

The plan was simple. Olivia and her girlfriend to pose as a couple house-hunting, to see if Ruth Crozier was aware of the empty properties. Using a civilian in an undercover operation was not permitted but as Jaz, Olivia's partner, worked in the courts, Mandy reasoned she knew enough about criminals and was aware of the risks.

Josh wasn't so sure. "Do you think we should run it past the Super? Get clearance."

"Do you think he'd agree? By the time we'd got through all the red tape Ruth Crozier will be taking retirement."

"It could get Olivia into trouble."

"Relax. It's no big deal. They're thinking of hitching up together anyway, so it gives them a bit of an insight into the market. That's right, isn't it Olivia?"

"You can't," Josh said. "If he," indicating the Super's office, "finds out…"

"Well, we'd better keep quiet about it then, hadn't we?"

CHAPTER TWENTY-SIX

THURSDAY

Another burglary on Thursday morning was not a welcome start to the day. The call came from a man who saw two young men enter the back of his neighbour's house.

"Right, Let's go and have a word, Josh. See if he can give us a description."

The burglars had gone by the time they got to the house in Penylan and the elderly man who had alerted the police was only able to give the vaguest of descriptions. Young men in hoodies, jeans and trainers. It could have been anyone. He'd shouted at them, and they'd done a runner, he thought, as he could hear car wheels spinning seconds after they'd scarpered.

"Let's have a look around the corner. See if there are any cameras or if anyone saw anything suspicious," said Mandy.

"Long shot. No speed cameras along here. Only at the lights on the main road. We might get some pics if they went along there," he pointed. "My guess is they went through the lanes at the back of the houses. Or up the hill. I'll take a look."

"Waste of time," said Mandy.

Ignoring the comment, Josh walked around the corner and scanned the road and the houses. He hoped some of them would have security cameras. Nothing. His foot caught on a folded-up piece of cardboard. Litter. Unusual here. He picked it up. A list of some sort, misspelt and written in untidy capital letters.

PARK – CORNER BLAR RD.
57 EGGWARE (THURS)

———————

PARK – END WITCURCH LANE
24 OSPAY (FRI)

———————

PARK – TY COCK RD
33 CURCH PLACE (FRI)

At first, Josh glanced without interest. Some delivery guy had dropped his list was his immediate thought. Then, it clicked.

"Look at this."

Mandy read it, turned it over to see if there was anything on the other side before a questioning, "And?"

Josh pointed to the first line on the paper. "Where are we now?" He watched as Mandy looked at the street name.

"Blair Avenue," she said.

Her eyes lit up when she realised the significance of the note.

"And the house where there was an attempted break-in was fifty-seven Edgeware Road. It's their hit list." He waved it in the air. "We've got their hit list." His smile was the most natural Mandy had seen from him for a long time.

They were a step ahead for once.

CHAPTER TWENTY-SEVEN

Mandy's bogus house-hunting plan was set for Thursday afternoon. Jasmine arrived before one, looking every inch the young executive with her long wiry hair tamed into something between a bun and a chignon. Patting her own wild mop, Mandy contemplated growing her hair longer then figured she couldn't cope with the in-between stage where she had more hair than head. She liked Jasmine's smart suit too, navy blue pinstripe with a simple raspberry t-shirt underneath. Should fool Ruth Crozier, especially when she saw Olivia dressed in a similar style instead of her usual jeans, slogan t-shirts and sloppy jumpers.

"Well, doesn't she scrub up, nicely? God, Olivia, I didn't know you even owned respectable clothes," said Mandy, eyebrows raised.

A giggle from Olivia seemed at odds with her appearance. "Mam bought this for me. She was afraid of me going to my cousin's wedding looking like a tramp. Nice, though not really my sort of thing. Weddings and funerals, like. What's the plan then?"

"I'm pretty sure Ruth Crozier knows something about these empty houses on the dodgy website. I'm afraid if we go in heavy, then whatever is going on, will stop. Bloody Withers won't give us the time for surveillance, so a bit of subterfuge. Act as if you're looking for a house together."

Olivia wriggled up closer to Jasmine and linked arms, gazing up into her partner's face with a mischievous grin. "Oh, we can do it. No problem. Right, Jaz?" A more restrained smile flitted across Jasmine's face as she agreed.

"Get her talking about what she has on her books and then tell her you'd been driving around and noticed this house," Mandy pointed to a photograph and the Google search results with its location, "and you wondered if it was for sale as it looks empty. Ask if she knows who might own it or if it's available. Clock her reactions. Don't arouse suspicions."

"Should we make appointments to see any houses? Give us a chance to see her in action, like?"

Mandy considered. "A good idea. Not now though. Take details of a couple of houses and say you'll be in touch if you decide to view."

Josh was sitting watching them with a face like a chewed plum. "Why can't we go and ask her straight out? Why all the amateur dramatics?"

"If she's involved in something, then going in and telling her we suspect her is like having a bloody big alarm going off. We need evidence. All we have so far is her dead husband was a director of a company which appears to own some empty houses. Big deal."

"And a house where a young lad was assaulted and drugged. What if...?"

"What if nothing, Josh. Facts. Evidence. If she reacts, we know we're on to something. Then we can bring her in for interview. Tell you what. Little task for you. Find out who the husband's solicitors were and ask them if Ruth is fully aware of all her late husband's assets."

Josh grunted at her then went back to his desk. Mandy planned their strategy for Friday. If the list they found was linked to the burglaries, then they had a good chance of catching the lads involved. On the other hand, it could be a whole day wasted.

"Helen, did anything come of the possible link to the golf range? Was the little toerag in with this gang, do you think?"

Resting her hands on the file on her desk, Helen nodded. "There were several links which pointed to a connection. Thirty-four robberies so far this month. Ten of those the houseowners were at the golf range at the time. It seems a high percentage to be chance."

"And Lee? Has he been seen with any of his old mates? Who's the one with his neck tattooed? Terry something or other. Always on the edge of trouble those kids were."

"Information says they've gone their separate ways. Terry did three months inside and then moved north. Lee has a girl and a job, baby on the way."

"No way. God help it," Mandy said. "Pickpocketing while still in pissy nappies."

Helen shook her head. "He's not a bad kid, thinking about it. Just in with the wrong gang. He worked in the local shop for a while. Always polite when I went in."

"Yeah. I bet." Josh intervened. "The solicitor dealing with Crozier's estate is in court this afternoon. Ring back tomorrow."

"It's always tomorrow. Why can't we get answers today? I was hoping Olivia and Jasmine would be back by now. Where the hell are they? I suppose their report will be tomorrow as well."

A phone rang and Helen picked up.

"Yes. Send it over now, please. Thanks for pushing it to the top of the queue. I'll tell Olivia she's had special treatment."

She put the phone down and grinned. "Olivia worked her magic on Stevie. Speeded things up. He's given us the DNA results from those butts you collected. There's a positive match to Cinderella man and a partial match too."

"Partial?" asked Josh.

"A close relative. Could be a sibling or parent. They have other evidence, but they haven't processed everything yet. The cat hairs are the same though. A match to those found on the clothing of the dead man."

Mandy whistled. "Our super-clean Cinderella man was living in that house? It doesn't quite fit with the body, does it? He was still smelling of shampoo and clean nails. He must have been somewhere else that morning. I wonder where?"

"And the last meal. Fancy stuff which certainly wasn't cooked in the squat, was it?" Josh added.

The clock on the wall ticked around to five o'clock. Although the temptation to stay on and work through the paperwork was strong, Mandy knew Friday was likely to be an interesting day. Besides, Tabitha was making savoury pancakes for their evening meal.

* * *

"We can't stay here. It's dirty. No running water. How long has this place been empty?" Paskal asked. Igor was by an open door, smoking, keeping watch on the road. Every time he heard a car or footsteps he closed the door, making the space seem even more gloomy. The other three men sat on their bags on the floor, whispering to each other.

There was no furniture, a few empty crates; black bags full of what looked like old wallpaper stripped from the walls, and some offcuts of wood. It looked as though, at some point, someone had intended to renovate, then abandoned the idea and the house. The windows were boarded up and damp penetrated the walls, staining them green. And everywhere the smell of it so strong you could almost taste the rot. Paskal spotted a rat running along the skirting board and shivered. Why the hell had he ever agreed to come here? He should have gone to the police when they knew about Elio. Prison couldn't be worse than this.

As Paskal watched him, Igor finished smoking his cigarette and threw the butt into the garden. He took the packet out of his pocket and shook it. Only one left. It wasn't good. He'd been smoking almost non-stop for hours. Tensions were high enough as they'd been told not to go out, even for food. When the phone rang, Igor answered. He listened, rubbing his hand over his forehead. The call was brief and when it ended, Igor swore and shoved the phone back into his pocket. His temper had got worse over the past couple of days. He was unpredictable and morose.

"We move again, tonight. It's not safe here. I told the boss about those other boys and how this is shithole." Igor spat on the floor and started to gather their things together. "The one we left in the other house. He told police and now they have pictures. On the news." He prodded Paskal in the chest. "You and me, pretty boy. Told you we should have killed him. We lie low for a couple of days. Wait and see. No work. We rest."

No work seemed good – at first. No work meant no money. What did the boss intend to do with them if they weren't working? Paskal couldn't take much more of this. Elio was the lucky one. He didn't have to worry about any of it, not anymore. He slumped down on to his bag and waited. It wouldn't be long before they knew where they were going. Maybe to work in the fields. He wouldn't mind too much. Better than this dungeon of a place. He leaned against the wall. The damp seeped into his clothing and he shivered. He offered another silent prayer for the soul of his brother and for his own deliverance. But all he heard was the wind whispering and the branches of an overgrown tree tapping on the boarded-up window.

CHAPTER TWENTY-EIGHT

FRIDAY

Torn between the desire to see their faces when they were caught red-handed and needing to find out how Ruth Crozier had reacted, Mandy decided on the latter. She sent Josh out on the stakeout for the burglaries. She waited to see what Olivia had to say. It was disappointing. Ruth Crozier appeared indifferent to their questions.

"She sort of shrugged. Said she knew nothing about it, she'd make enquiries if we were interested, like. We took details of a couple of houses."

"And what did you think?"

"Hard to tell. Bit of a smooth operator," said Olivia. "I did notice she was on her mobile soon after we left. She went out about ten minutes later and all. Shut up shop. Though it was lunchtime."

"I think we've rattled her cage a bit. Let's see what happens next." It was a pity she hadn't asked Olivia to follow Ruth.

An hour later Josh came in and gave the thumbs up sign. Terry and his mates were caught red-handed breaking into the house they'd targeted. Success. At least Withers would be off her back for a little while.

"So, it was Terry after all, the little bugger," said Mandy. "Thought Helen said he'd moved north?"

"Seems he moved back to Cardiff at the beginning of the summer. Kept a low profile."

"About the same time the burglaries started. Fits. What's he got to say for himself? Was Lee involved after all?" asked Mandy.

"No. Seems as though the connection to the golf range was a coincidence. New facility attracting a variety of people." Josh looked at his notes. "He asked Lee to store things for him. When Lee discovered it was stolen, they parted company. He's pulled his little brother, Jimmy, into the gang and Gazza Evans. He's known to us as well."

"Have their houses been searched?"

"Yes. Nothing to be found and Terry's mother screaming about police harassment, false accusations and the rest."

Helen intervened. "She's downstairs creating holy hell."

"They must have things stashed somewhere. They can't have got rid of everything. Let's have a little chat with Jimmy, shall we? See if we can shake him up a bit. He's not been in trouble before, has he?"

"No and he looks scared to be in custody. He was the driver. We can throw a lot at him. Driving without a licence for starters."

"Good. Let's rattle the little shit's cage, shall we?" Mandy nodded at Josh and smiled at Helen as she took the file of notes from her.

The lad was sitting in an interview room huddled in conversation with someone Mandy took to be either a duty social worker or duty lawyer. It was the former. She introduced herself as Chrissie. A responsible adult. Jimmy had straightened when the door opened, turning towards them with a startled expression. He might be sixteen, but he looked about twelve. His dirty blond hair flopped over one eye and his chin was pock-marked with pimples in various stages of eruption.

After switching on the recorder and detailing who was present, Mandy fixed Jimmy with a stare.

"Well then, James. Your brother's got you into a right pickle this time, hasn't he?"

Jimmy chewed on a dirty thumbnail, shooting frightened glances between Josh and Mandy. His mouth opened but no sound came out.

Taking her time, Mandy opened the file. She tutted at it and passed it to Josh. "Doesn't look good for him, does it?"

"No. But it's the first time he's been in trouble," said Josh. "The judge might be lenient. Let him away with community service, instead of a custodial."

With a shake of the head and jutting her lower lip out Mandy replied, "Can't see it happening unless he cooperates with us. Bit of help here and we could put a good word in."

"I ain't saying nuffin'. I ain't no grass." Despite his bravado, Jimmy was shaking, and he moved from chewing his thumbnail to picking his spots.

Mandy ignored him, still addressing Josh. "His mam's downstairs. She'd be gutted if he got put away." A pause.

"And that old boy didn't look too good to me. If he had a heart attack and didn't recover…" She tutted, shaking her head again. "Really bad. Could be accessory to all sorts of other things. A few years inside."

Josh sighed, nodding in agreement. "Really bad."

Jimmy swallowed. He was shaking more now, panic in his eyes.

"If Jimmy here doesn't want to help, then we'll throw the book at him." Mandy closed the file again and stood. Josh did the same. As they moved towards the door, Jimmy spoke again.

"What you wanna know?"

It was hard to keep the smile off her face. They sat down again, waited. Stretching the tension.

"Where are you keeping the stuff you nicked? We know it's not in your house, or garage, so there has to be a lockup or something somewhere." Producing a map Mandy pushed it towards Jimmy. "You don't have to say a word, just point."

"I dunno where it is now."

With a grunt of frustration, Mandy moved to stand again, prompting Jimmy to speak.

"It used to be kept in the garage at an empty house. Then yesterday morning when we goes there to pick up the gear, there's somebody there. Some fat bloke, foreigner. Told us to fuck off. He had a knife."

A prickle of excitement made the hair on Mandy's neck stand up. "DS Jones, could you get those e-fit pictures?"

When Josh left the room Mandy leaned forward. "What happened then?"

"We scarpered. Terry went back later and kept an eye out. He saw the guy and some others get into a big van and leave." Jimmy was pale, although the trembling had eased a little. It was as if he was relieved to talk about it all. "Terry picked up his stuff and got out of there. He passed it on to a mate of his. I dunno who." He paused as Mandy had raised an eyebrow. "Honest. I dunno."

She believed him.

Josh came back with the e-fits from Daniel's descriptions. He spread them on the table in front of Jimmy. "Do you recognise any of these men?"

With one grimy finger Jimmy pointed. "Yeah. Him. He was proper pissed off. You won't wanna mess with him."

It was Igor. At last, they had a connection.

"Very wise. He's not a very friendly character. Last young man to make his acquaintance ended up in hospital." Pointing at the map again Mandy asked, "And this house – was it on this road?" She indicated the road where they had found Daniel drugged and tied up.

"Naw. Over by here it was." He placed a finger on the map. Llandaff. "Big empty house. All overgrown. Never seen those blokes there before." He sniffed and wiped the back of his hand over his nose. "What's gonna happen to me now?"

With a grin Mandy swept the pictures up and put them into the folder. She stood.

"Thank you, Jimmy. A great help. We'll tell the judge about your cooperation. Someone else will come and talk to you, take a statement. You'll be charged with illegal driving, aiding and abetting a robbery. I daresay your mam will be able to take you home in an hour or so."

They left him sitting open-mouthed.

"Aren't you going to push him for where they stashed it?" asked Josh.

"I don't think he knows. We could put the pressure on the other two. Later. We've got bigger fish to fry. A link to Cinderella man perhaps with the empty house"

"I can't say Jimmy looked too thrilled to be going home."

"Have you seen his mam?" Mandy grinned. "She'll hammer shit out of him. I expect he'd rather be in a nice quiet cell. Let's get over to the road in Llandaff, pronto. Warn Olivia we may need back-up. And ask her to check out who owns the property. We'll suss it out. Bet you a fiver it's–"

"Owned by the same company where Ruth Crozier's husband was the CEO."

Mandy grinned. "You got it in one." There was a spring in her step as she headed towards the ground floor and her car.

CHAPTER TWENTY-NINE

As soon as Mandy and Josh entered Movers and Shakers, Ruth ushered them into the back. They passed a couple deep in discussion with another woman, thirties, dyed red hair and earnest tone, undoubtedly Ruth's assistant.

The room she took them to was bright, everything in brilliant white, with a sink unit, fridge, coffee machine and kettle and coats hung on a stand in the corner. A sliding door was partially open revealing a cloakroom. Functional and compact. Although the smell of fresh-brewed coffee wafted in the air, she didn't offer them anything.

"To what do I owe the pleasure?" Ruth asked, gesturing for them to sit at a tiny round table with fold up chairs. She pulled up a chair and they sat almost knee to knee in the confined space.

"We wondered how much you knew about your late husband's involvement in Rollins Property Development?"

A slight tension in her shoulders was the only indication Ruth Crozier was unnerved by the question. She met Mandy's eyes as she responded with a faint laugh, "Goodness Inspector Wilde. Quite a leap. Last time we spoke it was about a pair of shoes. What does John's business have to do with any of it? I'm intrigued."

Despite her pretence at amusement, Mandy noticed Ruth had wrapped one arm around her waist. She certainly knew more than she pretended to know. Mandy waited, watching Ruth, before she replied, "We have evidence linking the dead man found in Nant Fawr woods with one of the properties in your husband's portfolio. The same property, in fact, where a young man was held captive and drugged. It's a bit of a coincidence, don't you think?"

"It may be a coincidence, Inspector. Mere coincidence. My late husband left me with quite a mess to clear up. The solicitor is dealing with most of it. I've found it all rather overwhelming. All I can tell you with certainty is John was not a good money manager. He had a finger in too many pies. The debts he accumulated as a result have left me with quite a number of problems. Now, if there's nothing else, you won't mind if I get back to work?"

"Do you have a list of the houses your husband had a stake in?"

"As I said, you'd better talk to the solicitor. He has more of a handle on things. I'm trying to survive and keep Movers and Shakers going. It hasn't been easy." The relaxed attitude had disappeared.

"And what are your thoughts on the fact one of those properties has been used to house men, possibly illegal immigrants, who attack and drug youngsters?"

"Obviously, I'm horrified. Do you have any idea how long they had been there? I know empty houses are targets for squatters…" She stopped and turned her head towards the door again. "I don't think there's anything else I can help you with today."

"Not today. We'll talk to your solicitor and request the information. It would help our inquiry if you told him to cooperate. Saves a lot of fuss with warrants and the like." They stood. Mandy's eyes held Ruth's. "Thank you for your time, Mrs Crozier. We'll be speaking to you again soon, I'm sure."

Ruth Crozier sat as if transfixed.

As soon as they were out on the pavement again, Josh smiled. "She knows something, doesn't she?"

"She does. How much? Get on to her solicitor again. We need a list of those properties. We need to dig a bit further into this but I'm damned sure Ruth Crozier is more aware of the goings on in the house than she wants us to believe."

"She put on a good cover, seemed a bit scared as well."

"Know what you mean. It's as if there's something hanging over her. Could be all the debt she mentioned. If it's true, then she's got a helluva lot on her plate. See what you can find out. How much truth is she telling us? Who holds the debts?"

* * *

"The Super's super happy," Helen said as soon as they got back to the office. "And Terry's singing. Told us everything except who bought some of it. They've gone to retrieve the stolen goods he hasn't sold on. Once I have the list, I'm going to go through the reports to see if I can reconcile the items with their owners."

"Sounds like a Monday job to me, Helen. What's happened to little bruv, Jimmy?"

"All three have been released on bail. Jimmy had a clout around the head from his mam and Terry had an earful as well. They'll both be in court. I confess I'm glad Lee wasn't involved. He's a nice lad."

"I think Jimmy could be too, given half a chance." Mandy sighed. "Remind me before it comes to court to see if we can put a word in somewhere, try and help him before he turns into a wannabe crook like his brother."

"Wilde. A word."

Mandy almost jumped. She hadn't seen or heard Withers approach. With a grimace he couldn't see, she turned and followed him into his office. He sat behind his desk leaving her standing in front.

"Well done on catching those little thieves. Good police work there."

"Team effort, sir. And it was DS Jones who found the vital clue."

"I've been told there's some connection to our mystery man and Daniel Levin's attack. Correct?"

"Yes, sir. There was a report of men fitting the descriptions of Daniel's assailants in the vicinity of an empty house in Llandaff. We're trying to establish who owns the property. Uniformed officers on patrol say the house in question is boarded up. DS Jones and I were going to have a look."

"Good. Don't let me keep you. It's mid-afternoon. Despite your success on these robberies, the Levin case needs answers." He peered at her, adding, "And there's no overtime remember."

"How could I forget?" Mandy mumbled under her breath as she left. She gestured for Josh to follow her out again. It wasn't so much the identity of Cinderella man the Super was interested in, more to do with Jacob Levin breathing down his neck.

CHAPTER THIRTY

Like the other house, the property they approached was well hidden behind a tall, overgrown hedge of laurel; thick, lush green foliage. This house however, looked as if it had been empty for years. The gutters were overgrown and broken, wooden window frames, flaking and soft with rot, were boarded from the inside.

"Doesn't look a likely place, does it?" Josh pushed aside a branch of sumac, dripping red leaves, as they made their way up the short drive.

Mandy was inclined to agree. A sense of desolation hung over the place. "Let's have a look at the garage where Jimmy said they stashed some of the stuff they nicked."

The garage door was a metal up and over. The lock had been tampered with and opened with an easy twist.

"Well, somebody's been here, recently too. Not a squeak or a moan. Bit of oiling been going on."

Apart from a few empty cardboard boxes, broken and rusted tools and a roll of old carpet, nothing was left in the garage.

"Waste of time. Might as well go home," said Josh.

"I don't know. Look at the door. What do you see?" She pointed away from the garage towards a door half hidden at the side, not the back of the house.

"An old door. Needs a lick of paint."

"And? What don't you see?"

It took a moment. Josh cast his eyes over the rest of the exterior before he turned towards Mandy. "No cobwebs. Let's have a closer look."

The door, when examined, gave them more clues. The cobwebs had been pushed to the side and smudges by the lock indicated it had been used recently. Pulling a set of picks out of her pocket, Mandy proceeded to prod at the lock.

"What are you doing?"

"An old door, Josh. Easy to pick. Not like these new five bolt double-glazed things. I've locked myself out a few times and these little beauties," She jangled the set of picks, "have been lifesavers."

"It's breaking and entering, again." Josh reminded her, with a grin.

"I'm going to have a quick look. Why don't you have a scout around out here and see if there's anything else?"

The lock opened with ease, and a film of grease on the pick told Mandy someone else had been in there recently. She used her torch to sweep light around. Nothing significant. No sign of occupation. Wait. The beam picked up an empty cigarette carton which, in contrast to everything else, looked new. She put it into an evidence bag, took a last cursory glance around and went outside again locking the door behind her. It was dusk, and Josh was waiting with an evidence bag in hand.

Holding her bag aloft, Mandy said, "Snap. What've you got?"

"Fag ends. Look recent. Same brand as the others we found."

"Fag packet. Let's drop these to the lab and see if there's any DNA matches with the others. I don't think they were here long. It's a pit in there."

"The other place wasn't exactly the Park Plaza, was it?"

"In comparison it was. I wouldn't put my dog to live in there."

"I didn't know you had a dog."

"Only an imaginary one. Let's get rid of these and bugger off for the weekend. Woman cannot live by detection alone and your stomach is rumbling like a volcano again." They climbed into Mandy's Juke. She revved the engine, crunched it into gear and headed towards Cardiff centre, joining the queues snaking around the city. She was tempted to put on her mobile siren, decided against it, turned to Josh and asked, "Plans for the weekend?"

Josh shrugged. "Whatever Lisa has decided. There's a friendly on at Ponty. I doubt if it'll be on the cards. What have you got on?"

"A bowl of steaming soup and crusty bread followed by feet up in front of the telly. Tomorrow is drama group."

A snort from Josh. "You belong to a drama group? Priceless."

"Not me, idiot. Tabitha. I wonder if Daniel Levin will have recovered enough to be there."

"You know your niece texted him several times, don't you? Her number showed up when we looked at his records."

"I noticed." Mandy sighed. "I think she's got a crush on him. Oh God. As if there's not enough to deal with. Drama in work, drama at home. Think I'll spend the weekend under the duvet." It was a tempting idea.

CHAPTER THIRTY-ONE

SATURDAY

Deep in a dream about empty houses, rats, high-heeled shoes and scrambled eggs, Mandy was startled by a knock on her bedroom door. With a grunt she pulled herself upright as Tabitha entered holding a tray with a mug of green tea and a slice of wholemeal toast, buttered and with a thin layer of ginger preserve.

"Breakfast in bed. What have I done to deserve this?" Mandy yawned and stretched.

"I didn't hear your alarm and it's drama group this morning." Tabitha glanced at the clock. "The auditions."

"Oh dammit. I forgot to set the alarm. Stick the tray on the side and I'll munch as I get dressed. Don't worry, sweetie. We'll get there in time."

It was a frantic dash to leave the house and as they drove across to the hall, Mandy was cursing under her breath. It was like being in some sort of game where every obstacle was thrown in your pathway. Red traffic lights, cyclists, double parking and pedestrians walking out between cars and vans, coupled with a drizzle misting the windscreen. They made it with a minute to spare.

"See you later, Tabs. Break a leg."

Tempting though it was to return to the warmth and comfort of her bed, Mandy went shopping first to stock up on food. It was at these times Mandy ruminated over her life and her situation. Parenting Tabitha, since Joy had cleared off last year, had been okay. Then she thought about Daniel. Everything a child could want or need in a material sense but distant parents. And Terry and Jimmy's mother. Terry had gone off the rails. Jimmy had a chance to make a better life, if he wanted it. Mandy sighed, causing the assistant at the check-out to ask if something was the matter.

"Sorry. Lost in thought."

She gathered up the shopping and beat a hasty retreat. She'd be talking to herself next. By the time she'd unpacked everything and prepared a meal for later it was time to wend her way back to collect Tabitha. She noticed Daniel's bike wasn't there, so he was probably still too sore to attend. Tabitha would be disappointed.

The doors opened and, with the other parents, she drifted into the room. Kelly was in a corner talking to some girls while Tabitha stood with the teacher and Daniel Levin. For once Mandy wasn't sure what to do. Should she approach them or wait? Ms Thomas was talking with some animation and Tabitha was alight, almost glowing with what? Excitement? Embarrassment? As she stood watching, Mandy could hear the click of heels on the wooden floor behind her and a familiar voice greeted her.

"Inspector Wilde. I didn't expect to see you here. You have a child?" Mrs Levin's tone was so incredulous

Mandy was tempted to say something biting. She resisted and gave a false smile instead.

"My niece. I see Daniel has recovered."

"Not entirely. He's still sore and traumatised. He's very independent. He wanted to ride his bike. I insisted on a lift. This week at least." She tilted her head to one side. "And have you found the men who did those awful things to him?"

"We're following some lines of enquiry. I think they may have gone to ground. We'll find them, sooner or later." It was like being interrogated by Withers.

The supercilious lift of the lips and "Really?" indicated Mrs Levin didn't believe a word of it. She turned away from Mandy and glanced over to where her son was still engaged in excited conversation with Tabitha.

"Who's the pretty girl with Daniel? He hasn't mentioned anyone."

"Tabitha, my niece. Daniel's been texting her." Mandy walked away from Mrs Levin, aware that she was standing, frozen, glaring, at her. As soon as Tabitha spotted her aunt she dashed over, followed at a more leisurely pace by Daniel.

"Guess what, Auntie Mandy? We're doing West Side Story and I'm Maria. Dan's going to be Tony." Tabitha was almost dancing on the spot and Daniel had a sort of sheepish look. As predicted the bruising under his eye was an impressive range of colours, mainly purple and blue.

"Daniel. I'm ready. We need to go now. I've a hairdresser's appointment." Mrs Levin's imperious tone cut across the gap between them. She hadn't moved from the spot where Mandy had left her and was tapping her handbag with one hand, impatient.

"Gotta go. I'll ring later." He gave Tabitha a squeeze on the arm and a cheery smile before following his mother out of the hall.

"Isn't it cool, Auntie Mandy? I'm going to have to rehearse a lot. It'll be fun. Oh, and can you give Kelly a lift, please? I said we could."

"Sure."

As she drove back towards home with the excited teenagers in the car, Mandy's heart felt like lead. She knew what was going to happen. Tabitha was already half in love with Daniel. How on earth was she going to deal with her when it all went pear-shaped? At least she knew how to deal with work problems. It might take time, but she knew she would find out the truth about Cinderella man. Tabitha was another matter. A much more difficult one.

* * *

Paskal surveyed his surroundings. This hiding place was as bad as the last one, worse in some ways. It was cold, so cold he could almost see his breath. If the boy hadn't come snooping, they could have stayed in the first house. It wasn't luxury. But they had a television, and could get out, go for a walk, go to the shop. The boy had changed everything. Now they were wanted men. The boss told Igor their pictures had been on the news. That was why they needed to keep out of sight. Not being able to get out into daylight was proving stressful. Igor was pacing up and down, a caged animal about to explode. No cigarettes they'd been told. Something to do with security and sprinklers. Igor didn't have any cigarettes left. It hadn't helped with his temper. Day faded into night, the only light coming from a tiny slit above their heads where grey clouds drifted past, ghost-like. The rain pelted down, so loud on the roof it sounded like gunfire.

They had food, sandwiches and fruit, and running water to drink but there was no comfort. They'd brought their sleeping bags, with no mattresses, so the concrete floor dug into their bones. A tiny cubicle off the room they were in, had a toilet and washbasin, and they were confined until their fate was decided. Paskal had lost track of time. How long had they been in this prison? How much longer could he endure before Igor erupted and took out his frustrations on him? As if aware of these thoughts the older man stopped in front of where Paskal sat cross-legged on the floor and took out his knife, flicking it open and closed again with a click. Then, with a snort, he stomped off again on another round of the room. When would they be allowed out again? They knew nothing of what was happening in the outside world. Paskal hoped there would be some release from this half-life even if it meant joining Elio in the mortuary. He shivered at the thought. Had he come so far to end up dead in a foreign land where no one knew him, and no one cared?

CHAPTER THIRTY-TWO

MONDAY

There was a sort of anti-climax feeling to Monday after the excitement of catching the gang on Friday. Helen was sifting through the list of items found and comparing it to the list of stolen goods. Painstaking work and many of those items would need to be analysed for fingerprints and possibly used as evidence before being returned. Some items, like jewellery, held sentimental value so it was always a relief for the rightful owners to know they had been recovered.

Josh had taken Olivia to speak to Ruth Crozier's solicitor in the hope they could find some further connection or leverage. She denied knowing the property was being used and it seemed there was no direct evidence to link her to Cinderella man or the others. There had to be something.

"Well, I never. Come and see this."

Mandy wandered over to where Helen was pointing at the screen.

"Here's the list of people who reported thefts over the last month. On the day Cinderella man was found dead in the woods," she paused, "recognise this name?"

Mandy whistled. "Beverley Bowen. She reported two grand missing and then rang up an hour or so later to say she'd made a mistake. Not long before we found the body in the woods. Too much of a coincidence in my book. I think we need to have another cosy little chat to Mrs Bowen, don't you? Come on, Helen. You'll like her house as long as you don't have holes in your socks."

* * *

Mrs Bowen appeared puzzled at first when she recognised her visitors before inviting them in. She gave a faint smile of approval when Mandy removed her shoes without being asked. Helen slipped off her loafers and they followed Beverley into the same room Mandy had been in before.

Beverley waved a hand. "Do sit down, please. To what do I owe the pleasure?" Her lips curled into a smile despite a wariness in her eyes.

"You'll remember the last time I was here we were making enquiries about clothing as we had links to the body of the young man found in Nant Fawr?" More a question than a statement.

The smile still fixed on her face, Beverley said nothing, waiting for another indication of why the police were visiting her again. Mandy paused, allowing the tension to rise between them before getting to the point.

"It seems, from our reports, on the morning of the ninth of October you rang to report a robbery." Turning to Helen she asked, "What were those details again, DC Probert?"

Helen opened her notebook. "A call was received from Mrs Bowen at this address to report a theft of two thousand pounds."

"A lot of money. How distressing." Mandy's eyes never left Mrs Bowen's face as her breathing become more rapid as she clasped her hands together. She opened her mouth, closed it again.

Helen continued, "About an hour later Mrs Bowen rang again to apologise and explain she had forgotten putting the cash in her safe." She closed her notebook and they both waited while Beverley laughed nervously.

"A silly mistake. I did apologise. People must make mistakes all the time. I was distracted; not thinking straight. It's not an offence, is it?"

"No. However, lying to the police and obstructing an inquiry is."

"I… what do you mean?" The smile had gone, and she swallowed.

"On the morning in question a man's body was discovered in Nant Fawr woods." Opening her folder, Mandy took out the photo of Cinderella man without showing it to Beverley.

"This young man had two thousand pounds in his pocket. The exact amount you had reported stolen not long before he was found. In addition, he was wearing shoes previously owned by the husband of an acquaintance of yours. Not one. Two coincidences." Another pause before she continued, "Two too many in my book."

Beverley had paled, one hand clutched to her throat. The other hand was clenched to stop the trembling.

"I'm going to show you something, Mrs Bowen. I'd like you to look at it and answer my questions. Think very carefully before you answer." She handed her the picture of Cinderella man. "Take your time and consider what I've told you. I believe you know this man. Am I correct?"

Outside a neighbour was rattling with the bins. Inside the room no-one spoke. Closing her eyes for a second, Beverley Bowen sighed. Her shoulders sagged and she stroked the photograph. "Yes. His name's Elio Dibra. He's an immigrant, I believe."

Bingo. "And how did you know Elio?"

"He… he did some work for me. Not having a man about the place has disadvantages. Just occasional jobs. He was very good with his hands." She didn't look up, seeming to be mesmerised by the picture.

"I see. So how did he know you had money and where to find it? Or did you give it to him?"

"Yes. No. I don't know. I suppose he saw me at the safe or something. Maybe after I'd sold one of the paintings. Some people still like to use cash." She handed the picture back to Mandy with a dismissive wave of her hand towards the artwork on the walls.

"Why did you ring up and say you'd found the money? Why not tell the police you knew who had the money?" Mandy was firm, her gaze fixed on Mrs Bowen's face.

It took a second or two for her to respond. "I didn't want to get him into trouble. If he… he wasn't here legally. I realised if it was investigated it would be very bad for him when he was caught. It wouldn't simply be extradition, would it? More likely a custodial sentence." She shuddered. "I couldn't do it to him. I'm trying to do some good with my husband's money. Elio was obviously desperate if he felt the need to betray my trust."

"Did you give him the shoes and clothes he was wearing?"

She nodded. "Yes, in a manner of speaking. He had horrible dirty trainers and tracksuit things. I didn't want him coming to the house dressed in such a manner. Not in this neighbourhood. I told him to rummage through the charity bags and take whatever he wanted. He took a bag of stuff. I had no idea what was in it. He may have sold some of it for all I knew."

Helen fidgeted and cleared her throat. Mandy widened her eyes at her.

"He must have been here very early in the morning. Are you an early riser?" asked Helen.

To their surprise, Beverley flushed. "Sometimes."

"So, did you see or hear Elio enter or leave the house? Did you see him take the money?"

"No. I was… I must have been upstairs."

"Why did you think *he* had taken the cash. Surely anyone could have broken in? Why assume it was the odd job man?" Helen was insistent.

"Who else could it have been?" She stood and smoothed down her skirt. "Now, if there's nothing else, I have a committee meeting in half an hour and I need to prepare. I'm finding this all very intrusive."

Mandy stood and thanked Mrs Bowen for her time. "At least we have a name which should help us to find his family. Thank you. You've been very helpful."

Retrieving their shoes Mandy and Helen left Beverley Bowen standing in her doorway looking less than happy about their visit.

"She knows something else," Mandy said as soon as they were inside the car again.

"Yes, very nervous. Should we have pushed it, do you think?"

"Hard to judge. We'll need to talk to her again. She's covering something. We should have shown her the e-fits of Igor and Paskal."

"We've got a name and we think he was an illegal immigrant. It's something, isn't it?" said Helen.

There was no reply. Mandy was deep in thought. At last, she turned the key in the ignition. "I think we could follow up and see if any of her friends can help with our enquiries. You and Olivia see what you can dig up on Beverley Bowen. I'm going to take Josh and have a chat with her friends, starting with Rebecca Hubert. Push her a bit and see what comes to light."

CHAPTER THIRTY-THREE

"Okay. Boss says we can work. Outside in the yard. No talking to the others. Got it?"

Paskal was relieved. Since the move the other three men with them had disappeared. Hustled out in darkness leaving Paskal alone with Igor whose temper had become worse while they'd been imprisoned. At least he'd be able to have a cigarette and it would help. What sort of work now? The car washing had been back breaking and the skin on his hands hadn't had time to heal properly, still red and angry looking. Igor went out of the room and came back with orange overalls, hats and gloves for them.

"What do we have to do? What's the job?"

"Whatever I tell you, pretty boy." Igor spat on the floor and patted Paskal's cheek. Neither of them had shaved for days and it made Igor look even more menacing – predatory and dangerous.

As they left the room where they'd been confined, the cold was more intense. They were in a warehouse with crates and boxes stacked high, a strange sort of metallic smell in the air and noise echoing in the space. A couple of other men were watching them from a distance, not saying anything.

"We move those boxes to the lorry. Got it?" Igor pointed, a sneer exposing a glimpse of yellowed teeth.

Paskal nodded. Oh yes, he'd got it and no mistake. As soon as he could, he planned to make his escape. He had no idea where he was. The journey from the house had been short, so he reckoned they were still within the city somewhere. The money he'd kept in his shoe wasn't much. Enough for a little time. If he could find his way back to the first house, there was more money hidden under the floorboards in the room he'd shared with his brother. Elio had been cautious, handing over most of his earnings. The extras he'd kept quiet about and secreted. "Until we need it, little brother." Well, he needed it now. He'd bide his time. Wait until things relaxed a bit and then he'd be gone.

* * *

A junior legal secretary had given Josh and Olivia a printout out of the documents available from Companies House and instructions on how to do further searches should they need more. A waste of bloody time, Josh had declared. Nothing apart from what was in the public domain. Olivia prepared to scour through again in case anything had been missed. On the way to Rebecca Hubert's house, Mandy gave him the information from Beverley.

"We've got a name. It's a start. Where he came from, or where he was going, is another matter. We think he was here illegally so would be keeping himself under the radar."

"Why approach Mrs Bowen?"

"She's known for helping people. Wants to use her husband's money in good causes. Perhaps she saw Elio as a needy person. Someone whose life she could change. An amount of money like that would make a difference to my life too. I should give her a sob story."

"And me." A long heartfelt sigh from Josh. Things still not settled in paradise then.

It took a few minutes before Rebecca Hubert answered the door. She looked a little dishevelled and distracted, narrowing her eyes at them before the moment of recognition.

"Ah, Inspector Wilde and Sergeant Jones again. Still looking for lost bags of clothes?" She arched one eyebrow at them and then stood to one side. "You'd better come in. It's much too draughty standing here."

They followed her down to the kitchen which looked every bit as haphazard as the last time they'd visited, although a mug stand on the table was now draped with necklaces of various designs and little net bags which looked as though they contained earrings. It seemed the creative side of her life provided more satisfaction than being houseproud. The contrast between this house and Beverley Bowen's home was startling.

"These are lovely." Mandy was genuinely impressed with the jewellery. "Are you intending to sell them?"

"I did think I might take a stall at a craft fair or try to flog them on the internet. You didn't come here to talk to me about my art though, did you?" She sat at the table, indicating for them to join her.

"No. We've been to see Mrs Bowen. She's been very helpful. She told us she knew the young man found in the woods. We wondered if, as her friend, you knew him too."

Rebecca leaned over, picked up the packet of cigarettes and took one out, taking her time lighting it and inhaling with a deep breath. She held it for a moment then blew out the smoke.

"We aren't exactly bosom pals, you know. Being widowed is all we have in common. You've been to her house," she waved the hand with the cigarette in a wide gesture, "it's not quite the same, is it?"

The woman's candour was refreshing. If only she'd say more. Give them something to go on.

"What did Beverley tell you?"

With a gesture short of a flourish, Josh took out his notebook. "She knew the young man was called Elio Dibra. She thought he was Albanian. He'd been looking for work, so she employed him on an ad hoc basis. She wondered if he was an illegal immigrant. She supplied him with the clothes and shoes we found him wearing as she didn't want him looking scruffy when he approached the house."

"Did she tell you what he did? What work?"

Another glance at his notebook and Josh replied, "We assumed odd jobs. She said something about how he was good with his hands."

With an unexpected burst of laughter Rebecca said, "Oh, I bet he was. Priceless. I'll put the kettle on. I think you might be interested in what I've got to say." She stubbed out her cigarette on an overflowing saucer of butts and was still chuckling to herself while making the drinks. She rattled around in the cupboard and then brought three mugs over to the table. Josh grasped his like a lifeline, breathing less deeply now the cigarette had been extinguished.

"Where do I start?" Rebecca considered her own question. "I think it began with the bereavement group. It was something suggested to all of us at some point after our husbands had died. A shared experience. For some strange reason, even though we are so different, Beverley, Ruth and I, shared a great deal of anger about it, I think. Ruth was furious for her husband leaving her with problems; Beverley angry as she thought she'd been robbed of her husband too early; and me, well, I wanted to kill the bastard for cheating on me and death had robbed me of the satisfaction." She took a sip of her coffee.

"What about Mrs Price-Williams? Was she part of the group?"

"Her bereavement is more recent, so she wasn't part of the original merry widows' group."

"The merry widows?" Josh asked.

"It's what we called ourselves. The three of us decided we'd go out for a meal now and again. Give us something to look forward to. Wine and more wine. We drank too much, talked too much and laughed too much. Isobel came a few times. Not really her scene, I think."

She paused and glanced to one side, remembering, her lips twitched.

"One evening Beverley surprised us by saying how much she missed having a man about the place. I joked about putting out the rubbish and she said no, it was more. She blushed and Ruth and I twigged she was referring to the more intimate side of things. We teased her about it. She denied it, of course." Rebecca chuckled. "She said she missed having someone in the house at night. Security. As if." A throaty laugh accompanied the last words.

It had been a good move to talk to Mrs Hubert after all.

"Beverley rang me one day about a week after that evening to say she'd had a very personable young man calling to do odd jobs at a reasonable rate. He had a sob story, she was a sucker for those, so she gave him some work clearing the garage. I suppose it was about the time Isobel was clearing out her husband's things, so she told him to take what he wanted as it was going to charity."

"Why didn't you tell us this the last time we called?"

"You didn't ask, did you? You wanted to know what I'd done with the clothes, and I told you." She shrugged.

"What else can you tell us? Did you know Beverley had either given a lot of money to Elio, or he'd stolen it? Has she said anything about it?"

Rebecca's eyes widened. "A lot of money. How much?"

"I'm not at liberty to say. More than an odd job man would expect to be paid. We also have reason to believe he was in her house earlier on the morning his body was found."

"Good God. You don't think she gave him something? Poison or... what am I saying? She's not nasty. A truly altruistic person. No harm in her. The opposite. I'd think if he had money, it was for services rendered." As she said it, Rebecca sipped her coffee to cover a smile.

"Services rendered?"

With a sigh, Rebecca placed her mug down and pulled out another cigarette, then, changing her mind, replaced it in the packet. "You want the whole story?"

"Yes."

"It was never actually vocalised at first but about a month after Elio started doing odd jobs, Beverley seemed to be brighter somehow. A sort of glow. You can probably guess what we thought."

"No idea."

A snort from Rebecca greeted the remark. "I think, Inspector, he was doing more than playing security man at night. She never said so, but she gave him a key to her house. He was often there at strange times. She's fastidious, of course, so the poor devil probably had to wear overalls or something before entering the room."

"Or shower?"

"Undoubtedly. Probably before and after playing her security man." The last words were accompanied by finger quotation marks.

People who did that really pissed Mandy off but she let it pass and smiled at Rebecca.

"Did you ever meet Elio?"

"No."

Josh opened the folder and passed the photo to Rebecca. "This is the man we found in the woods. We now know it was Elio Dibra."

She picked up a pair of spectacles and peered at it. "No. We never met. But…" She bit her lip, undecided it seemed. "He looks vaguely familiar. Something about the eyes reminds me…"

Josh took out the e-fit picture of Paskal and held it up as they watched her reactions.

Rebecca took a quick breath. "I… is he dead too?"

"Now why would you think that, Mrs Hubert? Have you not seen this on the news? We put out an appeal. A teenager was held captive and drugged by this man and another older man."

Josh passed both the picture of Paskal and Igor across to Rebecca. She held his look for a moment then slowly took out and lit another cigarette, inhaling long and deep, before placing it on the edge of the make-shift ashtray. Clearing more space on the cluttered top she set the pictures down, side by side.

"I don't watch the news."

"Do you know either of these men or their whereabouts? We know they were living, with three others, in a house in Llanishen. They moved from there to Llandaff where unfortunately we lost trace of them. If you know anything it's your duty to tell us, otherwise you could be charged with obstructing an investigation."

"Okay, I get it." A spiral of smoke rose from the ashtray. She ignored it and, setting the spectacles down, gave them a resigned look. "This guy," she tapped on the picture of Paskal, "must be Elio's brother, or related in some way. His name's Paskal. The other one I don't know. I've never seen him, and I don't know where they are now. I haven't seen Paskal since the day the body was found in Nant Fawr."

"How did you know Paskal?"

"He arrived one day saying Mrs Bowen had told his brother I might need a handyman." She laughed, a dry mirthless sound. "He did a bit in the garden at first. It was summertime so he worked bare-chested. Such a well-toned body. He was subtle, stroking my arm when I paid him. One day he arrived later than usual, and I'd had a glass of wine. I stumbled, he caught me, and I cricked my back. I was in some pain. He told me he was training to be a masseuse... let's say we had an arrangement from then on."

"An arrangement?"

"He came Tuesdays and Thursdays. We had sex. I paid him. He left. Occasionally I'd ask him to do other things like mow the lawn or wash the car. Basically, our arrangement was for the other reason." She paused. "It's why I thought Beverley had a similar arrangement with Elio. Knowing how fastidious she is, the overnight security aspect was probably genuine. Plus, one of the charities she supports is to help immigrants. For me, I enjoyed the young man's body."

Rebecca's frankness was unexpected. "Do you have any idea if these young men worked elsewhere? What about Mrs Crozier? Did she have a... handyman?"

"Oh, Ruth doesn't need one. She already has someone."

"Does she? Do you know who?"

"Good God, no. Ruth plays her cards close to her chest. Bit of a dark horse. She's never said anything about it. I'm guessing. When we've been out together, she divulges little but there is someone in her life. Little secret smiles when she gets a text message. Not her mother or bank manager, I'll bet."

When they got into the car again Josh seemed a bit distracted. "What's up, Josh? You got a problem?"

"She's about the same age as my mother."

"And?"

"With young men? It's all a bit…"

"It's bloody sex exploitation. Gigolos. Toy boys. Cubs. Whatever name you give them. What we don't know is if they were doing it voluntarily or being pimped by someone. It's every bit as bad as young women with older men. Some of them are in it for the money and some of them are smuggled into the country for prostitution. Sounds to me as if Elio and Paskal were being used in some way."

"Are we going to speak to Ruth Crozier now?"

"I think I'd like to have another scan through her financial details first. See what's come up. I'm not quite getting all the links yet."

CHAPTER THIRTY-FOUR

"Right. Cinderella man's name is Elio Dibra. We think he could be Albanian. Possible illegal immigrant. This bod here," Mandy stuck the picture of Paskal next to Elio, "is his brother, Paskal. They were both working for Beverley Bowen and Rebecca Hubert respectively. As gigolos we think. Rebecca Hubert was open about it. With Mrs Bowen we're not so sure. Male escort. Security man. It's a bit vague."

"Whoa, I'd never would have guessed now. How'd they do it then?"

"Do you need graphic detail? No sex lessons in school?" Mandy said.

"I didn't mean… Were they with an escort agency or something then?" asked Olivia.

"I doubt it. We've got a few things to check over. Josh, contact your mates in immigration. See if the names are familiar to them. Also see if they are aware of any undercover sex slaves, male, working in this area. I know they won't tell you," She held up a hand to stop Josh's protest, "just tell them what we've got and see what reaction you get."

"Helen, ring the Albanian embassy and see if there is any way of tracing the family. Somebody's missing them. Elio and Paskal Dibra. Early twenties. We're guessing they're Albanian so don't push it if they're reluctant to help. We don't need an international incident to add to our problems."

She turned back to Olivia. "See if you can find out if Beverley had made any enquiries about gaining legal status for an immigrant. It's a long shot. She may have given him the money to pay a lawyer. Check who is on the committee of the charity she's involved with. Do a bit of digging. See what shit you uncover."

Almost to herself, Mandy said, "I'm going to look a bit at Ruth Crozier's background. I'm not sure where she fits into this unless… unless she knows who sent those young men to her friends. Maybe she did. Now there's a thought. I'll have another look at the evidence we gathered from the first house, see if anything strikes a spark. We're missing something. I can feel it."

Mandy took a magnifying glass and scrutinised each photograph from the house where Daniel had been held. What was she failing to see?

First came the financial records for the assets Ruth owned since her husband's death. Mandy began to see the root of the problem and the reason Ruth Crozier was so unforthcoming. She had inherited huge debts. Behind the front of a successful businesswoman, the reality was stark. Peeling away the top layer revealed buildings worth less than her husband had paid for them. The house in Llanishen, where Daniel had been found, was one, as was the house in Llandaff. There were two in Radyr and a farm somewhere in Powys. Probably why Ruth Crozier was so disgruntled and unhappy. Having to downsize was one thing. Knowing, even if she sold everything, she would still be in debt must be quite overwhelming. Poor woman, in more ways than one.

It looked as though she'd had to sell her house at a reduced cost to get a quick sale. The question remained. Was she aware of the squatters or was she involved in some way? It looked as though her husband had gambled on flipping the houses but had come adrift somewhere along the line. She delved further into the holdings and shareholders. She paused on the third page. Isobel Price. Could it be? The address confirmed it. Isobel Price-Williams had been a shareholder in the business owned by Ruth Crozier's husband. They needed to speak to Mrs Crozier and Mrs Price-Williams again. It appeared they were more than ex-neighbours. Had there been discord? If Mrs Price-Williams had invested in the estate agency, was she pushing for some return on her investment?

* * *

Music was playing when Mandy got home. Tabitha and Kelly were giggling, dancing and singing along. Mandy felt herself relax. Their little episode earlier in the year, when they'd been groomed and almost sexually assaulted by older men, hadn't dampened Kelly's spirits or damaged the girls' close friendship. She hoped Tabitha's crush on Daniel wouldn't cause any disharmony either.

"Hey, you lot. How's things and what's cooking? I can smell something suspiciously like banana bread."

"And moussaka. A new recipe." Tabitha seemed pleased with herself. "It's okay if Kelly stays, isn't it?"

"Of course, as long as her mam knows. We can walk her home after. It'll be dark by then, but I need to stretch my legs a bit." Plus, teenagers roaming around in the dark wasn't a good idea.

CHAPTER THIRTY-FIVE

Progress had been so slow. Nothing from the Albanian link, yet. Josh's contacts knew nothing about the Dibra family, so it was assumed the group of men who had been involved with Daniel's detention and drugging were not part of a bigger ring of immigrant workers. The fact remained though, if what Rebecca Hubert had told them was true, the men were, in effect, sex slaves. It seemed more than coincidence when a meeting of the merry widows had resulted in a young man arriving at Beverley Bowen's door. Everything seemed to point to Ruth Crozier's involvement. And what was it Rebecca mentioned about Ruth having a secret lover? All clues and suspicions, nothing concrete. Time to talk to Mrs Crozier again.

She turned to Olivia. "See if you can dig up anything else about those properties and Ruth Crozier's business interests. Where's Helen this morning?"

"She rang in. The kids have a bug. She's running late."

"God, let's hope the rest of us don't get it. Could be the reason why I've been a bit grotty. Come on, Josh. Let's get cracking. I want to talk to those women, and I want another look at the houses we know Paskal and his cronies camped out in."

Ruth Crozier was less than pleased to see them again. She was about to leave the agency when they arrived.

"DI Wilde, DS Jones. If you want to speak to me then it will have to wait. I'm on my way to a viewing. I'll be about forty minutes or so. Was it something urgent?" Her tone was impatient as she jangled her car keys in her hand, folder held close to her chest.

"Perhaps you'd prefer to call into the station. We have some further questions for you. Or we could come back in an hour." Mandy fixed her with a stare.

With a sigh the woman agreed. They watched as she stepped into her car and accelerated away.

"What now?" asked Josh.

"Let's go and talk to Mrs Price-Williams. See what she has to say about the money. We need to get her side of the story anyway."

As they approached the house a woman came out of the gate, got into a van with the logo Fab Flowers and drove away. They parked in the space she'd left. Mrs Price-Williams was at the door surrounded by boxes of flowers. A slight frown was the only sign of her displeasure when she saw them coming up the path. She picked up the flowers, shaking her head when Josh tried to help. "You'd better come in." They followed her to the kitchen where she proceeded to put the flowers into several buckets of water. Mandy watched her.

As if reading her mind, Mrs Price-Williams said in explanation, "The church, St Patrick's. It's my turn to do the flowers. Normally, it would be a Saturday. There's a special service tomorrow, so we want to make sure everything is right."

She took her time. Mandy worked hard not to show it, but her fuse was getting short. She had to fight the urge not to react to Price-Williams childishly showing she was in control, and they would have to wait until she was ready. She held the woman's eyes long enough for her to look away to Josh. A small point made.

"We now know the identity of the young man we found wearing your husband's shoes. We thought you'd like to know."

"It's taken you long enough."

It felt like an accusation. Isobel Price-Williams didn't ask them to sit and seemed uninterested.

"The young man was called Elio Dibra. We think he was an illegal immigrant." She waited for a reaction, but Mrs Price-Williams had her social mask in place. Not so much as a flicker of concern, just mild surprise.

"An illegal? Good gracious. How did he get George's shoes?"

"It appears your friend, Beverley Bowen, gave them to him."

Isobel stiffened. "Mrs Bowen is an acquaintance, through the bereavement group, not a close friend. How did she get… Ruth Crozier. Of course. Clare asked her to take the bags to charity. I suppose she couldn't be bothered."

No love lost between Isobel and Ruth then. Had there been a falling out, a rift?

"Mrs Crozier thought it would be more efficient to dispose of the bags in several places and asked her friends to help." There was no response. "The house where we believe Elio Dibra was living was owned by a property development company, which could be linked to the estate agency. Do you know anything about it?"

"And why do you think I would have any idea of her business?"

Was she bluffing? Mandy took a deep breath. "Because your name is on documentation relating to the company – Rollins."

Mrs Price-Williams didn't blink. "My husband had many different business interests. Sometimes he used my name to... diversify his holdings."

"Tax avoidance," said Josh.

"Possibly. It was all legitimate, I'm sure. Tax avoidance isn't illegal. I didn't become involved in his business."

Josh glanced out of the window. In the garden a starling was picking bugs from the ground. The bird flew off with a flutter of wings. Beyond was the home office they had noticed last time. He looked back to Price-Williams.

"Who deals with the business now?"

"The solicitor has been sorting things out and Simon, my son, has taken over management of the wine business. I think I mentioned it the last time you were here."

"It seems Mrs Crozier owes you a large sum of money. Can you explain how it happened?"

"Bad management. Ruth's husband had grand ideas and he didn't have the capital to fund those ideas. Somehow, he managed to persuade George to invest. I believe the idea was to buy properties either repossessed or needing some work, do them up quickly and cheaply and 'flip' them I think it's called." She looked puzzled. "Goodness knows how he persuaded George it was a good idea. Anyway, the market changed, and house prices plummeted, so when Ruth's husband died the business was in trouble."

"And you wanted your money back."

"George tried to talk to Ruth, but she was in such a state. She said everything was with her solicitor." She gazed out over the garden. "Then, when George died suddenly, our solicitor suggested we rationalise and call in some of the debts. I have a feeling Ruth sold up and downsized to minimise the debt. I haven't asked her about her financial situation. It's not really my concern."

"There is still money owing?" Half question, half statement. They knew the answer. Mandy wanted to see what Mrs Price-Williams would say.

"You'd have to speak to Simon or the solicitors. Now, if you excuse me, I really need to take these flowers to the church."

"What do you think?" asked Josh as they got back into Mandy's car. "Bit of a cool customer, isn't she?"

"Yes. She's astute. I don't really believe she knows nothing about her husband's business affairs. She's an intelligent woman. What did you make about her relationship with Ruth Crozier? They were neighbours and, I thought, friends."

Josh pondered. "I got the impression there was no love lost. The way she said Ruth's financial situation wasn't her concern. It implied it wasn't her business and she didn't care. Not a very friendly attitude, is it?"

Mandy shook her head. "There seems to be a tension between them. I wonder why and what it means for Ruth Crozier. Is it solely the money? Let's find out."

CHAPTER THIRTY-SIX

By the time they got back to Movers and Shakers, Ruth Crozier had settled behind her desk and was clicking on the keyboard. She glanced up as the door opened, sighed, finished what she was doing and stood.

"Lucy, keep an eye please. We're going into the back room. I shouldn't be too long. Any problems then shout. Okay?"

With a "Yeah, sure," Lucy carried on scanning the screen, seemingly oblivious to the fact the police were there.

Mrs Crozier offered them coffee and biscuits which Josh accepted, and Mandy refused. They sat around the same table in the cramped room. As there was no point in doing anything except getting straight to the point, Mandy plunged in.

"We've been scrutinising your finances. It seems your husband left you in quite a bit of debt."

Ruth Crozier didn't meet their eyes and carried on stirring her coffee. At last, with a sigh, she glanced up, "A mess. An awful mess. It's overwhelming."

"And those empty houses. Do you want to tell us about those? We believe your husband and the late Mr Price-Williams had bought the houses as a joint venture."

She held her hands around her cup. "My husband was a charmer. One of those people who could get around anyone. He was also full of bright ideas on how to make money fast." She smiled weakly. "He had a relatively successful business buying and selling luxury cars. I had Movers and Shakers. It was my father's business and when he passed away, I took over. I used to be a Saturday girl here; making the tea; filing papers; sending out leaflets to clients; all before the internet took over things."

She cleared her throat, eyes back to the coffee. "John wanted to expand things. Buy houses, do them up and sell on as a profit. Perfect idea except he wanted to mortgage the business and these premises to do so. I wasn't happy with that. So, he went to George, full charm offensive, and borrowed." A small shake of her head. "It might have worked if he hadn't made several mistakes along the way."

"What mistakes?"

"He bought a couple of cars where he trusted the paperwork and didn't get them properly checked over. They were less than perfect; the buyers wanted their money back and that caused financial problems. His reputation also suffered." She sighed. "And he didn't get proper surveys done on all the houses. The cost of repairs was double his estimate. More debt. Then, when the market slumped, he was in over his neck. It made him ill."

"And what was Mr Price-Williams' reaction?"

"George was a sweetheart. He refused to put any more money in. They had an agreement where John was to pay back at low interest. It was barely manageable. Then John died." She swallowed, took a sip of her coffee and licked her lips before continuing. "It... I can't begin to describe how difficult things have been. When George went too, their solicitor started putting pressure on to pay the debts. I couldn't even afford to do up the houses and rent them out. It's why I sold my home and moved. I was forced to downsize to pay back part of the debt."

A crunch beside Mandy. Josh was demolishing a biscuit.

"Did Isobel Price-Williams have a disagreement with you?"

Ruth frowned. "She was cool towards me. We've never been best buddies anyway. I don't think she approves of me. She's a bit of a cold fish. I've tried my best, inviting her to the bereavement group, trying to make sure she's not isolated, being helpful." She looked away. Whatever had happened between her and Isobel Price-Williams, she was not going to tell them.

"If we can go back to the houses. They became your responsibility. Could you not sell them? Pay debts off?"

She sighed and shook her head, "I wish. John had paid well over the odds, and they are in poor condition. Negative equity."

"You have a duty to maintain them." It was a statement more than a question.

"They're money pits. I tried at first to renovate. Builders who looked at them were talking about me spending huge amounts. There's a farm in mid-Wales. I've been told it is little more than a ruin." She put her head in her hands. "Overwhelming. I've lost sleep over it."

Josh put the pictures on the table. Elio, Paskal and Igor. "Do you know any of these men?"

Her eyes were hooded as she looked down, appearing to study the pictures carefully. "I've never met any of them. Who are they?"

Picking up the picture of Elio, Josh said, "This is the young man found dead in the woods. We know this," he tapped Paskal's picture, "is his brother who may be suffering from a genetic condition." He let it sink in. "And the third man is wanted in connection with the unlawful detention and drugging of a teenager they held captive in one of the houses you own."

A sharp inhalation of breath from Mrs Crozier.

"It's something of a coincidence isn't it when Elio, the dead man, was working illegally for your friend Mrs Beverley Bowen and Paskal, his brother, was providing sexual favours for your other merry widow, Mrs Hubert. What can you tell us about it?"

Mrs Crozier played with the teaspoon. "Nothing. What my friends do in their own time is not my business."

Mandy leaned forward a little. "Mrs Crozier, this young man was living, squatting, in one of the houses you own. He appeared on Mrs Bowen's doorstep less than a week after a conversation about how she missed having a man in the house. It strikes me as more than chance. You are the link between those pieces of information. I think you know more than you're telling us."

"I don't know what you expect me to say, DI Wilde. Coincidences are more common than people think."

Lucy stuck her head around the door, blinking through her long fringe. "Sorry Ruth. I've got Mr Batts on the phone insisting he speaks to you. Something about rearranging the viewing."

Ruth Crozier seemed relieved. She stood up. "I have to take this call. I'm sorry. I'm not quite sure how you think I can help or what you are looking for."

"We're trying to find the whereabouts of Paskal and Igor and the other men we believe are with them. It's part of an ongoing investigation into the illegal detention and drugging issue we told you about. We have reason to believe they are still somewhere in the area, in hiding. We think they're illegal immigrants. If you know anything it's your duty to tell us."

"Of course." Ruth kept her eyes on the floor as they left.

As soon as they were out of earshot Mandy said, "She knows something. More than she's letting on. We need to keep an eye on madam here."

"Bit of a rough deal with the husband. Do you think she's involved with something else? Dodgy business transactions?"

"God knows, Josh. Let's go and have a poke around the house where they held Daniel. There's something there niggling at me. And this time I've got the keys." She grinned.

The house smelt worse than the last time they'd been in. Musty and damp. No wonder Ruth Crozier had a problem on her hands. It would take more than a lick of paint to get this place marketable, unless as a builder's project. The price she would get for it now would be substantially less than her husband had paid. It looked as if someone had made a half-hearted attempt to improve things. The wallpaper in the hallway had been stripped, in places, exposing cracked plaster which was also coming off in lumps. God knows how much time, effort and money had already been invested. Not for the faint-hearted, for sure. They went straight through to the kitchen. The utilities had been switched off so there was no water, and the light was dim due to the boarded-up windows. However, a scuttling announced the building had new residents.

"Bloody mice. Or rats. It didn't take them long. I thought there was a cat around here."

"It probably cleared off when it realised there was no chance of food."

As she peered into cupboards, Mandy said, "I suppose forensics have taken everything of note from here. There wasn't much but something is bugging me. I'm sure we've missed evidence of some sort. I wish I knew what it was."

They moved into the lounge area and Mandy prodded around the furniture, frowning, unsure what she was hoping to find.

"Not exactly luxury, is it?" asked Josh. "Still, I suppose it's better than some of the places they put illegal immigrants. I've heard they are worse than prison."

"Yeah. I read stuff as well. Noisy, dangerous and in limbo, the poor buggers. Not knowing what's going to happen to them. We don't know what the situation was for Elio. We do know he lived here. DNA evidence and those cat hairs from the animal prowling about outside."

They moved upstairs. They were almost in darkness with a pencil light of sun filtering through the gaps. Mandy caught her foot on something and stumbled.

Josh was using his phone as a torch. "Looks like another one of those wooden crates. Furniture substitutes. We used to have old apple crates at home in the shed for my dad to sit on when he went out for a smoke. These are smaller." He peered at it. "Says Montagny. Produit de France."

"I've got it." Mandy was elated. "It's what's been ticking away in my brain. Josh, you're a bloody genius."

"What?"

"They're wine crates. Don't you see?"

Silence before Josh responded, "Ah. You mean someone with a wine habit furnished this house."

"Or a wine business. It's what's been playing havoc with my head. I simply didn't make the connections. And who do we know with a wine business?"

"Mrs Price-Williams. You don't think… could she be involved?"

"No idea, sunshine. Let's go and find out."

It didn't take long before they drew up outside the Price-Williams house for the second time. Isobel's car wasn't on the drive.

"Looks as though she's still at the church," said Josh, as Mandy switched off the engine and opened the door. "Where are you going?"

"I'm going to have a little look around while we're here. I want to see what's in the home office."

"What if one of the neighbours rings the police?"

"We are the bloody police. You stay here while I have a butcher's. Anyone asks, show them your warrant card and make up some bullshit about burglary in the area. Give them the stuff about making sure everything is secure."

"Okay. What if Mrs Price-Williams comes back?"

"Then you might have to use your imagination. Tell her I went to speak to her son in the home office. It's where I'm heading. Don't worry. If she's doing the whole church with flowers, it will take a while. Besides, if she catches me peering into her home office, so what?"

"True. She's unlikely to offer us a viewing, is she?" Josh grinned. "And Simon might be there."

Mandy went round the side of the house and down to the home office. Up close the building was bigger than she realised. It was almost like a granny flat or an Airbnb rental place. The blinds were closed but not completely so she could see inside. She took a couple of photographs.

"Right. Let's go." Mandy jumped into the car, revved up and was out of the street before Josh had fastened his seatbelt.

"Any good. See anything?"

"Well, for starters it's more than a home office. It looks like three rooms minimum. There's a bedroom with bunkbeds at one end. A sort of open area in the middle and then an office. Computer, filing cabinet and safe. There's a door leading from there to the back so I'm assuming a toilet or whatever else. If all the utilities are connected that is. A home from home."

"Does the son live there?" asked Josh

"I don't think so. It looks more of a stop gap. Weird."

"A sort of summerhouse for the grandchildren to play in? You know, camping without the bugs."

A snort of laughter from Mandy. "God, I used to hate camping. The great outdoors. No thanks."

"Where to now?"

"A little chat with God, I think."

CHAPTER THIRTY-SEVEN

Isobel Price-Williams was finishing the floral arrangement around the base of the pulpit when Mandy and Josh entered the church. It was hushed in the building so the clunk of the door closing behind them alerted her to the visitors. She straightened, flinching when she saw who it was.

"Twice in one day. Really Inspector, if I didn't know better, I'd think you suspected me of something."

"Of what? In charge of a dangerous weapon perhaps?" With a slight smile Mandy indicated the secateurs the other woman was holding. "We're still interested in the connections between you and Mrs Crozier."

"I've told you. We were neighbours. Her husband managed to embroil my husband in some hare-brained scheme which proved to be a disaster."

"You don't like her." Mrs Price-Williams made no response to deny it. There had to be a reason. "Was it always the case? I mean your husbands seemed on good terms so I'm assuming you ladies socialised too."

A definite drawing up of the shoulders indicated the question did not find favour with Isobel.

"We socialised for a time. I wasn't sorry to see her move out."

"Why?"

"I have my reasons." Her lips tightened. She wasn't going to say any more on the matter.

"Your son manages the business, you said. Does he live at home?"

"Goodness, no. Simon is almost forty. You wouldn't expect a grown man to be living at home, would you?" Her tone bordered on sarcastic.

"Of course not. I wondered as he was there the other day. Now you are on your own, he may have moved in on a temporary basis to keep you company."

"I may look like an old woman to you, but I can assure you I am more than capable of looking after myself. He sometimes uses the home office. Most of the time he's at the warehouse. He works hard at keeping the business going." Almost a touch of anger. It told Mandy some of what she needed to know.

"The flowers look beautiful. So sorry to have disturbed you." Mandy said before they left the church again.

"So, we're none the wiser," said Josh as they emerged into the fading afternoon light.

"On the contrary, Josh, we know Ruth Crozier pissed off Isobel Price-Williams, big time. There's no love lost there, despite what Ruth said about wanting to support Isobel." She glanced back at the church. "Something is going on under the surface. They've had a falling out. I think it happened before Mr Price-Williams popped his clogs."

"Do you think the son will enlighten us?"

"Only one way to find out. Let's go and have a word with him. Get Googling. Where's the warehouse? I'm assuming on one of the industrial estates."

Scanning his phone Josh grunted and showed Mandy the map. "Looks like it's one of those units near the old tax office in Llanishen."

"Not far then. We've got time to have a quick word. See if he can tell us more. If he's running the business, then he'll be aware of the money side of things."

The units on the patch of land behind the small shopping centre at Llanishen were signposted but it still took them a while to locate the warehouse.

"There it is. Bottom on the left. I can see the logo, WWW on the wall," said Josh, pointing. Mandy put her foot on the brake. Josh was thrown forwards and then backwards. "It didn't need an emergency stop. It's not going anywhere."

"I've had a thought. One of the pieces of paper from the house had www scribbled on it. What if it wasn't a website address? What if it was a logo? What if Paskal was trying to give us a clue? Daniel said he wasn't keen on Igor and the way he behaved."

"And maybe Paskal left Daniel's phone under his pillow so he could call for help." Josh mused. "Do you think he was trying to tell us the wine merchant is involved in some way?"

"Mmmm. Maybe. Or I'm crazy."

"Well… you said it." Josh grinned at her. "Do we go in or do a bit more digging first?"

"I think a quiet little conversation won't go amiss. You do the talking and I'll do the snooping. Pretend you're interested in wine. You can bullshit about it a bit, can't you? You must have had friends in uni from posh backgrounds who knew about wine."

"Not the circles I moved in. We drank whatever was the cheapest, topped up with vodka. Hangovers like you wouldn't believe."

"Oh, I'd believe it. My sister ended up having her stomach pumped due to alcohol poisoning at one point. Puking up blood." She grimaced. "It wasn't pretty."

A lorry was parked outside, the doors open and men moving about. It seemed they preferred to do things the old-fashioned way with the men carrying crates from the lorry into the building, rather than using a pallet stacker.

They approached the driver who was waiting by the cab of the lorry, cigarette in one hand and ham roll in the other. He was wearing a beanie hat and they could see weary eyes and stubble-covered chin as they got close. No doubt he'd driven over on the morning ferry and was desperate for sleep.

"Where's the owner?" asked Josh.

The man indicated, by a flick of his thumb, they should look inside the warehouse. The place was much bigger than Mandy expected with shelving high above them in regimented rows. Inside they had fork-lift trucks to raise crates above their heads. Mandy noticed the crates being brought in from the lorry were placed in a different area. It was noisy with the chatter of the men and the machinery echoing off the roof. Worker bees. It was a random thought. Mandy remembered her uncle Huw with his bees. He'd told her all about how the hive worked and how the queen was dependent on the workers. Not so much different from this. Men running around doing the hard graft while someone else reaped the benefits.

"Mr Price-Williams?" asked Josh, when he could get the attention of one of the men.

The man, hard-hatted and florid complexioned, pointed to a staircase. "Office if he's not outside. He might be checking the consignment."

It looked as if a couple of small shipping containers had been set, one on top of the other, to make an area separate from the rest of the warehouse. A window had been cut in one side and they could see lighting and shelving although no sign of Simon Price-Williams.

They were about to climb the stairs when someone shouted, "Hey. What the hell do you think you're doing?" They recognised the man himself. They flashed their warrant cards, and he waved them up to the office, a scowl on his face.

Josh wasted little time getting to the point.

"We wondered if you could help us, sir, as you are obviously an expert in the wine import business."

"What are you looking for? Recommendations for the Christmas bash? Or even a raffle donation." Simon Price-Williams had a smirk on his face. "We've done it in the past. In my father's time. I think he was golfing chums with a few of the high-ranking officers."

Typical, the old boys' club. Still, if doing a bit of dick swinging made him happy it was fine. Josh had taken out his phone with the photographs of the crates.

"We've come across some wine crates and wondered if you would be able to give us some information about their provenance. What sort of wine? Who would be likely to use those crates? I noticed most of your shipment is in cardboard boxes."

"The future. It used to be wooden crates and corks. These days it's as likely to be screw tops and cardboard boxes. Even some of the more famous brands are looking towards screw tops. It avoids wines spoiling through corkage."

"So, these would be historic?" Josh had his phone ready but hadn't shown Simon anything.

"Possible. Not necessarily. Some of our more distinguished customers like to have the wooden crates. They perceive it as more prestigious. If you pay forty-five quid or more for a bottle of wine, you want to feel you are getting something out of the ordinary." A rueful laugh. "Insider secret, sometimes we actually take bottles out of the cardboard and put them into wooden crates."

"Could you have a look?"

As Josh was about to pass the phone to Mr Price-Williams, Mandy interrupted. "Do you have a toilet?"

With a "what the fuck" look, Josh paused, phone still in his hand.

Mr Price-Williams appeared startled by the request. "Downstairs. Almost directly below here." He swallowed. "It may not be very clean. We're all men here."

"Don't worry. I'm not the health inspector. Thanks." With a cheerful grin she descended the metal staircase. From upstairs she could see most of the warehouse. Downstairs, underneath the office area, she reckoned there was more than a toilet. The door creaked on the hinges as she opened it. A door to the right said storeroom. She tried the handle. Locked. Okay. Fine wines or other valuable stuff, no doubt. The door in front was ajar so she entered a sort of hallway with a couple of doors leading off. The one to the right had a toilet sign so she ignored it and opened the other one. Somebody was living here. Sleeping bags, mats and discarded clothing but no sign of the occupants. The sound of water flushing told her someone would soon be leaving the toilet, so she closed the door again and waited as a young man came out. For seconds they stared at each other and then he made to brush past her. Mandy spread her arms wide to prevent him, hoping he wasn't into blood sports.

"Paskal," she said, "we've been looking for you."

CHAPTER THIRTY-EIGHT

He didn't resist. Or run.

Within minutes after Mandy's call, one patrol car arrived, then another. The warehouse was sealed. The workers, confused and uncertain about what was happening, were held back by uniformed officers. Simon was put under caution on suspicion of harbouring an illegal immigrant and men wanted in connection with a crime. Igor was nowhere to be seen.

Paskal seemed to accept his fate, sitting hunched in a cell, knees drawn up to his body. Price-Williams was vocal. Demanding his lawyer, refusing to answer questions, ranting endlessly about his connections and his rights. It was going to be a long day and a longer night.

"Olivia, get a warrant to search the warehouse and Simon Price-Williams' home. Plus, I want someone to check out the office at his mother's house." She paused. "In fact, get a warrant for her house as well. Now we've got Paskal's fingerprints I'd like them to test for prints there. I've got a feeling the cosy little home office was used as more than a playhouse for grandchildren."

She turned to Helen. "I think we've got a strong enough reason now to bring in Ruth Crozier. Make sure she gets a glimpse of Mr Price-Williams and watch for reactions. I think they're in this together, despite all her protests." As Helen turned to pick up her coat, Mandy added, "And contact Daniel Levin's parents. They need to know we've made some progress. Stop them creating hell again. I don't blame them. If somebody had treated my niece the way Igor dealt with Daniel, I'd want to pulverise them."

"Are we ready to talk to Paskal now?" asked Josh.

Mandy nodded. Time to unravel the mystery.

Paskal regarded them with interest. Introductions made and procedures explained, Josh asked him if he needed an interpreter or a lawyer. He gave them a smile and with a shake of the head addressed Mandy. "I expect my English better than your Albanian, Inspector." His stubble was the start of a curly beard and Mandy was thankful they had caught him before he became almost unrecognisable. With a full beard and a beanie hat he wouldn't look much like his e-fit picture, older and more rugged. He'd shrugged when they read him his rights. In fact, he seemed relieved the cat-and-mouse game they'd been playing was over at last.

"We need to question you about the detention and drugging of Daniel Levin. We believe you were there when it happened? Do you know the whereabouts of the man known as Igor?"

With another shrug, Paskal replied, "He's at warehouse with me. Don't know. Run away when he see police come. He smoke a lot. Round back of building where no-one see him. Boss not like him leaving butts at front door. Is wrong impression for customer." He met her eyes. "My brother, Elio. When can I see him?"

She hadn't been expecting it so soon. It was a reasonable request and one she would ensure was followed up. For now, though, Paskal was a conspirator in a crime and had to be treated as such. Immigration would want a word as well, so she'd try to organise for him to see the body before then.

"As soon as we clear up a few things. We need to find out what you know about what happened to Daniel. You were there, weren't you?"

"The boy? Yes. Is he alright? I stop Igor. He want slit his throat. Igor is madman. Something not right," he prodded the side of his temple with his long fingers, "up here."

"What about the others? Daniel said there were three other men. We haven't found them either so do you know what happened to them?"

A shrug of the shoulders was the response at first, then, "We work in warehouse, they go somewhere else. Igor say they get money, clothes, passports. Told to go. Not for us. Our faces all over screens. All very on edge. Lock us up at first."

"In the warehouse?"

A nod. "Yes. First move to bad house. Cold. Rats. Then room in warehouse. Cold, no rats. Then we work."

There was a whole complicated story here and Mandy wanted to hear it all. "Let's go back to Daniel. What can you tell me about what happened? As many details as you can, please."

Paskal tilted his head to one side and began. "I sleep when I hear big noise. Loud. Shouting. I think it's fight. I go downstairs. Igor has boy tied to chair. The others stand, do nothing. The boy has blood on him, here." He placed a hand on his nose and cheek. "I think Igor do something more to harm boy."

"Did you try to intervene?" By the puzzled expression on Paskal's face, it was not a phrase he was familiar with, so she added, "Did you try to stop Igor?"

"Yes. I say, 'What are you doing? Are you mad?' Igor look at me and I think he is going to hit me too. He wants to kill boy. Boy very pale. Scared. I say, 'Ring boss.' It's what he do then."

It fitted with what Daniel remembered and Mandy was satisfied he was telling the truth. There was an added urgency to find Igor. He was dangerous. If he knew he was being hunted, he'd be on edge. A threat to the public. If cornered, God knows what he would do.

"Boss say we need to leave boy. Not harm. We got move to other place. Igor gives him something and boy goes to sleep. He ties boy's hands. Puts in bed. I take boy's phone and put under pillow. When he wake he can ask for help." He took a breath. "Is boy okay?"

"Yes. Daniel was shaken and had a few nasty injuries. He's a strong lad. He said you had been helpful to him, but you could still be charged."

"For…?"

"You may be seen as the party to an offence. Secondary liability in committing a crime although you were under duress."

Paskal looked confused.

"It means you were involved in Daniel's kidnapping and assault."

Paskal opened his mouth to protest.

"I'll tell Daniel's father and the CPS about your intervention and hope we won't have to press charges," said Mandy. "After all, you probably saved Daniel from another beating, or worse." Thank God he had been there, otherwise they could have found a body. She knew Paskal wouldn't understand all the words although he'd have the gist of the meaning. He knew he was in trouble.

"Then, there's your immigration status. I take it you are not here legally." She knew the answer and watched as Paskal reacted.

He leaned forward and stared at the floor. "We thought it better in UK. Safer. Now Elio dead. How I tell my parents this?" Tears filled his eyes.

"The authorities are trying to trace your parents. They'll be glad to know they have their other son, safe and well. Do you have any idea why Elio was in the wood? It wasn't exactly the most direct route back for him, was it?"

Paskal shrugged a little then said, "Elio like trees. Says he talks to them. Tells his secrets. They whisper back to him." He put a finger to his temple. "A little crazy. We lived near a forest when we were young. He was always there, climbing. Talking to trees."

She regarded him with sympathetic eyes. He was so young. Not much older than Daniel in years; decades in experience. His parents must be frantic with worry. Mandy thought about her own reactions when Tabitha and Kelly had been the victims of crime earlier in the year. Fear, despair, anger and a desire for justice. Even though Elio had died from natural causes the way he had been living and working was something his parents didn't need to know.

"Tell me, Paskal. How did you get here? To Wales?"

"On lorry. We hear man comes. He want workers. Hard workers. Builders."

"You didn't work as a builder all the time, did you?"

He said nothing, looking directly at Mandy as if gauging what she knew or what to say to her. She waited, knowing he would break the silence first.

"We did jobs, my brother and me. Some building."

Determined to get to the point Mandy continued, "Then you offered sex to lonely older women. Did Elio too? How did it come about? Why bother if you were earning with the other jobs?"

He shifted in his seat and wiped a hand on his trouser leg. "We owe money. It paid well. Woman happy to have man about. Not big deal."

Was he blushing? He certainly looked flushed.

"Owed money for what?"

"Money for travel. Money for room. Money for food. Money to buy back passports."

"They took your passports and you had to work for them at whatever was required." A statement more than a question and Paskal nodded.

"Can you speak for the recording, please."

"Yes. We do what boss says."

She wanted to punch hell out of Simon Price-Williams. What a bastard. Keeping a calm exterior, the questions continued. "What sort of jobs were you asked to do? And the others? Did they also have sex with women for money?"

Paskal laughed. "You see Igor's face. You think woman like? No way. He do different things. Building. Car wash. We paint, outside and inside house. Fix broken things. Then boss say we can earn other ways." He made a gesture with his hands, finger poking into his balled-up fist. "Not such hard work. Good money. Women sometime give extra. Elio's woman want him in house. Like guard dog." He flicked his fringe out of his eyes. "Elio, he have plan. We go to London. Big city. New life."

"Did you know your brother had stolen a lot of money from the lady he was involved with?"

The startled look on Paskal's face told her the answer.

"Your brother was found with two thousand pounds in his pocket."

"How…?" Paskal held his hands apart, bewilderment written all over his face. "So much money." He appeared to be shaken. "How did he die? Someone attack him? For money?"

"He had a massive heart attack. It's called Sudden Adult Death Syndrome. It's a genetic condition so there's a chance," she paused but there was no other way to say what needed to be said, "you might have the same condition."

Paskal gasped and put his hand over his heart. "I die too?" His eyes were huge, his distress almost comically over-dramatic.

"There are treatments. First, you'll need to be tested to see if you're in danger. It's one of the reasons we've been so anxious to find you. Your brother wouldn't have suffered. It was quick. Plus, he was found not long after he died. Daniel was one of the boys who found him. He told us he'd seen you one day with your brother. Near the house where you were hiding. The reason why he was snooping around."

"Snoop?"

"Searching. Looking for something, not in an obvious way."

Another silence descended. Paskal closed his eyes but not before Mandy saw the glint of tears.

CHAPTER THIRTY-NINE

Simon Price-Williams was huddled with his lawyer in the interview room. He looked up when Mandy entered with Josh. He had the same patrician features as his mother, without the arrogance. He straightened up, leaned back in the chair and crossed his arms. Although he looked confident, Mandy noticed one leg was twitching under the table.

After the formalities, Mandy waited, her eyes on Price-Williams.

The lawyer, Chivers, a large, overweight man with red cheeks and thinning hair, greying at the temples, coughed, and addressed the detectives.

"My client admits to harbouring illegal immigrants. He felt sorry for the men and was in discussions to find ways to gain legal status for them." His words, in a surprisingly high-pitched tone, seemed to indicate he thought it was the end of the matter.

"Oh, I think there's more to it than that."

"What do you mean?" Chivers was taken aback.

"Two of the men Mr Price-Williams was hiding in his warehouse were wanted in connection with the unlawful detention and drugging of a young man. You may have seen the pictures on the news." With a nod towards Josh, she watched to see the reactions as Josh removed the e-fit pictures of Paskal and Igor and placed them on the table. Simon swallowed and looked away as the lawyer flushed. After a moment he cleared his throat.

"I've seen these of course, on the news. I'm sure Mr Price-Williams had no idea the men were suspected of anything of the sort."

"Really?" Mandy raised an eyebrow. And I'm a duck with three legs. What crap these lawyers talked at times.

Chivers coughed again. "I think I need a little more time with my client. This rather changes things. I didn't expect anything like this and I'm sure my client didn't either."

"Rubbish. Mr Price-Williams was told why he was being arrested. You read the brief. Now can we all stop playing games and start talking? This man," Mandy tapped the photo of Igor, "was at the warehouse and somehow managed to escape. We believe he could be dangerous. So, we'd like you to tell us where he may be hiding out. We have reason to believe you may have other boltholes in the city he may know about, so we'd appreciate your co-operation."

Simon's leg seemed uncontrollable now. He put a hand on it to try and stop the movement and mumbled, "No comment."

Mandy took an audible breath, her eyes narrowing "It's not very helpful, Mr Price-Williams. We know you moved the men from an empty house in Llandaff to the warehouse. We also know before Llandaff they were living in a house in Llanishen. A house where some of your wine crates were found as make-shift furniture."

Waiting for it to sink in Mandy turned to Josh. "DS Jones, have they found fingerprints matching those of Mr Price-Williams in the Llanishen house?" Mandy was acting on instinct again. They had taken Simon's fingerprints during his arrest. A link with prints found there would be further proof of his involvement. Josh was quick on the uptake.

"I'll go and check." They stopped recording as Josh left the room. Mandy sat in silence. How long before he broke? How long before he gave them the information they wanted? She tapped her fingers on the table, watching, waiting.

After a few minutes Josh returned. "Under analysis now."

They were both sure some of the fingerprints found in the house would belong to Simon. No matter how many "no comments" they had from him the evidence would stack up. The interview continued.

"What's your connection with Mrs Crozier?"

Simon almost jumped at the question. "She was our neighbour for a number of years. She moved recently."

"And you have business interests. Mrs Crozier has inherited debt from some of her husband's unfortunate investments. She owes your family quite a bit of money, doesn't she?"

"I… yes, I… my father lent her husband money."

"And your mother wants it back. I wonder why the urgency? Your mother must have known about her husband's investments. It seems a little, how can I put it, unneighbourly, to pressurise Mrs Crozier to the extent where she has to sell the home she lived in for many years to pay back a loan."

"It was R… Mrs Crozier's idea to sell up and use some of the capital to pay back."

"How's business?"

The change of direction threw him. "What? I don't understand."

"We'll be looking at your finances. My guess is the sort of wine company you are running is a bit niche. I think your business is in trouble and you've been looking for ways to save money."

"No… I… things have been a bit slack as there's been a recession and everyone is feeling the pinch." He looked away.

"Let's go back to the houses. Why those houses? How did you know about them? Is Mrs Crozier involved in the business too?"

"I don't understand. Mrs Crozier has her own business. An estate agency."

"Oh, we know. We also know the empty houses where your illegal immigrants were living belong to her company. Or should I say your company. Your mother's name is registered as part of Rollins. How do you explain it?"

As if on cue, a knock on the door announced Olivia. "A word?"

They noted the time for the end of the recorded interview and exited the room, leaving the door ajar. Olivia was waiting at the end of the corridor with Ruth Crozier. Mandy stood where she could be heard and said, "We'll be back soon, Mr Price-Williams. I suggest you have a heart to heart with your solicitor and listen to his advice."

Then, "Perhaps you could escort Mrs Crozier to room two, DC Wyglendacz?" Her voice was a little louder than usual. She wanted both Simon and Ruth to know the situation, before leaving them to stew for a while.

* * *

Superintendent Withers was waiting for them.

"I hear you've caught the men in the Levin case. Well done." He didn't exactly look delighted at the news. When did he ever show much enthusiasm? Except when they found Daniel. Even arranged for coffee and cakes for the team. Bit random but perhaps he had his reasons.

"We've got one of the men here, sir. Paskal is the brother of Elio Dibra, our Cinderella man. He's the one who helped Daniel. The other one, Igor Shabani, is still at large. He escaped during the raid."

"Have you informed the press to alert the public?" A deep frown creased his forehead. It was a worry if the man wasn't found.

"We have, sir. I was wondering if a television appeal might be in order?" He'd love that. "He could be dangerous if he's cornered, and we don't know if he's got a weapon."

"Hmmm." Withers consulted his watch. "Bit late for the six o'clock news. Suppose they could do one of those breaking news things. I'll get the press office on to it now. Have the Levin family been informed?"

"Yes, sir. We're interviewing Simon Price-Williams. It was his wine warehouse where the men were working."

"Good grief. Not Simon Price-Williams from Williams Wonderful Wines? I hadn't made the connection. I suppose if he's jailed the business will fall apart. Pity. Some good wines stocked there. None of your supermarket rubbish. I knew his father. Nice chap. Gave up the golf a couple of years ago. Still the wife was the driving force there I should have thought. I suppose I'll have to find my wines elsewhere if the company closes."

With another grunt he left to ready himself for a possible television appearance. Mandy shook her head. What a prick. More worried about his wine than the fact Simon Price-Williams was sheltering illegals. Unbloodybelievable.

Olivia was animated. "Thought she was going to wet herself, I did, when I told her we wanted to see her at the station. Recognised me too. She's not under arrest, is she? I mean, I haven't cautioned her. Said we needed a bit of a chat like, about the houses."

"How did she react to knowing Simon was here?"

"Well, when you called out his name she sort of tensed. She didn't say nothing. I could tell she wasn't expecting it. What do we do now?"

"Good question, Olivia. She's involved. Has to be. After all, her husband's company owned the properties. And Price-Williams. It's too much of a coincidence. He just happened to know there were empty houses where he could hide illegal immigrants, keep them as slaves and not worry about possible viewings or sales."

"And they were neighbours. John Crozier and Price-Williams had financial dealings," Josh added.

"It's all too cosy for my liking," said Mandy. "Let's see what she has to say."

Olivia nodded. "Told her she could have a solicitor but she seems a bit baffled about it all. Dunno if it's genuine or an act."

"Well, let's find out." She inclined her head towards Josh. "Let's rattle her a bit, shall we? We can't detain her without reason, so let's see if we can dredge up some link." She turned to Olivia again. "Anything from Helen?"

"The Levins are going to assess the situation and will be in touch tomorrow. She said there was a bit of a barney going on there. The mother wants to press charges. Daniel was adamant Paskal helped him, and he'd refuse to give evidence if pushed."

Mandy could feel her shoulders relax at the news. If Daniel was refusing to give evidence against him, it was a huge step in his favour. Sometimes, people did the right thing, and she had a new respect for the boy, standing up to his parents over this issue.

Anything on the fingerprinting?"

"Too early. We'll have everything by the morning."

"Okay. Thanks, Olivia. Best if you get some sleep. It's been a long one and tomorrow is likely to be as bad. Tell Helen I'll see her report in the morning. And I think we'll have a closer look at the finances of Williams Wonderful Wines first thing."

Mandy cast a glance at Josh. "Best tell Lisa we've got a tricky one. Sorry. Blame it all on me. I can carry it. I'll give Tabs a ring. She'll probably go over to Kelly's."

Josh wandered off into a corner to ring his wife. Mandy guessed his reception would be far from warm and within minutes he was back at her side, looking pained.

He squared his shoulders. "Ready. Let's do it."

CHAPTER FORTY

Ruth Crozier fiddled with the wedding band she still wore. Interesting how some widows dispensed with their rings as soon as their husbands went underground, while others hung on, clinging to a rosy image of the deceased. Perhaps Ruth Crozier was insecure in her singledom. A cup of coffee sat untouched in front of her.

"We'd like to talk to you a bit more about your involvement with Mr Price-Williams and his business interests." Mandy took a seat opposite Mrs Crozier, her chair scraping the floor as she moved it. "We're going to record the interview and you are entitled to have a solicitor present, should you wish."

"A solicitor? My involvement?" Mrs Crozier clasped her hands together. "What do you mean? And why is Simon here? Has something happened?"

Mandy leaned forward. She waited, the delay increasing the tension. "Mr Price-Williams has been arrested for harbouring illegal immigrants. What can you tell us about it? I should remind you, although this interview is voluntary, you are under caution. This is an ongoing investigation."

Ruth Crozier swallowed. "Why should I know anything? I've already told you about my business dealings with the Price-Williams family."

Shuffling a file of papers Mandy said, "Yes. Your husband owed quite a bit of money to Mr George Price-Williams, Simon's father. You had no idea illegal immigrants were using your buildings. Am I correct? It's what you told us."

No response, a slight incline of the head.

"You need to speak for the recording Mrs Crozier."

"Yes." It came out as little more than a whisper.

"You also thought it was a coincidence when two of those young men, living in your so-called empty houses, offered to work and provide paid sexual favours for at least one of your friends."

Ruth Crozier was fiddling with her ring again, still silent, her, her mouth tight.

"We now discover your erstwhile neighbour's son has been harbouring the same men who were previously living in your properties." Another shuffling of paper. "Both the house in Llanishen, where Daniel Levin was held, and the house in Llandaff, are properties you own. It strikes me, Mrs Crozier, there are too many connections here for you to be totally ignorant of what was going on. Frankly, I think you have misled us and you've been lying to us."

Drawing a deep breath and meeting Mandy's eyes, Ruth Crozier said, "I haven't lied."

"You haven't told us the truth either, have you?"

"Not everything, no."

At last, they were getting somewhere. If Ruth thought Simon was co-operating with them, she could shed new light on the investigation.

243

"What do you want to know?" Ruth asked, her shoulders dropping.

"Let's start with the nature of your relationship with Simon Price-Williams, shall we?" Maybe it wouldn't be such a long night after all.

With a deep sigh, Ruth said, "Simon and I are lovers. We have been for some time. Before John died, in fact. It wasn't intentional. Simon makes me laugh. I can relax with him." She glanced away as if considering what to say next. "When his business ventures started to go downhill, John became very morose and difficult to deal with. He drank too much and blamed me. If I'd lent him the money. If I'd mortgaged Movers and Shakers. If I was a proper wife and supported him then we wouldn't have this financial mess, and so on. You get the drift."

After a nod of agreement Mandy waited.

"Simon was so sweet. He saw me in the garden one day, crying, climbed over the wall and sat and talked to me. Listened to my side of things. Then he started turning up outside the shop. We had lunch a couple of times, talked a bit about the strains of owning and running a business. It... progressed from there."

"Was anyone aware of this? Your friends said they thought you had a secret lover. Did they know who it was?"

"I hinted to Beverley and Rebecca there was someone in my life, but Simon and I were very discreet. At least we thought we were. I'm sure John didn't suspect anything. I felt guilty as hell."

"It didn't stop you."

"No. I was completely enthralled. When you get to a certain age you start to feel invisible as a woman and the attentions of a younger man… it was flattering to say the least." She flushed. "I don't know what Simon's motives were… it's an arrangement which suited us both."

"No strings?" Josh asked.

"In a nutshell. Simon isn't married. He was when he was in his twenties, and it didn't work out. We are both adults so…"

"How does this relationship impact on your business ventures? How are you involved with his illegal immigrants?" asked Josh.

Mrs Crozier examined her hands while it seemed she was considering how to answer the question. Then she lifted her head again. "We talked about the houses a while back. Simon said he knew of some guys looking for building work. They'd do the job for peanuts if they could live there while doing the place up. I didn't ask too many questions. I had enough on my hands with trying to keep Movers and Shakers together, selling my home and downsizing." She raised one hand to her cheek, her little finger pressed against her lips. "Now you're telling me he betrayed my trust and had illegal immigrants living there. Appalling." She shuddered.

Was she telling the truth? Could they detain her? There was reasonable suspicion considering her links to the other women. Bloody woman. They couldn't arrest her for being Simon Price-Williams' lover so they'd have to let her go.

"I have no doubt, Mrs Crozier, we will need to speak to you again. For now, we have no further questions.

Please don't leave the country. DS Jones will see you out."

Ruth leaned down and picked up her bag from the floor beside her. A slight tremble in her hand was the only indication she was feeling under pressure.

When he returned to the office Josh asked, "What now? Do you believe her?"

"About Simon being her lover? Yes. About not knowing she had illegals in her properties? You must be bloody joking. If she wasn't aware, then she must be stupid. Ruth Crozier is not a stupid woman. I'm going to follow her and she what she does next."

"What do we do about Price-Williams?"

"We can hold him for twenty-four hours. He's been arrested for harbouring illegal immigrants and under suspicion of aiding and abetting the unlawful detention of Daniel Levin. We need to question him further. Stick him in a cell. Give him a taste of what's to come."

"And his lawyer?"

"Tell him to come back in the morning as we're still searching for the other man, Igor. Until we have the slippery bugger in our hands, we aren't quite sure what's going on here. Once Mr Wonderful Wine is banged up take yourself home. Grovel." She grinned at Josh and sprinted down the stairs and out through the door in time to see Ruth Crozier drive off.

* * *

Mandy followed Ruth's car at a safe distance. She expected her to go home so was surprised to see her heading towards Cyncoed. Curious. Who was she going to see? It wasn't long before she found out. Another piece in the puzzle. If Ruth Crozier and Isobel Price-Williams didn't like each other why was she visiting her at this time of night and straight from the police station? It wasn't a long visit. Ten minutes later Ruth emerged while Mrs Price-Williams watched her leave. There was no doubt about the body language of the two women, and it wasn't friendly. Ruth went home and Mandy decided enough was enough. Time for her to go home too.

Tabitha seemed to be full of bounce when she got in, not even waiting for Mandy to take her coat off before she announced, "Mum rang. She's coming home next week. Not December. For good." The glow about Tabitha was obvious and Mandy forced herself to respond in a positive way.

"Hey. Fantastic. Did she say anything else?"

"No. She'll ring and let us know when. She'll be able to see our play and meet Daniel."

Oh God. Two bloody problems at once. Mandy could hardly wait. Although she loved her twin sister, Joy's return was like trying to stop a fire with a watering can. Plus, Tabitha's crush on Daniel was a worry. She was going to get her heart broken and there was nothing Mandy could do to stop it. Her whole body felt heavier than usual as she climbed the stairs to bed. It seemed the case would soon be solved. The problems in her personal life would take more than a bit of detective work to unscramble.

CHAPTER FORTY-ONE

WEDNESDAY

What had started out as a search for Cinderella man's identity had turned into a right mishmash. Illegal immigrants, modern slavery and male sex workers. She left for work early, after a quick goodbye to Tabitha. She couldn't face seeing the glow of hope on her niece's face.

Olivia was already at the station. She was often early. Perky and chirpy like a little bird in the morning and a party animal to boot. The energy of the young. It was obvious something had happened Mandy didn't know about.

"Hey, whose party is it? Or have you got fleas?" Mandy still had a fuzzy head.

"They got him. Pulled up outside Cardiff Central railway station an hour ago. Trying to get a train to London, he was, and bashed one of the security guards. If it hadn't been for an SAS bloke returning from leave, who knows what might have happened. He had a knife and was waving it around and shouting. It'll be on the news by now. They got him in the cells. Doctor on the way. The Army guy didn't take no nonsense."

"Olivia. You're gabbling." Mandy shook her head. "Who got pulled up? What army guy? What the hell's going on? I don't get it."

"Igor. The other bloke. The one who ran away–"

"And attacked Daniel Levin. They've caught him. An SAS bloke caught him?" Olivia nodded. Mandy asked, "Where's Helen?"

"Here." Helen had walked in behind them.

Mandy swung round. "You did liaison with the Levin family. Give them a buzz and see if Daniel can come in and identify Paskal and Igor this morning." She turned back to Olivia. "Immigration haven't come to get Paskal yet?"

"No. I did what you told me. Told them we were still interviewing him in connection with a crime."

"Good. Let's see if we can get him over to the mortuary sometime to formally identify his brother. Then we can see what the next steps are. I should imagine the parents will want the ashes."

"What if they want the body?"

"God knows, Olivia. Wait and see what Paskal has to tell us. Not my problem. Immigration guys can unravel all the crap. Where's Josh?"

"On the way in. He was parking," said Helen.

"His battered Corsa? He'd be better leaving it in the middle of the road and having it towed away."

"What?" Josh had caught the tail end of the conversation.

Helen coughed, Olivia found something fascinating on her computer and Mandy gave Josh an innocent look.

"Just saying the traffic guys sometimes remove vehicles if they look as if they've been dumped."

A strange little snort came from Olivia which she tried to cover up with rustling papers. Josh sat down and leaned over to switch on his computer.

"No time now, Josh. Let's see how our latest guest is doing."

"Huh?"

"Igor was picked up creating hell at Central Railway Station this morning. Let's see if the doctor has finished with him."

"Doctor? What happened?" asked Josh.

"According to the oracle here," she gestured at Olivia, "he tried to get the London train and then started getting a bit violent."

"Bloody hell."

"Indeed. Has Igor been processed, Olivia?"

"Yeah. We've got his fingerprints and mug shot."

"Good. Helen, let me know when Daniel comes in. I want to be there when he does the identity thing."

"Sure. I'll ring the Levins now. It's turned eight. We've got mobile numbers as well, including Daniel's."

"Josh and I will visit our guests and decide who we want to talk to first. Then we'll come back and regroup. We should have the fingerprint stuff back to check prints. We need to look at the Williams wine business records. And I can tell you what I saw last night."

Mandy strode off. The doctor was coming out of Igor's cell when they got there. A thin man with gold-rimmed spectacles, he peered at them.

"How is he doc?" Josh asked.

"A bit the worse for wear. He's going to have a bit of a shiner tomorrow and possibly a couple of cracked ribs. I've done what I can and given him some pain relief."

"Is he fit for questioning?" Mandy didn't want any further delays if possible.

"Yes. But not for long periods. He needs rest."

Mandy wrinkled her nose. "And a bath."

The doctor agreed. "If he gets worse, ring me. Good day." With a nod he left, no doubt glad to escape. The cells were not the most salubrious part of the police station and in the mornings with the smell of vomit from the inevitable drunk arrested for disturbing the peace, plus other noxious odours, it was not the place to linger.

Mandy stepped into Igor's cell. "Good morning. Igor, isn't it? We've been looking for you. The doctor says you're well enough to talk to us, so we'll get you some breakfast and then we'll have a little chat."

There was no doubt the man in the cell was Igor. The e-fit picture Daniel had described was accurate down to the bushy brows and scar on one cheek. He sneered at them, one lip curling upwards. "No English." Then a laugh, which he stopped almost in seconds as he grimaced, holding his side.

Mandy hoped it hurt like hell.

On the way back up to the office, Mandy almost collided with a tall, muscular man. He had a tanned face and the bluest eyes Mandy had ever seen.

"Sorry," he said, "My fault. I was in a rush. I'm hoping to get the London train. I wasn't expecting a little detour to the police station on my way. How's the shitbag?"

Pulling herself up to her full height, shoulders back, Mandy still wasn't on a level with him. "I beg your pardon."

The pompous remark was so out of character that Josh made a quick getaway. She could hear him chuckling when he thought he was out of hearing.

The giant grinned at her. "Sorry. I should have introduced myself. Sergeant Dave Travis." He held his hand out as he continued, "You must be DI Wilde. I've been giving my statement to your colleague, Helen. I'm the one who gave our friend downstairs a bloody nose."

As she shook his hand Mandy felt her face form a stupid grin.

"Have we met before?" he asked. "You look familiar. You haven't got a twin, have you?"

It broke the spell. No doubt Joy had met him somewhere. She was always drawn to a uniform although he looked damned good in civvies too.

"I do have a twin. If you've met Joy, I'm sure you'd remember." She pulled her hand away after she realised it was still clasped in the warmth of his huge fist.

His eyes crinkled at the corners, and he said, "I hope we meet again, DI Wilde. I'm glad to have been of service." He gave a slight bow before walking out of the door. Mandy stood transfixed. She was still a little dazed when she got back to the office.

Helen said, "I see you've met the hero of the day. Gorgeous, isn't he? Almost tops Cillian Murphy with those eyes… He can rescue me any day."

"Helen. You're a happily married woman."

"I can look, can't I?"

With a muttered, "God's sake," Josh plonked himself into a chair. "What next?"

Mandy went over to the whiteboard and started to make a list. "Okay. We've got Igor. He's playing the "me no understand" card so we have to wait for a translator. Olivia, can you get on to it, please? No rush, we can hold him for a while. Give him a little time to think about things."

She wrote his name down, and then arrows linking to Paskal and Daniel Levin. "Once we have Daniel's confirmation these two," she ringed Igor and Paskal, "were involved in his detention, then we can charge Igor, and possibly Paskal, although my feeling is, he was a victim too. Without his interference we might have found a body instead of a live boy."

There was a murmur of agreement. Paskal Dibra had lost his brother and been exploited by Simon Price-Williams in his sordid little games. He didn't need a criminal record on top.

"Helen, gauge the mood if Jacob Levin comes in. He may be amenable to not pressing charges on Paskal." Helen nodded.

"Next up, financial records for Williams Wonderful Wines. What have we got? Olivia, any headlines yet?"

"Yeah. From what I can see the balance doesn't look too healthy. It's been going downhill since Simon took over, it has. I don't think he's got a handle on it yet."

With a flourish, Mandy wrote "money worries," and a question mark next to Simon's name.

"Fingerprints? Any matches? Surprises?"

"We need to chase those. Nothing yet." Olivia answered, making a note.

"Well, get your arse in gear and get down there. Tell them we need info yesterday. We must have something more if we're to get this bloody mess sorted." She turned back to the board. "I'm convinced Mrs Crozier is up to her scrawny neck in all this. Guess where she went last night after she left here?"

"You didn't follow her?" Josh seemed surprised.

Mandy smiled. "Course I did. What do you expect? The woman has too many connections to this to be as ignorant as she claims. Expect me to believe she knew nothing? Total bullshit. She's as tough as they come. If we can break Simon Price-Williams, my money's on her playing a major part. Little Miss Innocence she bloody well isn't. When she left here, she went straight to Isobel Price Williams. From what I could see when she came out, it wasn't a friendly chat."

CHAPTER FORTY-TWO

When the telephone rang, Helen answered. "Okay. I'll be down now." Replacing the phone she said, "Daniel Levin and his father are downstairs. I'll take them up to the interview room, shall I?"

"Please. I'd like a word with them first. Test the waters. See how the mood is with regards to Paskal."

"Going soft?" Josh asked.

"That's me. All heart."

"Yeah, right."

As Daniel entered the room with his father, Mandy thought he looked nervous. The cocky teenager she'd met in the woods after they'd found the body of Elio was probably still in there, but his brush with Igor had knocked some of the edge off. He was still pale. Jacob Levin was as bombastic as ever.

"So, you've made an arrest at last? You've got the bastards who hurt my son?"

"We believe so, sir. We've made a couple of arrests including Igor Shabani, the man who assaulted Daniel."

"And the others? There were five men present, weren't there?" He demanded as he stood, rigid, giving Mandy a "don't mess with me" look.

"There were, sir. However, only one of those men was responsible for causing bodily harm. Three of the men have disappeared. We have reason to believe they may have gone to London. The authorities have been alerted, countrywide. The other men were witnesses. One of the men we arrested intervened and probably saved your son's life." She didn't refer to a possible charge of joint enterprise for the others. Her implied plea for Paskal went unheeded by Mr Levin who made an indistinct sound in response.

Daniel was more aware, regarding Mandy with a quizzical eye. "What happens now?" he asked. "Do I have to see them? Pick them out of a parade?" He appeared a little anxious at the thought. No wonder. Having to face the man who wanted to kill him would be hard under any circumstances. She was quick to reassure him.

"No, Daniel. We use a system called VIPER. It means Video Identification Parade Electronic Recording. See the screen over there," she pointed at a screen on one wall, "on there you will see a series of videos. When you see the man, or men, you recognise in connection with your assault then tell us. No physical contact needed."

Daniel took a deep breath. It wasn't clear if it was relief, or nervousness. He was sensible enough to know the importance of his witness statement and correct identification.

Mandy directed him to a chair opposite the screen. "You sit there so you have a clear view. We'll be behind you, so you have no indication from anyone present. Each person will have a number. You make a note of the number. If you are unsure at all then you can watch again. Any questions?"

"What will happen to the men?"

The poor bugger was worried about it. Was it a surprise? Mandy wondered what was going on inside his head. How to reassure him?

"Regardless of your witness statement, both men we have in custody have committed crimes by entering the country illegally. They will be deported, in any case, as undesirable aliens. Igor assaulted someone at the railway station. We have witnesses so he will be prosecuted for that offence at least."

"And Paskal? If I recognise him on the screen what happens to him?"

"For God's sake, Daniel. Does it matter? He was there with the other brute." Jacob Levin's impatience was apparent.

"He tried to save me. He did save me. He doesn't deserve the same punishment, does he?" asked Daniel.

As Jacob Levin frowned at his son, Mandy wanted to hug the lad. He knew the issues. The questions he was asking showed insight and empathy with Paskal. If only his bloody father was of the same mind. She tried to remain neutral when she replied.

"If you recognise Paskal then your father is right. He was present when the crime was committed. There may be leniency in view of the circumstances and your testimony of how he helped you."

"Let's get on with it. I haven't got all day." Jacob Levin interrupted the silent message Mandy was trying to impart. Daniel held Mandy's eye before he glanced at his father and took his seat. When he said, "Ready," the video began. Photographs of a line of men fitting

Daniel's description of Igor, made slow progress across the screen. Each man paused, stared at the camera, turned to their left, then the right before returning face on.

"Number Four. The one who hit me."

"Sure?"

"One hundred percent."

"Great. Well done." Mandy gave him a pat on the shoulder. "Now, you'll see a different set of pictures to see if you recognise Paskal."

Daniel sat immobile, watching. When Paskal's face appeared a slight movement of his fingers was the only sign of recognition. When the video parade was over, he said nothing, stared at the blank screen.

"Well? For God's sake Daniel. Come on. Was it one of those men?" By this point Jacob Levin was becoming flustered, irritation written all over his face.

"I'm not sure. Should I watch it again? I was a bit shaken when the bloke stopped Igor from killing me. Blood in my eyes and stuff. I wouldn't want to make a mistake, would I?" Daniel turned towards his father. The question hung in the air.

"Better to get the main man, don't you think, sir?" Mandy addressed Jacob Levin, waiting and hoping.

In the background Mandy could see the trace of a smile on Helen's lips.

"I suppose we have to go with it. Seems a pity when there was a gang of them."

"Igor was the only one who hurt me," said Daniel. "The police have got him. He'll be punished. Won't it be enough?"

A period of silence held everyone in the room as Jacob Levin considered the question. It was difficult to know which way he would swing. After what seemed an age, he said, "Well, it's not what I would have wanted but I suppose we need to make sure this Igor Shabani gets the punishment he deserves. If I got my hands on him..."

"Undoubtedly better you don't, sir. We don't need to complicate matters, do we?"

In her quiet and calm way Helen added, "The important thing is Igor will be punished for what he did to your son. Don't you agree?"

Although he looked uncertain about it all, Mr Levin gestured for Daniel to follow him and, with a glance at Mandy, left the room. Helen followed them out, talking in her measured tones. Mandy sank into a chair. Paskal would still be punished. It would be a lessor offence and deportation. Now to sort out the other problem. Immigration would want to take him to a detention centre. He needed to see his dead brother first. Only one way to do it without getting into deep shit.

* * *

Withers was in his office with a pile of paper in front of him when she knocked his door. He looked up and frowned when he saw Mandy. He looked weary. She wondered how long he'd served. How long to retirement. For all his faults the Super was fair and honest. No bent coppers under his watch. He missed nothing.

"Wilde. This paperwork never ends." He sighed and rubbed his eyes. "I hear you had the Levin lad in this morning. All go to plan? We've got positive ID?"

"Yes and no, sir."

"What do you mean?"

"Daniel identified Igor Shabani as the man who assaulted him. He was unable to make a positive ID on Paskal Dibra."

"Damn it. He'll be charged with entering and working in the country illegally anyway." Withers was peering over the top of his spectacles.

"It's with regard to Mr Dibra, I wanted to speak to you, sir." Keep it calm. Keep it measured. Make sure he doesn't guess what you're trying to do.

"What about him? Immigration will deal with it now, won't they?"

Deep breath. Here goes. "Yes sir. However, it struck me we don't have a formal identification of Elio Dibra's body. The person most qualified to do so is his brother. I wondered if we should take him to view the body? Make it a formal identification. Just in case. We don't want to find we have the wrong man at some later date, do we?" Pause. "Sir."

Withers sat, as if contemplating the issue then with a grunt he conceded. "Not like you to go strictly by the book, Wilde. You're right. Sort it. Pronto."

"Yes, sir." Mandy turned away so he wouldn't see the grin on her face. Tick. Objective achieved.

* * *

After Mandy had left the room Ross Withers took off his specs. He'd wondered how long it would take before she asked for Paskal Dibra to see his brother. Did she not realise he'd read the files and seen Paskal's request? Wilde might be a bit of a maverick, but she got things done. Reminded him of his early days. All that energy and dogged determination. And clever, too. Framing the request as an identification. He almost chuckled. He'd seen it all.

CHAPTER FORTY-THREE

Simon Price-Williams looked less than happy when he entered the interview room. He hadn't slept well judging from the shadows under his eyes. The rough stubble didn't enhance his appearance either. A night in custody had given him time to think and his lawyer had been briefing him again. Isobel had been ringing and complaining about invasion of privacy. She had not been able to speak to her son. It was obvious he would do time. How long depended on his involvement and the judge. No doubt they would engage a high-profile barrister to plead the case, but they had the evidence to prosecute regardless. There was more to come. Mandy was sure of it.

Simon gazed at them through bleary eyes. Was he ready to talk? He'd made a huge mistake and he'd pay with his freedom. Now to see who else was involved. Was Ruth Crozier telling the truth?

"Good morning. I trust you slept. Have you had breakfast?" The smile Mandy gave him didn't reach her eyes. He grunted in response. Josh flicked on the tape, stated names, glanced at Mandy.

"Well, Mr Price-Williams. We are awaiting the results from the search of your home, your mother's home and the garden office. I wonder what we will find. Care to enlighten me? We know you harboured illegal immigrants and exploited them by making them work for you. In fact, your list of misdemeanours grows by the hour. Once again, I should like to advise you co-operation is the best way forward."

Another grunt and a glare from Simon.

"Shall we recap? We have in custody the two men who were living and working in your warehouse. Men wanted in connection with the illegal detention and drugging of a young man. We have the statement from one of those men, employed by you as a sex worker, whose brother was also working illegally for you. Later this morning we shall be interviewing Igor Shabani who assaulted and threatened to kill Daniel Levin. He has been positively identified as such and in connection with a serious incident at Cardiff Central railway station. This is a man you harboured, knowing his involvement in criminal activities. From where I'm sitting you are in deep trouble."

The lawyer leaned over and whispered in Simon's ear. A startled expression crossed Simon's face, followed by resignation.

"What do you want to know?"

"Let's start from the beginning, shall we? How long have you knowingly been involved in employing illegal immigrants?"

"About a year, perhaps less. I... when I took over some of the responsibility for the wine business, I could see things were not going too well. I tried talking to my father about it. He was still involved, gradually letting go so he could retire." His eyes wandered to the corner of the room as he recalled. "I wanted to diversify. Buy in wines from other countries. I did a couple of trips abroad to get samples. He objected. Wanted to stick with the French stuff and the expensive quality wines. He wouldn't see reason."

"And things got worse? We've looked at the financial records. No wonder you were pushing Ruth Crozier for the return of the loan." She watched as Simon blinked at the mention of Ruth's name.

"It was my mother's idea. I told her we were sinking. She's never liked Ruth anyway. Thought she was after Dad." His lips curled at the edges.

"Ruth was involved with you. For some time. Before her husband died, in fact."

"You… she told you?"

"Oh yes. Mrs Crozier told us quite a lot about your involvement. Quite illuminating."

Josh inhaled as Simon bent forward, hands and elbows leaning on the table.

"What did she say?"

To lie or not to lie? With the lawyer present how could she make Simon believe Ruth had said more? Ruth had given them very little to work with, denying knowledge of everything and putting the blame firmly on Simon's plate. As Mandy deliberated, letting his question go unanswered, a knock on the door disturbed them.

"Results, ma'am." Olivia's said, eyes wide behind her specs.

It was a welcome break. Gathering up their papers and switching off the recorder, Mandy and Josh got to their feet.

"We'll ask them to send in some hot drinks. You could use a few extra minutes with your solicitor anyway." She noticed Simon's leg was twitching again. With his nervous disposition he'd be eaten alive in prison. The best he could hope for was an open prison where he might not be picked on by the heavy mob.

"Forensics back." Olivia was grinning. It had to be good news. "Nothing in Simon's house but we've got fingerprints matching Elio, Paskal and Igor in the summerhouse as well as a couple of unknowns."

"Yes." Mandy punched the air. "We've got the bastard. Not only in the warehouse, his office space as well. I had a feeling about the summerhouse. What about Isobel Price-Williams? Did they find anything in her house?"

"Not a sausage. The place is cleaned to hell and back, it is. I don't suppose a speck of dust is allowed to land for more than five minutes." Olivia blinked. "She created an awful fuss, like, about the team even being there."

"Tough shit. She shouldn't have a son involved in criminal activities. I can't believe she knew nothing about any of it. What did he tell her? She must have seen men coming and going. She's not stupid."

"Could be they were only there at night. We can ask them."

"Is Paskal still with us?"

"Yeah," said Olivia. "Helen's going to go with him to see the body of his brother."

"What am I going to do? Apart from a trip to the mortuary?" Helen walked back into the room with papers in her hand. "That's sorted. Immigration is itching to get hold of Paskal."

"They'll have to wait. We need to know a bit more. Ask him about the summerhouse. Did they stay anywhere before they went to the first hiding house?"

"Oh, and there's a safe in the summerhouse." Olivia interrupted. "Forensics can open it, in time. They said it would be better if they had the number."

A nod towards Josh who was making notes.

"I'll ask Paskal about the safe as well. I can do it on the way to the mortuary. I'll let you know if there's anything to report." Helen glanced at her watch. "The transport van should be ready. I'd better go."

"What do we hit him with first, Josh? The fingerprints or Ruth Crozier?"

Josh's bottom lip jutted out as he thought. "He reacted when her name was mentioned. Go in slowly and then slap him with another reference. I thought for minute in there you were going to tell him she'd testified against him."

In mock horror Mandy threw up her hands. "DS Jones. Would I ever do such a thing? What a suggestion." Her raucous laugh filled the room. "We've got him and he knows it. His lawyer will have advised him on his best options. Let's see how things go. Play the game."

Someone had taken in drinks and both Simon and Chivers were sipping from paper cups. Coffee at the station was at best mediocre; most of the time unpalatable.

"Well, Mr Price-Williams. How interesting. We now know you entertained our friends from abroad in the summerhouse in your mother's garden. Plus, we need the combination for your safe, please."

"The safe? Simple. My birthday backwards. You've got the details on my sheet."

With a nod Josh scribbled a note and left the room to pass on the information. When he returned Simon was explaining about the summerhouse. Mandy's instincts had been correct. It wasn't solely for the grandchildren.

"I had to take the men somewhere at first. Until we got the houses sorted. They didn't stay there long. A couple of hours."

"And your mother? What did she think?"

"My mother doesn't need to be involved in this. I take full responsibility. I took the men there the first night they arrived. It was always dark. No-one saw them."

"Not even Mrs Crozier?" Mandy raised an eyebrow. "Of course, she knows nothing even though you used her properties and sent Paskal, and maybe, Elio, as sex slaves to her friends." Keeping her face blank, Mandy waited.

"She... what has she said?"

"Nothing much. Innocent by all accounts."

"I don't believe you."

Oh yes. Now a little seed of doubt in Simon's mind would get those wheels turning. He would talk. Her eyes met his as she spoke.

"What you believe is unimportant. The buck stops with you. How, and why, did you bring these men into the country? We have a statement from Paskal Dibra, so we know you drove the lorry. You smuggled him and his brother into the country."

Simon put his head in his hands. "The first time was Igor and another man. They managed to get into the lorry without me knowing until I arrived in Cardiff. Then, when I was going to turn them in, Igor threatened me. He told me if I went to the police, they would swear it was all my idea. He said they were builders and I had to get them work. I panicked. I knew the houses Ruth's husband had bought, with my father's help, were in a poor state. I figured if they stayed and worked on one house at a time then it suited everybody."

"And did it? Mrs Crozier thought it was a good idea?"

"I told her I could get some jobs done on the cheap. She didn't object or ask too many questions."

"Was this before or after you became lovers?"

It was obvious Simon didn't like the question as a little frown appeared between his eyebrows.

"I've had a crush on Ruth since my teens. She's not much older than me and her husband was an obnoxious prat. She trusted me."

"Your Mrs Robinson?"

Simon nodded. Josh missed the reference.

"And the other men?"

"Igor said he had others who would come and work. I didn't want to know at first. I figured if anyone found out then I was in enough trouble." He swallowed. "It got tough. He didn't want to carry on with the building work."

"You had their passports. It was your word against them. You could have gone to the authorities. You don't really expect us to believe you?" asked Josh.

"You've seen Igor. He wanted to be in charge. He terrifies me. I said I'd give them money and their passports back, but he had names. People he knew who wanted to come here to work."

It sounded like bullshit, and she was losing patience with whatever game Simon Price-Williams was playing.

A knock on the door disturbed them again. Mandy suspended the interview and went to find out what the latest developments were from the team.

"They opened the safe," said Olivia. "Got the passports. Elio, Paskal and Igor all in there. Forensics checking for fingerprints now. Might be there's someone else involved."

"Good plan. I think we need to get Ruth Crozier in again. Her houses, her friends. She's got to be up to her neck in it. Bring her to the station, caution her and let's see if we can crack her smooth exterior. Tell her she's likely to get time for conspiring to harbour aliens."

The ring of the phone interrupted. Olivia picked it up.

"Ta. I'll tell DI Wilde he's on the way." Putting it down again she turned to Mandy. "Interpreter's here."

"Right, let's see what the other snake has to tell us. I don't know what any of them think they are going to gain by feeding us a load of crap. It's bloody annoying."

"Oh, and Mrs Price-Williams has complained, she has. The search party left dirty marks on her carpet."

"What the hell? Her son is in custody, likely to do quite a stretch. Her summerhouse has been used to harbour illegal immigrants and she may be implicated. And she's moaning about a footprint on the carpet. These people." She shook her head in disbelief. "Get the guys to process those fingerprints asap, will you? I'm sure there'll be more there to help us sort this case."

"Yeah. I'm on it." Olivia scurried off and Mandy turned to Josh. "Ready for a dose of Igor? Charm offensive ready?"

Josh scowled, "Nothing much charming about him, is there?"

CHAPTER FORTY-FOUR

Despite his night in the cell, Igor Shabani looked refreshed. The duty solicitor, grey suited with a face to match, was in conversation with him when they entered. So much for not being able to understand. The interpreter sat a little behind the two men, taking note of the conversation, not participating. A rattle on the roof indicated the promised storm had erupted. The clatter of hailstones provided a distant drumbeat. Not enough to pause conversation, but enough to make Mandy wish she was at home in front of the wood burner with a hot chocolate. Tabitha would be soaked when she got in from school, poor kid.

They went through the preliminaries, the translator, Michel, doing his job now and Igor listening to him as if he hadn't understood anything Mandy or Josh was saying. Well, it was fine. If he wanted to play silly buggers, they could make sure they dragged things out a bit too. Mandy shuffled the file in front of her and tutted.

"It seems Mr Shabani… have I pronounced it correctly?" although she addressed the translator her eyes didn't leave Igor's. The translator, corrected her, putting more emphasis on the middle syllable. Mandy repeated and got Josh to do the same. She could see a twitch in Igor's left eye. Good. She'd annoyed the

271

bugger. How far could she push him before he exploded?

The interview continued. "Well, Mr Shabani, we have here quite damning evidence. You assaulted a guard at the railway station, drew a knife and threatened several people. If it hadn't been for the actions of Mr Travis, who knows what else might have happened?"

Igor waited until the interpreter finished and then sneered at Mandy and Josh.

"We have several witnesses, so prosecution is inevitable. That act alone will count towards a custodial sentence. However, it isn't everything we wish to talk to you about this afternoon. We also have a positive identification by the young man you assaulted, tied up and drugged, leaving him stranded in an empty house. Another offence."

Again, there was no response. Igor seemed unperturbed by the whole proceeding, tilting his head while the translator, Michel, rattled the words out.

"Would you like to tell us what happened when you found Daniel Levin, the young man in question, prowling around the house where you were hiding with Paskal Dibra and three other men?"

God it was tedious waiting for the exchange between Michel and Igor. Mandy had to avoid showing her frustration.

Eventually Igor spoke. "No."

Josh tapped the table, diverting Mandy's attention. What the hell was Josh up to? Did he have an idea? She blinked at him, allowing him to take the lead.

"Daniel Levin says you threatened to kill him. In fact, you drew blood. We have the evidence to prove your involvement, so you're going to be prosecuted. Not talking will not help your case so you might as well give us some insight into the situation. Were you afraid Daniel would inform the police? You knew you were breaking the law by being in the country illegally, don't you? Yet another mark against you."

"The tab is growing Mr Shabani," added Mandy. "What's the point in keeping silent? Are you protecting someone?"

The faintest of smiles touched Igor's lips. He still said nothing, waiting for Michel's translation. Josh intervened again.

"We want to know the motive behind attacking an innocent young man, a teenager. Don't you have family? Brothers, cousins, nephews? How would you feel if they had been treated in the same way? You'd want to know more, wouldn't you?" Josh was calm, persuasive. Mandy thought she saw a flicker of something in Igor's eyes. He leaned towards the translator and spoke.

Michel listened and then said, "Mr Shabani says he does have relatives and friends. He admits attacking Daniel Levin. He was defending the security of the other men."

"A teenager against five men? Daniel says you threatened to kill him. You made a gesture of cutting his throat."

"A joke," said Michel, "Mr Shabani says he would never have killed the boy."

Mandy let it go. They had enough evidence with the testimony of both Daniel and Paskal to indicate otherwise. She was about to ask about Simon Price-Williams and his involvement when Igor mumbled something. Michel listened, nodded and whispered to the solicitor who said, "My client is feeling unwell again. I must ask for the doctor to examine him."

Alarm bells. Time was running out. She could apply to have both Simon and Igor detained longer for questioning. Igor wouldn't make bail anyway and she was suspicious about his motives. Did he think he would be taken to hospital and escape from there? What game was he playing now?

"One more question before we call a doctor," said Mandy. "Mr Price-Williams says you threatened to expose him to the police. It seems unlikely to me. Was he your boss? Was there anyone else involved?"

A snort of laughter came from Igor. He leaned forward until his face was inches from Mandy's. She could feel his foul breath on her face as in English he said, "Puppy. Do what bitch says." Then he slumped back and crossed his arms. Nothing more from him until after the doctor said he was fit. Clever bugger knew how to play the system. She was half-inclined to believe Simon had been threatened and frightened by Igor. The man was unsavoury and simmering with anger.

"Told you he understood English," she said to Josh as they went back to the office. "We'll have to apply to detain him here for a bit longer if he's going to play the sick card."

"What about Price-Williams? Do we need to keep him here?"

"I'd like a few more hours trying to get to the bottom of all this. You heard what Igor said about Simon being a puppy. Spineless. If he's sleeping with Ruth Crozier, my bet is she's behind it all. Using his crush on her to manipulate him and then letting him take the blame. Bring her in, again. Time to play heavy."

CHAPTER FORTY-FIVE

Ruth Crozier was twitchy. Not so unconcerned as she tried to make out. She was told allegations had been made against her in connection with the illegal immigrants found in Simon's warehouse. Maybe they would be able to rattle her and see if she told them some more. What they had wouldn't stand up in court.

Groomed, well-dressed and scented with some floral perfume not from Aldi, she opened a bottle of water and took a sip, her lips hardly touching the rim.

She had declined a lawyer's presence. "I've nothing to hide. I've done nothing wrong, as far as I'm aware."

It was questionable and Mandy wasn't willing to waste time. "You're aware Mr Price-Williams has been charged with several offences and, if found guilty, which he most certainly will be, given the evidence against him, is likely to go to prison for quite some time?" It was to the point and Ruth stared at Mandy as if the thought of imprisonment was as impossible as a tourist trip to Saturn.

"I wonder if you'll visit him there. Are you willing to wait so long for a man who has potentially implicated you in his criminal activities?"

"What do you mean? How has he implicated me? I've been foolish, I'll admit it. I trusted him to do the right thing. I never guessed…" She looked down and twisted her ring.

"Did you know your properties were being used to house illegal immigrants?"

"No."

"You knew they were being used for something, didn't you?"

"I thought, I mean I wasn't sure, Simon said he needed some extra storage space from time to time and he'd manage the houses. He helped you know. He got someone in to sort one of the better properties and we sold it. Not much profit though it was a start. He told me he could turn the others around too if I let him take charge."

"And you didn't ask any questions?"

Ruth Crozier closed her eyes and leaned her head back. She sighed, opened her eyes again and said, "You must think me very stupid not to ask questions. I had more than enough to deal with. I was trying to keep the business afloat, move house and deal with the grief of losing my husband. Despite his fecklessness, and the financial mess he left behind, I still miss him. We had some good years."

There was a sincerity about her tone which made it seem credible. Change tack. See what happens.

"Why did you go and see Mrs Price-Williams after you left the station last night?"

A stiffening of her shoulders indicated Ruth had been surprised by the question. "I went to see how she was and to tell her I'd seen Simon."

"She wasn't very happy about it was she? It looked as if you'd argued. Why, I wonder? Seems a kind thing to do, check on your ex-neighbour when you knew there was trouble brewing."

It seemed Ruth was not going to respond, so Mandy pressed on. "What exactly did she say to you?"

"What you need to know about Isobel Price-Williams is she's a very controlling person. Jealous too. When her husband was alive, she suspected me of trying to seduce him. Fact is he was a lecher. She couldn't see it."

"Did she know about your relationship with her son?"

"She guessed or Simon let it slip. She didn't approve. She had her eyes set on a good match for Simon, some young thing who would do as she was told and produce more grandchildren. I didn't fit into the mould." She took another sip of water. The radiator gurgled as they waited.

"When her husband died, and she discovered the extent of my debt, I think it was the final step. Even though I've always tried to be supportive, helped by inviting her to come to the bereavement group, dinner out and things, she's still spikey."

It was all interesting background information. It didn't tell them what they needed. How was Ruth Crozier mixed up with the illegal workers?

"One of the men we arrested, a man resident in a house you own, has implied you are the brains behind the operation."

"Me?" She laughed. "You've got to be joking, right? What did I mastermind? These days I'm struggling to deal with my own life without managing someone else's. I swear I had no idea what was going on. Simon kept telling me it was all okay."

"And you believed him? Even when strange young men turned up at your friend's houses offering special services?"

A slow flush spread from Ruth's neck up to her cheeks. "I asked Simon about it. We'd been talking about things. I said I was lucky to have him. I told him one of my widowed friends was bemoaning the fact she didn't have a man in the house. We had a joke about it. Simon knows Beverley and her fastidious nature." She chewed the side of her lip. "When Beverley told us a young man had appeared I thought it was a bit odd. Simon said it was a happy coincidence. I wasn't so sure. I felt uncomfortable about it all, but who could I tell?"

Her gaze was direct. Either she was a bloody good liar or telling the truth. For once, Mandy was confused. Could it be true? Simon trying to shift the blame? Then there was Igor's statement.

"You had your suspicions. And you *still* believed him?" Mandy repeated her former question in disbelief. Ruth maintained eye contact and nodded, unshaken in her denial of any knowledge of Simon's side-line. Try something else.

"One of the men we detained, Igor, the older one, more or less puts the responsibility for the whole set-up on you."

"How? I swear, Inspector, I never saw any of those men." A hand flew to her throat, and she swallowed. "I gave Simon the keys to the houses, he dealt with it all. In the beginning I had bills for building materials for the first house. When I sold it, and then downsized as well, a large proportion of the debt was paid. Simon told me we could take it slower on the other houses. I thought if men were living there then they were working on the house. It's the truth." A touch of hysteria had entered and her whole demeanour had changed from almost resignation to panic.

"Have you been in the office in the Price-Williams' garden? Would we be likely to find your fingerprints there, if you gave us a sample? We may need those to eliminate you from enquiries."

"Not for a few years. Clare, Isobel's daughter, brought the children to stay about three years ago now. We were invited over to afternoon tea. The children were playing there. I've not been in since. I'm willing for you to take my fingerprints if it proves I'm not involved in all this mess."

Nothing. No reason for further detention. No real evidence. A mangled mess. Worse than a cat with a ball of wool.

Josh hadn't said a word during the interview. He arranged for Ruth's fingerprints to be taken and then compared notes with Mandy. She was sitting at her desk, scribbling.

"What do you think?"

"Gut feeling? I think she's telling us the truth. She's guilty of being stupid about her affairs and trusting a shit like Price-Williams," said Mandy, adding, "I think she's genuine. Crap. We aren't at the bottom of the dung heap yet. What did you think?"

"The same." Josh scratched his head. "I suppose we can charge her with allowing her properties to be used for illegal purposes. As the Price-Williams family are part-owners I don't know if it would stick. Igor's comment doesn't make sense."

With a sudden swift movement Mandy leapt to her feet. "Unless the bitch he was referring to was someone else. It's possible, isn't it? He said Simon was a puppy and the boss was the bitch. The mother. Let's get Isobel in and find out what's been going on."

Mandy spotted Olivia coming back in with a coffee in her hand. "Olivia, get a uniformed officer to pick up Isobel Price-Williams and bring her in, please. See if she'll give a sample of her fingerprints. She claims not to know anything about the business so let's check if they match any of those we've got from the summerhouse and office."

"And the passports," added Olivia. "They found a few good prints on those too. You'd expect her prints to be in the summerhouse now, not the passports – unless she knew, like."

"Bloody great. We've been looking in the wrong places. Let's see if a change of direction will shake things up."

"What's the plan?" Josh was watching her.

"We've got limited time and I want maximum impact so while we're waiting, we'll have a little chat with Simon. Let him think we've got more than we have," she smiled. "He's weak. I don't believe he's the brains behind the whole operation."

Mandy turned to Helen, back from the mortuary and clicking on the keyboard. "That's where you come in, Helen. Like we did with Ruth, we leave the door open, so Isobel Price-Williams sees her son and he sees her. Show him we are talking to her in connection with the offence. It might unnerve him."

"Or her," said Josh.

With the plan in place, they simply had to wait. Simon was surprised the questions they asked him were quite general at times. He knew, and his lawyer informed him, he would be charged, and bail would be set at quite a high premium.

Mandy needed to know about access to the summerhouse. It seemed inevitable Isobel would be connected now they were thinking along different lines. She asked Simon, "Who knew about the passports in the safe? Who else would have access? We have your prints on them and those belonging to Igor, Paskal and Elio. Were they left out at any point? When did you take possession of them?"

Although Simon fidgeted in his seat, his lawyer had told him about the benefits of co-operation. He knew his twenty-four hours in custody was nearly over.

"When the men arrived in Cardiff, I put their passports in the safe. They were too valuable to leave about."

"Mr Shabani says you kept them as security until they paid off their debts to you. A sort of blackmail, giving them no choice in what they did."

"I may have mentioned I expected them to work in return for the food and shelter."

"And transport into the country." Mandy raised an eyebrow. Simon looked down at the table before answering.

"They agreed to do the work. They were supposed to do up one house at a time. It worked at first and then Igor got fed up and greedy. He didn't want to be stuck in all day. I set them up with a car-cleaning gig instead, hoping they'd see how well off they were in comparison."

"In comparison to what? Virtual prisoners. No papers, living under the radar… then selling sex. How can you expect us to believe you did those things for their benefit?" She slammed the table which made Simon and Chivers jump. With an exasperated sigh, knowing she'd overstepped the mark, Mandy got to her feet and opened the door so she could get out of the room. If she'd timed it right, then her next interviewee should be on the way. She left the door ajar and paced along the corridor. It didn't take long before the click of footsteps approached and around the corner came Helen, followed by Isobel Price-Williams. Every inch of her face looked set in stone, except for her eyes which simmered with anger. Well, to hell with her and her anger. Mandy spoke louder than usual as she addressed them both.

"Interview Room Three, please, DC Probert." Then turning to Isobel, "Mrs Price-Williams I shall be with you presently. DC Probert will explain procedures and get you a drink if you require. Did you want your lawyer, to be present?"

At this point they were outside the room where Chivers was sitting with Simon. Although Mandy's frame blocked the doorway it did not prevent Isobel from seeing her son. A look passed between them, and Simon's eyes widened as his mother glared at him. If she hadn't been seeking a sign, Mandy might not have noticed the almost imperceptible shake of his head. Isobel's jaw tightened, she didn't utter a sound, allowing Helen to lead her further down the corridor into another room. Mandy caught Josh's eye, a twitch of her lips showing the encounter had achieved exactly what she had hoped. Both Price-Williams and his mother unsettled.

Now, to pit them against one another.

CHAPTER FORTY-SIX

Before they had time to continue interviews, Olivia came in search of Mandy.

"Call for you, boss. Woman says she's your sister. Tried your mobile and couldn't get through."

Joy? What the hell was she doing ringing the station? She knew Mandy would be in work and her phone was likely to be on silent. What was so damned important it couldn't wait? She strode back into the office and picked up the landline, ready to give Joy a rollicking.

"I'm in work, Joy. What's up?" Her tone was curt. There simply wasn't time for family problems unless...

"Sorry, sis. I'm at the airport and... I need your help with something."

Oh shit. She'd been arrested for drug-smuggling or something stupid. Could be gorgeous Georgio, or whatever his name was, had put stuff in her bag without her knowing. Mandy's legs buckled and she dropped into a chair, the colour draining from her face at the prospect of dealing with her sister's latest problem. Joy had kicked her habit when she'd been here in the summer. Back with the boyfriend could have proved too much temptation. With a mouth so dry she almost rasped, she asked her sister, "What have you done this time? Have you been arrested?"

The laugh from the other end of the line was loud and harsh. "Oh sis, it's not what you think."

"Well, what is it? I've no time for games. I'm in the middle of an investigation."

A sharp intake of breath and then Joy's explanation. "I'm coming home because I'm pregnant. It wasn't planned." She paused, then, "I'm sorry, sis. And can I... can I stay with you? I won't get in until late."

It was as if someone had punched Mandy in the stomach. A sense of relief her twin wasn't in police custody replaced anger. No time for the discussion now. "Sure, where else would you go? I've told you my home is yours. Tabs will be there. You can tell her the happy news. We'll talk later." She almost banged the phone down and rubbed a hand over her eyes. She thought back to when Joy was pregnant with Tabitha. She'd felt the same then – nausea, exhausted and moody. Sympathetic morning sickness the doctor told them. Joy had felt wonderful while Mandy was functioning on a low level. Damn. Damn. Damn. How stupid. And how would Tabitha react? God knows. Another bridge to cross. She was damned if she was going to do her sister's dirty work. Was Joy intending to keep the baby? Why was life so bloody complicated?

"Are you okay?"

Mandy was aware of three pairs of eyes viewing her with concern. She took a breath and pulled her shoulders back.

"Yeah. I'm good. Let's nail this. Come on, Josh. Let's get to the bottom of this and some sort of closure for Elio Dibra."

Simon or Isobel first? Making her mind up, she stuck her head around the first room.

"Mr Chivers, I wonder if you could accompany me, please? We'll be back to speak to you again, Mr Price-Williams, once we've clarified a few points with your mother. Unless, of course, you have anything immediate to tell us?"

His leg was twitching, and Mandy wondered again how he would cope in prison. He wasn't a tough guy. Igor had told her as much. The lawyer scurried out of the room, head bent, and papers gripped in one hand. He was more used to dealing with civil than criminal cases and, no doubt, he would be replaced before court. In any event, if Isobel was involved, he couldn't work for both her and her son.

Isobel was on the offensive. "I demand to know why I have been dragged in here like a common criminal. It's bad enough my son has been accused of goodness knows what without this indignity. I'm supposed to be in a parish meeting this afternoon."

The arrogance of the woman was astounding. How she had the temerity to sit there pontificating when her son was not ten yards away being questioned for serious offences was mind boggling. Did she not realise she was under suspicion too?

"Your parish meeting will have to wait." Mandy was firm. "Your son has been helping us with our enquiries and we expect to charge him with several offences relating to Immigration Law. We are, in this interview, trying to ascertain who else may have been involved in these offences. Are you aware that on several occasions, illegal immigrants, stayed in your summerhouse?"

"How could I know that?"

"The summerhouse is in your garden. It's in full view of the house. You would surely notice activity, such as lights or noise at night?"

"I sleep at the front of the house. I don't sit up all night watching the garden." A haughty response, as if Mandy was asking silly questions.

"Are you a heavy sleeper?"

"I have trouble sometimes. My doctor has prescribed pills. They induce heavy sleep."

As Josh scribbled away, Mandy flipped her eyelashes at him. A point they should follow up afterwards.

"Do you ever go into the summerhouse? Would you notice if anything was different or if anyone had been in there?"

"I sometimes go down with the business post and give it a dust if the grandchildren are coming to stay. It's been some months since then. I think Clare prefers me to go to her place. It's less disruptive for the children." She attempted a tight smile, her lips turned upwards, no warmth in the eyes which bored into Mandy's.

Another shuffle of paper while Mandy decided where to go next. "Thank you for giving us a sample of your fingerprints. It will help to eliminate you from our enquiries. We expect to find your fingerprints in the summerhouse."

"Of course."

"You have free access to the office and the safe, I expect?" Josh was trying to move things along. "Should we expect your fingerprints on those areas?"

"We could see if the report is back yet?" Mandy said to Josh. "I asked for immediate attention. It could help."

Josh was back within moments, a couple of sheets of paper in his hand. His eyes met Mandy's. She knew before looking at the paperwork, Isobel's fingerprints had not been found on the passports. Could she bluff it? Dare she? Isobel's fingerprints had been found on door handles and the desk. Nothing incriminating on the safe or the papers inside.

"How much interest do you take in the business?"

A little frown passed between Isobel's carefully shaped eyebrows. "I don't involve myself in the day to day running."

"You're a major shareholder so you must be aware of the losses?" Mandy asked.

"I am aware things could be better. Yes." She pursed her lips.

"Did you make any suggestions to improve matters? Simon wanted to diversify. He says you wanted to stick to the French wines."

"It's where we built our reputation. Our clientele expected it. I'm not sure what you are getting at DI Wilde. What has this got to do with anything?"

Was she rattled or pissed off? It was hard to tell. Mandy let the question wait. "What if I told you Igor Shabani said the whole illegal operation was masterminded by a woman? Simon was a puppet in it, taking his orders from elsewhere."

Beside her, Mandy could sense, rather than see, Josh stiffen. "What if I said he named you as the woman in charge?"

"How utterly ridiculous. You are going to take the word of an illegal immigrant against my testimony? Really, Inspector, I thought you were clever. It seems I was wrong. You need to speak to Ruth Crozier. Simon's infatuation with her has coloured everything. Do you know he broke off his engagement with a very decent young woman because of her? If anyone tells Simon what to do, it's that woman."

"Why did she visit you late last night?"

Fleetingly, Isobel looked startled. She recovered within seconds. "To gloat, I suppose. She knows how all this business will affect my standing in the community, with the church." She looked down at her hands, clasped on her knee. "Simon was never meant to be a businessman. Too lacking in imagination, hopeless with people and figures. It's been so difficult since my husband died. He's refused to let me help. I had a feeling there was something. I was too wrapped up in my grief to bother much. All this," she waved a hand in the air in front of her face, "this debacle is my fault for letting him have his head."

There was nothing more they could do. No solid evidence linking Isobel except her son used the office in her garden. They had to let her go. Helen confirmed in the search of the house they had seen medication for Isobel, including sleeping tablets.

They'd have one last shot at getting information out of Simon and Igor, if he had stopped playing the sick card, and then it would be back to the beginning. Sift through everything, checking what had been missed.

Weariness was setting in. Her body felt heavy and her heart too when she thought of Joy on the coach speeding towards Cardiff. Bloody sympathetic morning sickness. Couvade syndrome to give it the correct term. It was making her feel like hell. More problems. More tears. More headaches. And the day wasn't over.

CHAPTER FORTY-SEVEN

"The doctor says Mr Shabani is well enough to be questioned further although he'll need frequent breaks," said Helen.

"Thanks, Helen. You'd best get off home now."

"I want to run through something first. I won't be long." She tucked a strand of hair behind her ear and peered at the computer screen. They left her to it. It looked as though Olivia had left unless she was trying to get something out of the technical team.

There was no time to warm Igor up with irrelevant questions, so Mandy got straight to the point. "Describe the boss. I think it's a woman. What does she look like?"

He shrugged and muttered something incomprehensible. Mandy raised an eyebrow. The interpreter said, "Mr Shabani says he never saw her face. She kept hidden. He heard her, and he could smell her perfume. Flowery. Like your DC Helen wears."

No description, just a perfume. Mandy grinned at him and leapt to her feet, leaving Josh to carry on with the set of questions they wanted to ask. She hoped Helen was still there and was disappointed to find the computer shut down and the chair empty.

"Oh bollocks."

Helen came from behind. "I was in the toilet. Something you want me to do?"

"Your perfume. What is it?"

"Cheap alternative to Chanel. 5th Element from Aldi." Helen smiled. "I didn't think you were into perfumes."

"Who else wears the same sort of perfume? Probably the real deal. Somebody we've been talking to? Think."

Helen's face lit up. "Mrs Crozier. I recognised it when she came in. I remarked on it in fact, and she said something about a gift. Not her usual choice. Why?"

"That's it. The link. She's the boss. Igor never saw the woman. He remembered her scent. She's the clever bitch behind it after all."

"We've no evidence, apart from Igor's statement and it's a bit dodgy, isn't it?" said Helen, with a slight frown.

"What's a bit dodgy?" Josh asked. "Nothing more out of Shabani. Shrugs and grunts. Looks like we're at the end of the road."

"Not yet. I've one or two tricks up my sleeve."

"Oh God." Josh's groan was audible. "What next?"

"A little subterfuge, I think. Send uniform to pick up Ruth Crozier. No actually, I'd like to do this one myself. You up for it, Josh?"

"As if I had a choice." With an overdramatic sigh and roll of the eyes towards Helen, he trotted after Mandy.

Mandy had given Josh and Helen the impression she had a plan, when in fact all she had was a gut feeling and an idea. Ruth Crozier was a good actress, but Mandy knew a thing or two about playing poker-faced too. Game on.

A surprised Ruth Crozier opened the door. She was dressed in pale grey lounge pants and top and had a glass of white wine in her hand. Not exactly broken-hearted with the knowledge her lover was going to be imprisoned. No doubt she thought she'd got away with it all.

"Inspector Wilde. I thought we'd finished our little conversation."

"May we come in? We don't want to alert the neighbours, do we?"

"It's a little late." With a shrug, she gestured for them to enter the narrow hallway, Josh almost squashed against a table as they waited for her to lead the way to a square shaped lounge. The room was furnished with two blue velvet sofas, a flatscreen television in one corner and side tables in pale oak. A vase of lilies on the windowsill gave off a heavy scent. Mandy hated lilies. She always thought of them in connection with death.

"I suppose you'd better sit down," said Ruth. Then, with a hint of impatience, "What now?"

They took their time sitting down on one sofa, so soft Josh seemed to sink into the depths, while Ruth perched on the other. She had set the wine glass down and held her hands pressed together in between her knees.

"I'm afraid we need you to come back down to the station with us for further questioning." Mandy paused. "Mr Price-Williams has been co-operating with us. Things are not as clear cut as we thought." She cleared her throat. "Your involvement in harbouring the illegal immigrants, for example."

"Simon didn't…" She shook her head. "No, of course not. How could he when I wasn't there?"

Josh was rigid although Mandy could feel his breathing increase. She knew he hated it when she tried to force issues. Too bad.

"We also have a witness who is able to identify you as the brains behind it all."

"Nonsense. Impossible."

"How could it be impossible? We have two men in custody. Two men who formed part of an illegal workforce. Two men who were kept virtually captive in a house you owned and used for labour and sex services for your friends. Two men who will be able to identify the woman known to them simply as 'The Boss'." She made quotation marks in the air around the final words before saying, "We think it's you." Mandy hoped she sounded more confident than she felt. Josh sat silent beside her, his presence a support.

"They couldn't recognise me." She flushed, eyes blazing. "I wasn't there. I don't care what they say. I've been duped by Simon. I'm guilty of being blinkered. As if my husband wasn't enough of an idiot, I have to fall for another one."

"You'd better come with us now. I think we need to continue this conversation at the station."

CHAPTER FORTY-EIGHT

The journey back to the station was silent. Ruth sat in the back. It appeared she had lost her bravado and remained subdued, no doubt wondering what evidence they had amassed. Precious little if truth be told. The onus was on them to find more. Plus, the clock was ticking, and Joy would be back to Brithir Street and talking to Tabitha before there had been a chance to prepare her.

They were surprised to see both Helen and Olivia still there. Expectation that the investigation was drawing to a close had encouraged them to remain at work.

"We've an hour before we have to apply for more time if we want to detain Simon further," said Josh once Ruth had been settled into an interview room. "Is it worth trying to get him to squeal on Ruth? He didn't say anything before. Do you think he's going to talk now?"

"Worth a shot. Why not?" Mandy turned to Olivia. "Can you go and have a little chat with Mrs Crozier, please? Find out where she was the day after the men were moved. Check it out. Otherwise, we've haven't got much to hold her except the scent of a perfume and a gut feeling." To Josh she said, "You see if you can get him to talk. I'm knackered."

"You need some time off."

"Yeah, maybe. Let's see what simple Simon has to say to us."

It was possible Chivers had told Simon about his impending release on bail as he seemed less fraught than before. Not twitching at least. They sat down, switched on the recorder and Josh started questioning while Mandy watched for reactions.

"We've been talking to your girlfriend again." Josh leaned forward a little. "Women. Hard to please, aren't they?"

Disarmed by the remark, Simon tilted his head a little and didn't respond.

"We know you weren't behind it all now. We've a witness who has recognised your girlfriend. Says she's the one in control. Told the men what to do. Told you what to do. Like a little puppy. So, you might as well give us the whole story. The truth. How did she make you do it?"

Simon almost jumped out of the chair. "Who recognised her? They couldn't. They're lying."

Some reaction. Was he covering for his girlfriend? If she didn't feel so exhausted, Mandy would have felt like singing. As it was, she couldn't even raise a smile. Josh pressed on.

"We knew she was behind it. Too many coincidences. So, let's recap. How did this business all start?"

"It was Igor. When I discovered him and his mate in the lorry, I was going to report it."

He looked earnest enough. "You've seen Igor. He threatened me. Said I had to help. I was going to give them some money and turn a blind eye."

"That is in itself an offence, sir," Josh reminded him.

"He said they were builders and would work hard if I gave them a chance." Now he'd started to talk, Simon seemed relieved and even eager to tell his side of the story. "I thought if they worked on refurbishing the houses it would be a way of helping them and helping Ruth."

"What went wrong?"

"I brought in a couple of young men to help. The first house was done on the cheap and it was all good. But Igor decided it wasn't enough. He started pushing for more. As I told you, I thought I'd show them what hard work was all about and got them cleaning cars instead."

"And they agreed to that? Or was it because you had their passports, so they were trapped?" asked Josh.

Simon looked flustered at the question, glancing at Chivers and then back to Josh and Mandy.

"They wanted a change of direction. It would have worked out. They'd soon have changed their tune again. Elio and Paskal knew how to earn extra. If Igor hadn't grabbed that boy and mucked everything up..."

"I've just remembered something." Mandy said. "The morning Elio died he had two thousand pounds in his pocket. He'd stolen it from Beverley Bowen. Did you know about that?"

"I think it may have been mentioned at some point."

"Pillow talk no doubt." They had connections.

After being charged, Simon had to surrender his passport and was released on bail. His mother would make his life hell for him. Prison for somewhere between five and fourteen years was on the cards, depending on the ability of the defence lawyer. He'd better hope for a sympathetic judge and jury when it went to trial.

"Result," said Josh, with a yawn. "It's been a long day. Let's hope Olivia has something positive from her chat with Mrs Crozier."

"It has been a long day and it's not over yet. Come on."

"Where to? Thought we were going to interview Ruth Crozier."

"Yes. Half an hour isn't going to make a difference. We're going to see Beverley Bowen. We need to get evidence from her. Make the case against Ruth more solid. Simon hasn't exactly named her, has he? In fact, he's been non-committal."

"Can't it wait until the morning?" asked Josh.

"No. It can't bloody wait. We've dragged Ruth Crozier into the station and left her dangling. I want this sorted now before she drives us down another pathway. All smouldering acquiescence and 'poor little me' isn't going to work anymore. I want her pinned to the wall with no way off."

Mrs Bowen's house was alight, and a porch lamp streamed across the front pathway, drive and lawn. Security no doubt. No burglar could avoid those beams. Beverley opened the door a notch, a chain securing the gap.

"Oh, the police. Has something happened?"

She rattled the chain, released it and allowed them to enter. They didn't need to be prompted and removed their shoes in the hallway. Josh's socks were intact this time.

The lounge looked different in the evening, table lamps providing subdued lighting and jazz playing in the background. Although a fire was lit in the grate there was no smoke or smell. Probably gas. Realistic and expensive no doubt. Similar to the one in Isobel Price-Williams' house. A paperback lay opened on one chair, spectacles on top. Beverley indicated for them to sit, glancing from one to the other, waiting for a cue.

"My apologies for disturbing your evening. A couple of questions if you don't mind answering?" It was polite, although clear the questions were to be answered.

"Of course, Inspector. How may I help?"

"It's about the morning after you discovered Elio had stolen two thousand pounds from you," Mandy paused as Beverley took a breath, "After you reported the theft to the police, what did you do then? Did you ring anyone else?"

"I wandered around in a daze for a little time. I was quite shaken."

"And then?"

"I rang Ruth."

"Why Ruth?"

Beverley had gripped both hands together so tightly the knuckles were white. She swallowed and looked away before answering. "I thought she might give me some advice. She's very down to earth. Comes from running a business, I suppose."

"And what advice did Mrs Crozier give you?"

Beverley fidgeted, twisting her wedding ring and puffing a little.

"She wasn't there. The girl said she was out of the office. I was quite distraught. At a loss."

Damn. There went Mandy's idea of pinning Ruth down as the villain of the piece. Beverley wasn't quite finished though, and she seemed almost distressed at the memories of the morning.

"I really didn't know who to turn to. I left a message asking Ruth to ring me back."

"Did she? Ring you back?"

"Much later. The same evening. After you'd called and asked about the bags of George's clothes. I was going round in circles. Not so much about the money. More about the lack of security. Elio knew where the spare key was left outside. If he had stolen from me, I no longer felt secure. I was thinking I'd probably have to change the locks."

Mandy's limbs felt like lead. With only circumstantial evidence against Ruth, they were stuck. Beverley hadn't finished though and what she said next made them sit up and take notice.

"Then the phone rang, and it was Isobel. I blurted it all out. She was so good at listening and understood why I liked having Elio here overnight. Not judgemental at all. It surprised me as I've often found her quite cool."

"Did she give you any advice?" asked Josh.

"She reminded me if the police found Elio and what he'd been doing in my house it wouldn't look good. Plus, if the press discovered," she took a breath, "it would make a mockery of all my charity work. All the good I had achieved would be swallowed by scandal."

"Is that all?"

A shake of the head. "No. She told me not to worry. She was sure I would get the money back and then she changed the subject."

"How?

"She told me the business would be able to sponsor an exhibition I was planning. I'd been lamenting about lack of sponsorship. Isobel said she might be able to get some raffle prizes as well."

A bribe in effect. They could have probably charge Beverley for obstruction of justice. What was the point? Humiliation for a woman who was trying to do some good in the world. Punishment for being foolish and naïve. It wasn't worth it. They would double check phone records, make sure of the facts and CPS would take over.

"Did Mrs Price-Williams give you any money to replace the two thousand?" asked Josh.

"She made a donation. It was about that amount."

Good question, Josh.

Back in the car Josh said, "If she'd told us all that in the first place, we might have got to the answer sooner. Obstruction?"

"I was thinking the same thing as she was talking. We didn't ask her the right questions though, did we? She told us what she knew. She identified Elio and was open about it. I don't think, in fairness, we can drag her through the mud over an omission. She does a lot of good work for the charity. Destroy her reputation and hundreds of homeless people will lose out as well. My bet is the CPS would think it's not in the public interest to press charges."

"Yeah. Suppose so. What now?"

"Back to the station. Release Ruth. Brief word with Igor and then home." The streetlights illuminated Josh's profile as she turned towards him. "How do you fancy leading the team for a week. I need some time off."

"Are you feeling okay? I... em... you've been looking a bit peaky for a couple of weeks. No offence."

"No worries. I feel knackered and nauseous a lot of the time. Courtesy of my sister."

"Joy? Thought she was off in sunnier climes."

"She was. She's back. Tonight. For good this time according to the latest message. I'm going to need some time to help her sort her shit." With a thump on the steering wheel Mandy continued, "I'm fed up clearing up after her and if she hurts Tabitha again by buggering about, I'm going to clock her one."

"Right."

She laughed. "Don't worry, you won't be called to a scene of domestic violence. Though we do have a hell of a lot to work out. I may tell you sometime. Not now. Let's get in and get this done."

* * *

Withers was waiting for them, a face like the Grim Reaper and tapping his watch face.

"How many hours overtime have you lot clocked up today? What's going on? Do you not think about how I'm supposed to justify the extra hours?"

Biting her lip to avoid saying something she might regret later, Mandy said, "Sorry sir, we needed another thread of evidence. DS Jones was about to charge Mrs Crozier but there's been a further complication."

"Humph. Good. Been a bit of a blinder, hasn't it?"

"Sir." Mandy hesitated before adding, "I wonder when this is sorted if it would be a good time for me to take some leave? I've a few personal things to sort and DS Jones could do with a bit more experience leading the team. Of course, if there's anything urgent…"

Withers stared at her for longer than was necessary. "Life and the job don't always mix, do they?" It was unexpected. Insightful. Of course, the old bugger had been doing the job for years and knew the costs. "Go through the channels. I'll approve it. We all need time away." He turned away and then swung back. "Get this sorted first."

* * *

Igor was slouched in a corner of the room. He was wary when they entered, watching like a fox surrounded by hounds.

"We know you can speak English so let's not go through all that rigmarole again tonight. It's late, I'm tired and I want to get this sorted. Okay?" asked Mandy. "If Price-Williams isn't the boss, who is? Do you have any description at all?"

He sat staring at them, not speaking and then he sat more upright. "Why I tell you anything?"

"So we get the person behind all this. Justice. For Elio. For Paskal. For you. You've been manipulated and treated badly. Locked up, forced to work. A judge could be more lenient if he knows you helped us to find the mastermind."

Igor considered it. "I go to prison."

"Yes. You harmed a boy and threatened people at the station. Criminal offences. You've also been working illegally. We can say you were forced to do so. They had your passports." She let it sink in. "Who is the boss? Where and when have you seen her? What can you tell us? Anything."

He cleared his throat and Mandy thought he was going to spit at them. Josh was fidgeting beside her, unsure what was happening.

"No face. I see her at warehouse. Dressed in black. Shouting at him. 'Stupid boy. Get rid of them. If you get caught…' Then she leave and I go to see him. Perfume fill room."

"It's not enough to convict someone. There must be something else. Was she wearing rings? Did she have an accent? Anything?" A wave of despair filled Mandy. They were so close and yet so far.

"She old." said Igor.

"How do you know if you didn't see her?" Mandy was beginning to suspect he was leading them on, wasting time.

"Walk like old. Hip hop?"

"With a limp? Like this?" She hobbled across the room.

Igor smiled, displaying discoloured teeth. "Is like. You good act. Think going big screen?" He held his arms wide, and his laugh was somewhere between a grunt and a chuckle.

Josh whispered, "The mother," under his breath and Mandy agreed. "Get them to give our friend here a hot drink and some chocolate biscuits as a treat. Here we go again on the merry-go-round."

She checked the time. It could wait until tomorrow. Isobel Price-Williams and her son were probably at each other's throats. Let them simmer and then see what crawled out of the shit.

CHAPTER FORTY-NINE

Laughter greeted her as she entered her terraced house on Brithdir Street. Tabitha's and a deeper, rowdier laugh. She kicked off her shoes and opened the door to the lounge. It was like looking in a mirror, except Joy's skin had darkened with the sun in Greece and she had a softer edge to her cheeks. Her eyes were alight with laughter and so were Tabitha's. Whatever her reasons for returning, whatever the future brought, these people were the reasons Mandy got up in the morning. She thought of Paskal and his dead brother and hugged Joy to her, emotion almost overwhelming her.

"Welcome home. Good to see you, sis."

"Hey, it's really good to be back. Family. Nothing like it. You two are the centre of my world. I'm sorry it's taken me so long to see it," said Joy.

Had she told Tabitha about the pregnancy? Mandy examined her sister for signs. How many months? She'd gone back to Greece in early July so how far gone? Not enough to show, that was for sure. Joy looked the same. Lithe, toned and tanned. If there were bags under her eyes, she'd managed to cover them up with make-up.

"Have you eaten, Auntie Mandy?" Tabitha's question broke the reverie.

"No sweetie. I'm over-tired and not the slightest bit hungry. It's been quite a day. And I'll have to go in early tomorrow."

"I'm bunking on the sofa tonight. You need your sleep, sis," said Joy. "Frankly it looks as though you've not slept for weeks."

Irritation made Mandy respond in a terse way. "I haven't been feeling great and we both know why. Have you told Tabs your news yet?"

The warmth in the room was replaced by tension as Tabitha glanced from mother to aunt.

"What news?"

"You haven't, have you?"

Joy shook her head. "Not yet. I was hoping–"

"That I'd do your dirty work for you? No bloody way. You clear up your own shit. Tell her. Now."

Joy opened and closed her mouth, but no words came out.

"What's happened? Tell me?" Tabitha was getting worried.

"Your mam's come home because she's up the duff again. I just hope this time she knows who the father is."

"Are you really?" asked Tabitha. "A baby?" Her eyes widened as she glanced at her mother's stomach for evidence.

At last, Joy found a voice. "Yes. It's true."

"Are you keeping it?"

Tabitha seemed overwhelmed by the situation, blinking rapidly. Mandy knew the signs. Tears would follow.

"That will be for your mam to decide but we'll stick together, won't we?" She put one arm around Tabitha, pulled her close and kissed the top of her head. Her niece smelled of verbena, fresh and lemony. Time to defuse the situation.

"I'm sorry. It's this bloody case." Mandy rubbed her forehead. "It's got to me, and you know what I'm like. A complete bitch until I've got the baddie."

"Now there's a confession. Did you record that, Tabs?" Joy laughed and the friction dissolved. "What about a nice cup of tea and a cheese sandwich?"

Mandy's stomach heaved. "Tea and toast, please. I don't feel like cheese." She exchanged a glance with her sister. They both knew why she'd gone off cheese. They needed a heart-to-heart, without the aggro and without Tabitha present. Another sodding problem to deal with. Weariness made Mandy groan. "I thought you had a test in the morning?" Her remark was addressed to Tabitha with a pointed look at the clock on the shelf.

"I do. I'd better revise and get to bed. Are you two okay now?"

"Yeah, we're good. Sorry. It will all be fine. Cross my heart and hope to die."

Tabitha grinned. "You're silly." She gave her mum a hug. "It's so nice to have you home, Mam. I'll bring you some toast in the morning." Then another hug for Mandy. "Night, Auntie Mandy."

Mandy and Joy waited until they heard Tabitha in the bathroom.

"What now, Joy? Where do we go from here?"

Her twin met her eyes, tears threatening to overflow. "I don't know, Mand. It was another mistake." She cradled her stomach. "All I know is – I want to keep this baby. I had nowhere else to go and no one to turn to. You will help me, won't you?"

Mandy closed her eyes hoping it was all a dream. Time rolled back sixteen years. Joy swearing she wasn't sure who the father was, and asking her sister to support her. Bringing her bloody problems back for Mandy to sort out every sodding time. As if she didn't have enough to deal with or any choice. Bugger.

* * *

THURSDAY

They didn't waste any time on Thursday morning, sending a car to collect Isobel Price-Williams at after eight. They checked the CCTV in the warehouse and spotted Isobel entering the day after the men had been moved from the Llanishen house. Although her features were indistinguishable and her head was covered with a scarf, the limp was obvious. They also had the camera footage from the road leading to the warehouse, and the security camera from the front of the building. She couldn't deny the evidence. Visiting her son at his place of work wasn't enough to convince the CPS so they'd have to push and hope she'd crack.

Mrs Price-Williams seemed bleary, unprepared and less imperious, having been caught without her make-up and still in her dressing gown. Simon was nowhere to be seen. No doubt he had scurried back to his own home and drunk himself into a stupor with expensive wines. Chivers would have told him what to expect in prison. They'd need to speak to him again as well.

Helen had gone with the uniform officers to collect Isobel, assuring the woman she wasn't being arrested while making clear it was in her best interests to answer some further questions. Helen reported back. Isobel was not pleased. She'd grumbled, dressed in haste and even put on some make-up and perfume.

Isobel was walking with a stick when she got to the station. Mandy enquired after her health and was met with a disdainful comment.

"When you get to my age you will find, Inspector, it takes one a little longer in the morning to enable one's body to move with the fluidity of youth, especially if one has been cursed with arthritis."

She limped into the interview room, refused a drink and waited for the solicitor to arrive. They watched her through the two-way mirror.

"Seems relaxed, if a bit narked," said Josh.

"That's how I feel every morning," responded Mandy, swallowing as another wave of nausea hit her. She tried to remember, couldn't recall details, of how long the queasiness had lasted when Joy was pregnant with Tabitha. Whatever, she needed to wrap this case up and have some time off.

Chivers arrived, a tiny speck of tissue still attached to his cheek where he'd cut himself shaving. Any other time, Mandy would have found it amusing. She wasn't in the mood to find anything humorous and wasted little time. They went through the usual proceedings including cautioning Isobel Price-Williams who viewed the recorder with disdain.

"Thank you, Mrs Price-Williams, for agreeing to help us. As you know we've charged your son, Simon, in connection with several counts relating to–"

"I know." Isobel cut across her. "Stupid boy."

"Stupid for harbouring the men or stupid for getting caught?" asked Mandy. No response.

"Do you take an interest in the wine business? Visit the warehouse to check upon things? Make sure it's all running well?"

"Simon runs the business. He took over from George. It was a gradual move and when George died," she touched her wedding ring, "he took over. Why would I need to go there? I leave it to Simon. I suppose I'll have to find a manager or sell the business now he's got himself into trouble."

"You've never been to the warehouse?" asked Mandy.

"No. Never. I'm not even sure where it is."

A lie. Why would she lie to them unless she was covering up her involvement? Mandy stroked the cover of the file. Inside she had the photographs from the warehouse, both inside and out, plus the traffic camera pictures of Isobel driving her car on the road to the warehouse. All dated and irrefutable evidence. She'd probably claim she'd forgotten. It wasn't enough. If they could unnerve her a little … Best to keep digging.

"One of the men we found hiding at the warehouse, a Mr Shabani, claims a woman was in charge of the whole thing."

Apart from raising one eyebrow, Isobel didn't react.

"He couldn't identify who it was as he didn't see her face." Was there a slight relaxation of Isobel's posture? Hard to tell. Mandy carried on, watching for a reaction. "He recognised the perfume, though. Almost the same as our DC Probert wears. Except my guess is the woman in question buys the real deal. Chanel No 5, not 5th Element from Aldi. Chanel is your signature perfume, I believe."

"Why are you telling me this, DI Wilde? I'm sure you didn't bring me here to discuss perfumes. I like Chanel No 5. My husband always bought me a bottle. Just because some immigrant says he can smell something like something else is hardly criminal. Do get to the point."

"We've spoken to Mrs Crozier about this as well. She wears the same perfume, a gift from Simon. Do you think she could be the woman in question – responsible for the whole thing?"

Something like relief crossed Isobel's eyes, the straight line of her lips curling a little. "Well, it could be possible. She's had her claws into my son for quite some time. I wouldn't be surprised if she's the one Igor saw at the warehouse. She's not as sweet as she makes out."

A mistake. They hadn't given a first name.

"She tried to seduce my husband and then bewitched Simon. He's besotted by her," said Isobel.

"You think it's possible Mrs Crozier was at the warehouse the morning in question and she's the one in charge? Do you think she's clever enough? I mean, it was quite an undertaking. It took brains, organisation and quick thinking to sort it all out. Quite a woman to be able to do that as well as run a business."

"She's not so clever." Petulant.

"So, you don't think she's the leader? Would Simon do as he's told? Does he do what you tell him? An obedient son?"

As if realising the trap Mandy was setting, Isobel held her head higher and closed her mouth in a tight line again. Time to go in for the kill. Mandy opened the folder and took out the photographs, placing them in front of Isobel, one at a time.

"As you can see this is evidence of your visit to the warehouse after the men disappeared from the house in Llanishen. The warehouse you said you never visited because you didn't know where it was. Your car driving there. You, entering the building and seen speaking to Simon. We know some of what was said, thanks to Mr Shabani."

Isobel had turned pale despite the make-up. She twisted towards the lawyer whose eyes had widened when the photographs were placed on the table. Chivers shook his head. Out of his depth.

"It could be anyone. Ruth could have taken my car. Simon has the spare set. It's probably her in the picture."

"We've checked. Mrs Crozier was in a meeting at the same time and there are three people who can corroborate it. You were supposed to be at a committee meeting at the church. You failed to turn up. The film footage shows a woman with a limp. You had us running around in circles, Mrs Price-Williams. Very clever. You almost got away with it."

"Stupid, stupid boy. I told him to give them their passports and money so they could all clear off." Isobel's nostrils were flared, and she was beginning to breath faster. "If he'd done what I told him instead of pandering to Igor. Too soft. It's always been his problem."

She seemed almost proud. Chivers placed a hand on her arm to try and silence her. She shrugged him off.

"You are right, DI Wilde. I was the brains behind it all. When those men smuggled themselves into the country in Simon's lorry, I could see the potential. They wanted work and we wanted cheap labour. It worked until Igor got greedy. I showed him not to tangle with me. They didn't like washing cars, did they? I made sure Simon kept their passports. Control. It's the key to managing people. Show them who is in command. If Simon had done as he was told, we wouldn't have this mess."

It was probably true. Mandy left Josh to charge Isobel while she went to tell the others what had happened.

"I never thought it was her," said Olivia. "She pimped out Elio and Paskal to her friends and all, did she? She always seemed above it, like."

"Sex and money, Olivia. Big motivators. Beverley will probably install more locks and cameras, so she feels safe. It's unclear if Elio provided sexual favours for her. I daresay Rebecca will find someone else to take Paskal's place. This little business will have shaken the merry widows."

Helen coughed. "Storm approaching." Whispered words as Superintendent Withers had entered the room.

"What's this I hear about the Price-Williams family? Both mother and son? Is it true?"

"Yes, sir." Mandy could feel herself swaying with fatigue. Sort the paperwork and then home early for a nap. She'd need all her strength to get through the next few days with Joy and Tabitha.

"Pity. Good wines. I suppose the daughter will take over the business now. Or sell it. I'll have to find somewhere else to order from. No matter. Good work." He turned his head to encompass all of them in his view. "All of you. Wilde, I suggest you take time off when you've filed your report. DS Jones can take charge. Good experience for him. You look like a corpse, and we don't want Rishi to get his hands on you, do we?" He laughed at his own attempt of a joke and marched out again.

"We've had Paskal's medical information through. He doesn't have the same condition as Elio," said Helen. "He's been moved to a detention centre and will be deported along with his brother's ashes. The parents have been informed. It's all very sad."

Mandy sighed. "Let's hope they bury the ashes near his beloved woods so the trees can keep whispering their secrets to him. Case closed. Right now, I need to get home to my family."

On the short drive home to Brithdir Street she thought about Joy and Tabitha. Joy was a bloody disaster magnet. A baby on the way. Last thing any of them needed. How the hell was she going to sort out her mess this time?

THE END

Printed in Great Britain
by Amazon

10910519R00182